BONES
OF THE
EARTH

A Dan Courtwright Mystery

Other Books by Paul Wagner :

Danger: Falling Rocks
A Dan Courtwright Mystery

Artisan Public Relations

Wine Sales and Distribution

Wine Marketing and Sales

Lecture Series:
The Instant Sommelier (Great Courses)
A History of Wine in 10 Glasses (Audible)

BONES

OF THE

EARTH

PAUL WAGNER

A Dan Courtwright Mystery

Published by Albicaulis Books

For Liz and her real-life FBI agent friend.

BONES OF THE EARTH

<h1 style="text-align:center">chapter 1</h1>

Until they walked in with their photos, it had been a good day for Dan Courtwright. He had arrived at the Summit Ranger Station early, as he often did. It gave him a chance to walk around the building, tidy up any obvious trash, and take a few minutes to organize things in the office.

The car that was waiting for him in the parking lot brought a small smile to the tall ranger's bearded face. A VW that was well past its shiny new phase had been covered with best wishes, streamers, and a big "just married" scrawled across the back window. Inside, the little car was crammed full of camping equipment. Dan noted that the packs looked as if they had been used many times before.

The young couple in the car jumped out when they saw Dan arrive, and eagerly waited by the door for him to open it.

"We don't open until eight," Dan apologized with a smile that he hoped would lighten the impact of the news.

"We're just really anxious to get out on the trail," the young woman replied. She reached out and took the hand of the young man next to her.

Dan chuckled. "Give me a minute to get the lights on and boot up the computer and I'll see what I can do," he replied.

Once inside, Dan took a quick look around. There were four messages on the answering machine, but Doris would take care of those when she arrived. She should be here soon. And while there were plenty of emails, none of them seemed urgent, or came from Dan's boss. So far, so good.

Dan flicked on the radio, turned on the cash register, and scanned the area behind the counter. There was nothing that needed his immediate attention. He took a deep breath, glanced at the young couple outside the door, and waved them in.

"We really appreciate this," the young woman said.

"I saw your backpacks in the car," Dan noted. "Are you here for a wilderness permit?"

"Yeah," she agreed with an energetic nod. "We're going to Hyatt Lake."

Dan pulled out the form and slid it across the counter, holding out a pen with his other hand. He glanced at the clock. It said 7:54.

The young woman started filling out the form. She stopped to look at what she had written, smiled, and showed the form to her husband. "Cheryl Monez," she said quietly to him.

The young man smiled and then leaned over and kissed her softly on the side of her head, his lips just touching her hair. Dan checked the permit and asked them where they were going to camp.

"Oh, we're going straight to Hyatt Lake today, and we're just going to stay there for three days, then come back out," she said.

Dan noticed that she was wearing make-up—something that might not last over four days in the back country—but it made her glow more than the usual backpacker who stopped in. He found it charming.

Dan handed the couple their papers and briefly talked them through the regulations about fires, bears, and trash. Before he could finish, Doris swung open the doors and marched into the station. Her short gray hair and round face and body were all just a bit too bouncy today. The energy she brought seemed to explode into the office.

"Good morning," she practically sang, her face transformed into a collage of shining teeth, wire rim glasses and teary eyes, framed by short curly hair. She stopped to study the two young people. "Oh, you are so lovely!" she said to the girl, "and you are so lucky!" to the young man. "Do you have everything you need?"

The two nodded, still holding hands.

"Maps?" she prodded. Young Mr. Monez explained that they had a GPS.

Doris became serious. "Where are you going? A map or two doesn't weigh anything. And if your GPS goes dead, then what?"

"We're really fine," the young man assured her. His wife nodded.

Doris quickly thumbed through her charts and handed him two topo maps. "These are all you should need," she said.

Looking embarrassed, Cheryl started to open her purse. "Oh no, honey, these are on the house," Doris stated emphatically. "They are a wedding gift from the US Forest Service." The new Mr. and Mrs. Monez thanked her effusively and turned to leave.

"Wait!" Doris called out. "Give me your phone. Let me take your picture!"

A few minutes later, Doris came back inside, smiling broadly. Dan met her with a bemused grin.

"Don't worry," she reassured him. "I'll pay for the maps."

Dan laughed and pulled out his wallet. He was surprised to see fewer bills than he expected. Where had the money gone? "Here," he said, handing her a five dollar bill. "This will help."

The rest of the morning Dan spent listening to Doris hum happily. She hummed while he gave a permit to a troop of Boy Scouts leaving for their fifty-mile hike merit badge—even through his rules and regulations speech. From the look of their young faces, there would be a few tears before that hike was over.

She hummed while she waited on hold to tell Gretchen Turner that two of her cows were out on the highway by Long Barn.

When Dan left to take a quick tour of the lake and grab some lunch, Doris was humming. And she was still humming an hour later when he returned.

She stopped humming when a young family came in about 3:30 that afternoon. The mother and father ushered their two little girls into the ranger station.

The two girls, maybe five and eight, stopped and looked at Dan, then at Doris. The older girl watched carefully, her expression guarded.

"Good afternoon!" Doris greeted them with exaggerated enthusiasm, leaning over the counter to bring her face closer to the little girls.

"Do you have a question?" the father quietly asked the girls. He stood back to give them room.

The younger of the two wore thick glasses, and peered through them intently at Doris. Her dark bobbed hair gave her a perky look. With a lisp she stated seriously, "We want to know about the thquirrelth."

And with that, Doris was off and running, asking questions of the girls, describing chipmunks and squirrels, and which ones they might find nearby. This was what Doris lived for, and the girls did their part as they listened in rapt attention.

Dan let his mind drift. The older girl reminded him of Lisa, Cal Healey's daughter. But Lisa was older now; she must be a teenager. Cal was a Deputy Sheriff in Tuolumne County, and Cal's wife Maggie had invited Dan to dinner tonight. That alone was something to look forward to with pleasure. Maggie was a good cook. Nothing fancy, but everything she made was always delicious.

And when she invited him, Maggie had mentioned that she had also invited Kristen Gallagher. Dan wasn't sure if Maggie was playing matchmaker, but he was delighted to know that Kristen would be there. He'd taken her to dinner once last month, and they'd traded a couple of voice mail messages since then. He wasn't quite sure what the next step should be. And while he thought he might be falling for Kristen, Dan wasn't sure how Kristen felt about him. Maybe, if it all worked out, he could ask her out again tonight. Maybe to a movie, if there was a good one showing. Dan didn't go to movies much, so he would have to ask Kristen about it.

He glanced up when a couple in their fifties opened the doors and walked in. With one glance he guessed they'd been out on the trail for a while. The man's face had the look of someone who hadn't shaved in a few days, and his hat hid most of his hair—but the hair that was showing needed a good wash. His wife's shirt had a dusty smear across the front, and her hair was hidden underneath a red bandana. The huge amount of dust on their boots and socks made Dan think they had climbed up out of Pine Valley. That trail always had six inches of powdery brown dust on it by this time of year.

As Dan waited expectantly, the woman looked at Doris and the two little girls and leaned close enough to her husband to whisper something in his ear that Dan couldn't hear. The husband nodded in response, and the two of them turned to peruse the bookshelves on the far wall of the ranger station. It was as if they wanted to keep a secret. And it wasn't going to be a good kind of secret. Something in her face told Dan that.

The girls' mother noticed this, and stepped in to wind up their conversation with Doris. "Okay, girls. Let's buy this book that can tell us about the animals, and then let's let the rangers get back to work," she said. She glanced over at the older couple while her husband paid Doris.

Dan could see that the backpackers were killing time, waiting for the girls to leave. It seemed to take a long time for Doris to ring up the sale. And then she made the mistake of asking which of the girls wanted to carry the bag. That set off another discussion. Their mother eventually had to intercede and carry it herself, the two girls still arguing about it as they left the office.

Once the family was out the door, Dan turned to the two backpackers, raising his eyebrows expectantly.

"We didn't want to talk about this with the little girls here," the husband said quietly. "I'm Glenn Bartlett, and this is my wife, Martha."

Dan nodded in greeting.

"We were up above Yellowhammer Lake," he said, "a couple of days ago, and we saw some … um, well, we think we found some human remains."

Doris stopped humming. The sudden quiet in the office allowed Dan to hear a light breeze outside blow through the pines, and the slight hum of the computer fan.

"Where did you see this?" Dan asked.

"We were trying to go from Yellowhammer up to Leighton Lake," Glenn explained. "It was pretty steep, and we were getting pretty far up the ridge. It's all granite up there, and we started seeing a couple of bones …. Well, Martha saw them…."

Dan began to relax a bit. At least once a year a hiker would find deer or bear bones and mistake them for human bones. This was probably no different.

"What did they look like?" Dan asked.

Glenn noted the skepticism in Dan's voice. "We took some photos," he said, pulling out a small black digital camera from his pocket. "They were kind of spread out, but we took a lot of photos."

Dan waited patiently while Glenn Bartlett pushed the tiny buttons on his camera and beeped through his photos. Doris hovered nearby. "Okay, here they are," Bartlett said.

He handed Dan the camera and explained how to push a button to scan through the photos. The small screen didn't show a lot of detail, and it was hard to tell what the photos really showed. Doris peered over his shoulder at what looked like white sticks among pine needles.

"We didn't move anything, so some of them are not too clear," Glenn explained, with his wife nodding her agreement over his shoulder. They craned their necks to try and see as Dan clicked through the photos. Rocks, pine needles, something white on the ground—that one there did look a bit like a human rib, he had to admit. The tiny screen really didn't give Dan much help.

And just then Dan found himself looking at something that removed his doubts. In the tiny screen of the camera, Dan could clearly see the unmistakable image of two white bones. The bones were coming straight out of a high-top hiking boot.

Dan looked at the wall clock. It was 3:49.

<h1 style="text-align:center">chapter 2</h1>

Dan stared at the photo in the little camera and then looked up at Glenn Bartlett.

"So where did you see this, exactly?" he asked quietly.

Glenn nodded wearily and started to talk. "We were southwest of Leighton Lake," he said. "We'd camped the night before at Big Lake, and so we came into Yellowhammer from there. And from Yellowhammer, we were looking for a direct route to up to Leighton. It seemed like it might be possible from the topos."

"What day was this?" Dan interrupted. He had pulled out a notepad and was taking notes. Doris cleared off brochures and papers from the large topo map of the wilderness they kept on the counter, and encouraged Glenn Bartlett to show them on the map.

"It was two days ago," Bartlett replied. "So that would be Tuesday. We went in on Sunday."

Dan nodded and glanced up to confirm the date on the wall calendar. He wrote down the information and looked back at Glenn Bartlett.

"There was no trail, but I thought we might be able to get up there anyway. We were just bushwhacking, trying to find a way up those cliffs," Glenn said.

Glenn reached into his pocket to pull out his reading glasses, adjusted them on his nose, and leaned over the map. He hadn't needed to wear them just to look at the photos, but this was now more serious. Martha leaned in as well, as did Dan and Doris. Dan could smell the two backpackers, a combination of smoke, sweat, and dust. Mainly sweat and smoke.

"Yeah," Glenn said, putting his finger down on the map. "That's Yellowhammer there. And we followed this bench up towards Leighton here … I was hoping that there would be some kind of ledge or chute that would let us get up this cliff here."

"It was really steep," Martha spoke up. "It was just crazy to go higher."

Glenn agreed. "We got part of the way up it, but we had to stop. It's all granite there, and there just wasn't any easy way up."

"It was scary," Martha said.

Glenn looked at her and shrugged. "It was steep. We stopped before it got scary."

"You stopped before you got scared," Martha corrected him. "I was scared way before that!"

Glenn continued to explain. "So I thought if we could work our way a little west, along this little ledge …" His finger now followed a contour line on the map. Dan noticed the rough fingernail, edged in black dirt after five days in the backcountry. "We might find a way up."

He stopped and turned his glance away from the map, and looked at Dan and Doris. "There was a crack I started to follow …"

"It was too steep for us," Martha added. "I wasn't going to go up there."

"Well, it was steep," admitted Glenn. "But there was a tree growing out of the rock there, and I thought if I could just get to the tree, I could see beyond it—and maybe I could find a route from there."

Dan and Doris followed the conversation back and forth, their faces moving as if they were following the ball at a tennis match.

"That's when I saw the bones," Martha said. "At first I thought they were from a deer, but then they didn't look right."

"So she called out to me," Glenn said. "I was just up by the tree. Her voice sounded concerned, so I stopped for a second to see what was the matter. And when I put my foot down, I heard something in the pine needles crack. And then I saw bones under my feet."

The story the Bartletts told came tumbling out of their mouths. Dan tried hard to get it written down, but he realized that it wasn't all in chronological order. He considered trying to interrupt them, to slow them down, but decided that he could always ask them questions later. Now, he wanted to get their story as directly as possible.

"Did you see the photo of the boot?" Martha Bartlett asked Dan. "That's when we were sure. It was pretty unpleasant." Her mouth twisted down when she said that.

"Oh, my gosh, I can only imagine," Doris replied. Dan nodded slowly, both to answer Martha's question and to agree with Doris. He was already searching his memory, trying to find some clue as to what the bones could be. Who was the last person who went missing in this area?

"So we took lots of photos," Glenn explained. "At first we didn't know if these were old, like Native American, or more recent."

"But when we saw the boot, and then there is one with some clothing … some of it looks like denim. Well, that means that they aren't that old," Martha said. "And we didn't want to touch anything."

"They have to be pretty recent," Glenn admitted.

"So we didn't really touch or move anything," Glenn continued. "We figured that you'd want it the way we found it."

Dan agreed that they had done the right thing. "I'm sorry that this happened," he said. "We'll have to send a team in there to check this out." He pulled out a new topo map from behind the counter, and laid it out. Handing a pencil to Glenn Bartlett, he said, "Could you just draw the location as exactly as you can on this map?"

While Glenn drew carefully on the map, Martha explained, "We took lots of photos, from all different points of view, so that you could find it easier ..."

"Really?" Dan was impressed. "How so?"

"We took pictures from down below, so we can show you on those where the bones are," Glenn said. "We could see it ... well, the place ... it was easy once we knew where it was. So we took photos. If you print them out, we can show you. But you'd never go there on purpose."

Dan thought about this. "I don't suppose you have the download cable for the camera with you?" They didn't.

"We can post these online by tonight for you, or email them to you when we get home," Glenn offered.

Dan shook his head. "I'd rather not have these online," he said. "What I'd really like to do is print them out, and have you mark them up for us ... would you be willing to do that for us?"

The Bartletts thought this over. "Yes ..." Glenn said slowly. "We need to get home tonight, to Livermore. I have to be at work tomorrow. Do you have a cable?"

Dan looked at Doris.

"Why don't I give Ray a call in town and see if he can help us?" she asked.

"Ray is the local camera and computer guy," Dan explained. "A lot of people up here people buy online or down in Modesto, but then somebody has to help them figure out how to use it."

Doris was on the phone to Ray, full of importance. She told him it was an emergency. She listened for a minute and then covered the mouthpiece and asked Glenn, "Which camera is it?"

Glenn read the name and numbers off the camera to Doris, and she repeated them to Ray.

After a few moments they heard her say, "Oh, shoot. We really need to get these photos, Ray." Then she was listening again. "Okay … yeah, I'll wait …" Then to her audience in the ranger station, she explained, "He's looking to see if he knows someone in town with the same camera …"

Dan and Glenn found themselves taking a deep breath in unison. Martha asked Dan if it was all right for her to go outside and sit on the bench there. She looked tired, exhausted. Dan assured her it was a fine idea. "There's a drinking fountain around the corner, if you want it," he added.

Glenn watched his wife walk out the door. He turned to Dan and said, "That boot up there was a lot smaller than mine … it was just about the size of Martha's. That was pretty hard on her."

Dan nodded. He wanted to respond to the hint of tension in Glenn's voice. "Of course," he replied. "We'll try to get this wrapped up and get you on your way as soon as possible …"

"Hi, okay …" Doris' voice interrupted them. Her volume jumped an octave on the next word. "Really? Oh, you're kidding! That's great. Thanks, Ray!"

She hung up the phone and said, "My daughter bought the same camera a few months ago! I'll give her a call and have her bring it right over."

It was not so simple. Doris' daughter was not at home, and her cell phone wasn't answering. It was probably out of cell phone coverage up here. Doris tried another number, and managed to reach her grandson, Travis.

"Okay," she announced to Dan and Glenn Bartlett. "Travis is just leaving school and says he can run home and bring the cable up here right now. He said he should be here in about twenty minutes. Which means thirty minutes."

Dan shot a questioning look at Glenn. "That's fine," the hiker said. "Does that give me time to run over to the store at the lake and buy Martha a snack? I think she could use that." Dan assured him that it did.

When Travis arrived, Dan could not help but think that the slight boy with short curly hair and freckles was far too young to be driving. He realized that he was at least mathematically old enough to be Travis' father, and the sobering thought just added to the weight that had descended on his shoulders in the last hour.

Doris greeted Travis like a conquering hero, and within minutes they were all gathered around a computer in the ranger station as Doris and Dan tried to connect the camera and download the photos. The cable that Travis had delivered seemed to fit just fine, but the computer would not open the files on the camera.

Doris called Ray again, and put him on the speaker phone while he directed her to execute a few commands on the computer. With each command, Doris reported the reaction of the computer to Ray. But nothing seemed to work.

"Sorry, Doris, but you have a really strong firewall on that computer," Ray explained on the phone. "It won't let you open anything or load anything onto the hard drive. I'll bet someone at the Forest Service made sure you were completely protected."

Dan shook his head in disgust. His mind was searching for other options, but this was one of the problems of having your office in the mountains. Computers were one of the things that people were hoping to leave behind when they came to the Emigrant Wilderness. "I'm sorry," Dan apologized to the Bartletts. "They really don't want us to get hacked here."

Glenn Bartlett said he understood. He looked out at his wife, who had now leaned back on the bench and seemed to be taking a nap. Her eyes were closed and her head was rocked backwards. "I'm sorry, but I don't think I have any solutions either," he said to Dan. "I guess I'll try to send you the photos from our home."

Travis had been watching his grandmother follow Ray's instructions. He turned to her now and asked, "Grandma, can I try?"

His voice conveyed a hint of frustration. "You just want to print out the photos, right?"

Doris looked at Dan. Dan shrugged. "If the computer is so safe, I don't see why not."

Travis waited for his grandmother to rise out of her chair, then quickly slipped into position in front of the keyboard. He typed a few quick commands, then read the screen. A few more clicks, and new screens appeared. One of the photos glowed on the screen.

"Okay, I think I can do this," he announced. "I'm going to set up a system that just views what's on the camera, and then we can do a screen save and print from there." Doris stared at him in amazement. "It's avoiding the whole hard drive problem with the computer—this way we don't have to worry about what's protected by the firewall," Travis explained.

Dan and Glenn glanced at each other, and Dan gave the hiker a rueful smile. They watched Travis's fingers fly around the keyboard and mouse. The printer began to hum, then spit out document after document into its tray. Within minutes, the photos were all printed out and ready for Glenn's notes.

Travis sat back in his chair and looked up at Dan. "That should do it. I think I got all of them. When you need them, you'll just have to work off the hard copies. But if you need to print them out again, I guess we'll need to save them on a USB drive or something …" He sat back in the chair and stared at the screen. "What are those bones?" he asked.

"That's what we're trying to find out," Dan said.

"I can blow them up for you, make them easier to see," Travis offered.

"That's okay," Dan replied. "We've seen enough to know that we're going to have to go up there and look at them anyway." Dan held out his hand to the young man. "Thank you, Travis. I still don't know what you did there, but I am really grateful."

"Isn't he amazing?" Doris insisted. "Travis, you are amazing!" Travis blushed and looked down at his feet. He was clearly not prepared to be embarrassed by his grandmother in front of strangers. He shook hands with Glenn Bartlett, reluctantly gave his grandmother a hug and kiss, and then shuffled out the door.

Dan turned to Doris and said soberly, "Doris, we are relics of a bygone age."

"Isn't it nice that the next generation is in such good hands?" Doris asked him. She brought the printouts from the printer and spread them out on the counter in front of Dan and Glenn Bartlett. For the next twenty-five minutes, Glenn talked Dan through the photos, numbering each one, pointing out where it had been taken on the map, and explaining how and why they were organized the way they were.

By the time they were done, the light outside had softened. Martha Bartlett walked back into the ranger station to see how they were doing. "Are you finishing up?" she asked.

"I think we have enough here to find the place," Dan agreed. "I really want to thank you for taking the time and trouble to do this."

Glenn looked at Martha as he answered. "We didn't really feel that we had a choice. Once we saw those bones in the boot, we knew we had to take care of this." Martha nodded in agreement.

"I wish I could do something for you," Dan said, "but I know you want to get home, so I'll let you do that."

Glenn thanked him. "Looking at the time, is there some place you would recommend for dinner tonight? What's the latest on the local restaurants?"

Dan's heart gave a leap at the mention of dinner. He looked at the clock. It read 5:35. While Doris ran through a list of restaurants that the Bartletts would pass on their way back to Livermore, Dan did some quick calculations. He wouldn't have time to go home and then make it to Cal's house by six o'clock. He'd just have to go in his uniform, and he wouldn't have a chance to shower.

He waved to Glenn and Martha through the window as they drove off, and then quickly helped Doris close up the office. While Doris shut down the computers and turned off the lights, Dan piled all the photos and notes from Glenn Bartlett into a file, and called down to the Mi-Wok station to talk to Steve Matson, his boss. Luckily, Steve was still there, although not happy about it. He had been delayed by a long meeting with a local resident who had complaints about cattle in the forest near his property.

"I'm afraid I have something that won't make you any happier," Dan said.

"Go ahead," Steve answered dryly. "I've already told my wife I'll be late for dinner. She's already grumpy."

Dan gave Steve a summary of the human remains near Leighton Lake. Steve wasn't one to interrupt something like this, and he waited for the full report, then responded. "So tomorrow I'd like you to take a team in there and check this out," he told Dan. "I'll let SAR know that we've got a situation and need their help, and I'd like you to run that for us."

Dan agreed. He had suspected that Steve would say that. In fact, he welcomed the assignment. It was his case now, and he felt an obligation to follow it through. Maybe even some excitement. It would, after all, get him out of the office and into the mountains.

As he was finishing up his conversation with Steve, Doris waved good-bye to him and left the station. Dan hung up the phone, took a quick glance around the office, and walked out the front door. As he locked the glass doors, he glanced at the clock on the office wall. It read 5:53.

He was going to be late for dinner.

chapter 3

Dan pulled off the street to park in front of Cal Healey's house, his tires making a crunching noise on the gravel of the road shoulder. A small cloud of dust rose in the late evening sun, and he waited for a moment for the dust to clear before he got out of the car. He was not pleased with the way the day had gone.

Dan had planned to stop and get some flowers for Maggie Healey on the way to dinner, but there hadn't been time. There wasn't time for a shower, or a change of clothes, and now he was twenty minutes late anyway. It wasn't how he had planned seeing Kristen again, and he was unhappy about it.

Cal's son Mark was in the front yard, tossing a football to himself on the lawn. When he saw Dan, he tossed the ball into the air one more time, really high, and then caught it and ran into the house, leaving the front door open. Dan assumed that Mark had been serving as a lookout for the last guest.

Cal walked up the steps to the porch and knocked on the frame of the front door.

"Come on in, Dan," Maggie called out from inside the house. "Everybody is in the back yard."

"I am sorry I'm late," Dan said to Maggie. "I hope I didn't ruin anything …?"

"Oh lord, no," Maggie reassured him. "Everyone's just having a glass of wine outside." She ushered him through the house and out the double doors onto the deck behind the kitchen.

"Hi, Dan," Cal called out from the far side of the yard, where he was talking to three other people by an apple tree. One, Dan saw immediately, was Kristen Gallagher. She was wearing a lightweight beige skirt that somehow managed to fit her perfectly and still float around her in the soft breeze. And a tailored white sleeveless blouse was set off by a sky blue scarf around her neck. Dan had a hard time pulling his eyes away from her to look at the rest of the group.

Cal gestured to the older couple standing next to him. "This is Tony and Janet di Conti, and this," he continued as he turned to the di Contis, "is Dan Courtwright."

Dan extended his hand toward Tony, and was surprised at the force of his handshake. Tony di Conti was about sixty years old and probably not five foot five, Dan guessed, and was wearing gray slacks and a polo shirt. Perhaps in some other part of the country this would have been informal attire, but in this neck of the woods blue jeans were much more common. And di Conti's wire-rimmed glasses were about ten years out of style, even for Tuolumne County.

Janet's handshake was so soft as to feel almost limp, but her flowered print dress and soft features fit the handshake perfectly. Her face broke into a bright smile as she greeted Dan. Even smaller than Tony, she seemed to balance him perfectly.

"And you know Kristen …" Cal finished up the introductions.

Dan greeted Kristen with a shy smile. He didn't know if he should shake her hand, or perhaps kiss her on the cheek, or a hug? In his confusion, he did none of these, and Kristen just smiled at him and raised her wine glass. "Hi, Dan," she said. Her eyes seemed to laugh just a little. He hoped she wasn't laughing at him.

"Sorry I'm late," Dan apologized. "I hope I didn't keep you guys waiting …"

"Not a problem. I heard you had a bit of excitement up there today," Cal said. He studied Dan's face as the others turned their attention to the tall ranger.

"Yeah … I guess we did," Dan replied. The others looked at him expectantly.

"Some hikers found some old bones," Cal explained. "Were they deer or bear this time?" While he talked, he pulled a wine glass from a tray and poured Dan a glass of white wine.

Dan shook his head. "Not from the photos. We'll go up there tomorrow to check it out."

"Yes, we will," Cal assured him. "I got the call about ten minutes before you arrived. I'll be part of the SAR team."

"Great!" Dan replied.

"There had better be some good fishing up there, somewhere nearby," Cal said. "Or I'm gonna be pissy the whole time."

"More than usual?" Dan asked with a grin. Dan wasn't sure how much information he wanted to share with the others at the party. He looked to the di Contis for support, but didn't find any help there.

"So where was this?" Tony asked.

"Do you know the area well?" Dan asked him.

Cal laughed. "Tony and Janet have been backpacking the Emigrant Wilderness for thirty years," he said. "They know it better than anyone I've ever met. They teach at Sonora High, and they spend every summer hiking in the mountains."

Tony smiled, and spoke slowly. "More like forty years, Cal." Then to Dan, "Yeah, we know the area pretty well."

"I thought your face was familiar," Dan said to the di Contis. "You must have come in for a permit … It's the area between Leighton and Yellowhammer Lakes." He studied Tony's face, wondering what kind of reaction that would cause.

Tony thought about it for a moment. "There's a lot of granite up in there," he said. "And not a lot of traffic. If somebody got into trouble, they wouldn't necessarily see a lot of passersby who could help." Then he turned to Cal, and stated with authority, "Red Can Lake. I'll bet you can catch some fish there. Yellowhammer might be good, too, but Red Can is a sure bet."

Maggie called from the house that dinner was ready. As they filed into the house, Dan waited at the door to allow Kristen to enter first. As she walked by, he caught a whiff of her perfume. It was lovely, warm and soft, just a little bit floral. Or was it spicy?

The table was set for six, which meant that the children wouldn't be joining them. "Lisa is at a friend's house, and Mark wants to watch the ballgame," Maggie explained. "I thought that I might get Lisa to help me tonight, but she saw through my plan," she added with a laugh.

With Cal at the head of the table, Tony and Janet sat on one side of the table, leaving Kristen and Dan on the other. Dan could just barely detect her perfume if he concentrated. Which he did.

Despite the distraction of the perfume, Dan learned two important things during dinner that night. The first one was that Maggie was a better cook than he had originally thought. The Mediterranean chicken and rice dish with lemons, olives and saffron was delicious, and even Kristen raved about it.

Dan could see that Cal didn't want Maggie to miss that compliment. "She's a professional, Maggie!" Cal pointed out. "She's cooked for some pretty important people. So when she says it's good, it's really good!"

Kristen laughed. "I've cooked for some interesting people over an open fire in the backcountry," she said. "The standards there are a little less demanding than in a restaurant. But Maggie, it is really delicious … of course, I love it anytime someone cooks food for me … that's my idea of a true holiday!"

The second thing that Dan learned was that Tony was a great storyteller—a true raconteur. A retired high school social studies teacher, Tony kept them all entertained with his tales of local characters.

As Maggie collected the plates and cleared the main course, Cal asked Tony if he knew of any stories about people disappearing into the mountains.

Tony sat back in his chair and thought for a moment. "Probably the best one is a guy by the name of Stan Dubcek," Tony answered. "Well, maybe that was his name. He was some kind of Eastern European, back in the 1950s. He came to town and started making friends. But nobody could figure out why he was here. It was all very mysterious. One of your predecessors in the Sheriff's office was pretty sure he was a Russian spy."

And there followed a tale. Tony explained that Dubcek was under almost constant surveillance, but that he was also trying to sell a few jewels that he supposedly smuggled out of Czechoslovakia after the war. He had a great story about being related to a count who had been assassinated, and the jewels were his family's fortune. And the first person he approached was the man who is today the best jeweler in Sonora. At the time, he was a young man who was just getting into the business, and his father was providing the money for the jewelry shop.

Dubcek sold an emerald to the kid but it turned out to be a fake. He almost got away with it, but the kid's father had the good sense to get it appraised by somebody in San Francisco and figured it out. But by the time he got back to Sonora with the news, Stan had already left town in a hurry.

"They found his truck up at Kennedy Meadows," Tony concluded, "but they never did find Dubcek. Some people said that he knew what he was doing in the mountains, and just hiked out of there to somewhere else. And other people swore they saw him hitching a ride over the pass and off into Nevada. At any rate, he disappeared, and the suckers tried to cover up the story because it made them look so bad."

"So how did you hear about it?" Cal asked.

"Well, I knew a lady up in Sugar Pine who was Czech, and she told me the whole story. The Sheriff went up there to interview her, and ask her what she thought of the guy. She said his accent was pretty good for a Hungarian!"

As the group chuckled over that story, "Don't forget Ike Rogers," Janet reminded her husband.

Tony grinned. "Well, that's one guy who really did go up into the mountains and disappear," he answered.

"Ike Rogers was a Korean War vet. This was also back in the fifties. He came to town straight from the war, and bought himself a complete mining outfit down at the hardware store. He didn't have a clue as to what he needed, and they took him for a bundle."

"This was back when that was really the only store in town where you could buy anything for the mountains," Janet added. "There weren't even any sporting goods stores."

"Yep," Tony agreed. "So this guy Rogers took a mule in through Eagle Meadows. He was telling everyone that he had a surefire map to a gold mine up there, but he was a little loopy. Anyway, he went in through Eagle Meadows, and that's the last anyone ever heard of him. Never seen again."

"So what happened?" Dan asked.

"They found his mule down in Cherry Canyon below Styx Pass," Tony answered. "This was about five weeks later. That's pretty remote country, even today, and back then it was even more so. The mule was damn near starved to death. And nobody knows what happened to Ike and his gold mine."

Janet asked Cal why he was interested in stories about missing people. Cal nodded toward Dan. "Dan got a tip today about some bones up in the back country," he said. "And I was just wondering what Tony knew about that sort of thing."

"Hey!" Tony laughed. "If I'm a consultant, you need to pay

me!"

"What kind of bones?" Janet asked.

"We're not sure," Dan replied. "That's why we're hiking up there tomorrow to see." He saw no reason to add to the rumors that must already be spreading through the county.

"Of course, back then, nobody ever registered for anything, so who knows how many people hiked in and didn't come out," Tony suggested. "Hell, I bet half the people who go hiking in there now don't register. And I'll bet nobody tells you when they come back out. Unless there's somebody at home waiting for them, you'd never know."

Dan reluctantly agreed. "You're right, but I'd like to think that we manage to get most of the folks to fill out a permit."

Tony was still mulling over the original question about missing persons. "What about Rebecca Ritter?" Tony suggested.

"That's a very different story," Janet replied, a tone of correction in her voice. "She wanted to disappear, and she did …"

"Maybe—but nobody knows that for sure," Tony answered.

Cal and Dan exchanged a glance over the table, and for once that evening Dan wasn't aware of Kristen Gallagher's perfume.

"Who is Rebecca Ritter?" he asked.

chapter 4

"Do you remember her, Cal?" Tony asked. "She went to Sonora High. A very bright young lady: model student. And really cute."

"I think she was a couple or three years behind me," Cal answered. "I don't remember very much about her. Wasn't she a cheerleader?"

"She was everything," Janet replied. "Excellent student, cheerleader, homecoming princess, National Merit Scholar. And she worked on the yearbook, too."

"So what's her story?" Dan asked. As the least local person at the table, he was pretty sure there was much that he didn't know.

"Well, it's an interesting one," Tony answered. "She was the perfect kid. As Janet said, she did well at everything she attempted. She's the kid that every teacher wanted to have in his class."

"Or her class," Janet added. "But in retrospect, I think she got along better with the teachers than she did with most of the students."

"Well …" Tony made a wry face. "Any kid who does that well in school is going to get a certain amount of grief from some of the other kids. Or envy. That's normal. But she did have a boyfriend."

"Well, I'm not sure how serious that was. And I really think that Rebecca didn't have a lot of close friends at the school," insisted Janet. "Her parents kept her out of some things, as I remember. They were very conservative."

Tony could see that his story was getting sidetracked. "At

any rate," he said, trying to bring things back on topic, "she was an exemplary student, and we all figured that she was destined for bigger and better things than Sonora High School. She was accepted into a bunch of colleges, and since her parents went to Berkeley, that's where she decided to go as well."

"That may have been a mistake," Janet suggested.

"Who knows?" Tony asked. He was beginning to show a little tension about Janet's interruptions. "But she was all set to go to Cal, and spent the summer working at her mother's office here in town. And she was still dating a young man here."

"Todd Walters," Janet reminded him.

"Right," Tony was nodding. "Todd wasn't quite in Rebecca's class, but he may have been the closest thing at that time. Good student, good athlete. Senior class president? That kind of thing. He was an all-league baseball player, and got a scholarship to the University of Washington? Is that right?"

"I think so," Janet agreed.

"But he wasn't really in her class. Okay, so all that's well and good." Tony held his two hands up, index fingers pointing to the ceiling, making a point. "But this is where it gets a little odd. The two kids decide that they are going on a last fling together, or something. They plan to go on a backpacking trip for the week before they are leaving for college."

"I think there were some people here in town who didn't think that was quite right," Janet interjected. "And I don't think that they described it as a fling. It was just a backpacking trip."

"Who cares what they think?" Tony snapped, obviously annoyed. "Those kids were out of school, and a week later they were going to be in college, where they could do anything they wanted." He let the silence hang, staring at Janet. She looked down at her hands, folded in her lap. Then he looked back at the rest of the group. "So they left to go backpacking together. One last long date before they were leaving town forever."

"That sounds kind of romantic," Kristen said. Dan could see that she was trying to defuse the situation between Tony and Janet. "Where did they go?"

"Sure, it was romantic," Tony agreed. "Considering that some people think Las Vegas is romantic. Hell, I'd much rather be up in the mountains. So they headed out through Crabtree… and I think made it as far as Deer Lake, or Wire Lakes. Somewhere in there. But here is the strange part. They take off on this adventure, and around town a few tongues are wagging. But that's nothing. Because about a week later, Todd Walters comes back from the trip. He's alone. And he's got a note from Rebecca saying she doesn't want to go to Cal, and she is not coming back to town, and her parents can go to hell."

"Tony!" Janet was shocked, or at least wanted Tony to think she was. "It didn't say all those things! It just said that she felt she was under a lot of pressure, and she didn't want to go to university."

"She specifically said something about not wanting to live up to her parents' expectations anymore," Tony insisted, his jaw tense. "And knowing her parents, I can understand why."

"So where did she go?" Cal asked.

Tony held up his hands again, this time palms pointing upwards. "Nobody knows. As far as I know, she's never been heard of again. She disappeared off the face of the earth."

"What did the boyfriend say about it all?" Kristen asked. Dan suddenly noticed her perfume again.

"He was angry," Tony said. "He said that he felt like he had been left holding the bag, and that Rebecca had left him without much food." He looked at Cal. "Her parents insisted that the Sheriff's office open an investigation, and they did. But with the note about how she was leaving and didn't want to be found, and no way of tracking her out of the back country, I don't think they got anywhere at all."

"They asked a bunch of people about it," Janet said. "But Rebecca had mentioned doing something similar to one of her friends. And they couldn't find anyone who had seen her at any of the trailheads …"

"Well, in those days, in late September, there weren't very many people up there," Tony said. "It's not surprising that nobody saw her. But there was no trace of foul play, and Todd Walters was a nice young man, good character references. There just didn't seem to be any other explanation."

"So that's it? She just disappeared?" Cal asked.

"Oh, people have said they've seen her in different places over the years," Tony continued, "but those were never confirmed. As far as I know, she never came back. And I don't think her parents have ever really recovered from the shock."

"What about the boyfriend?" Kristen asked.

"That's a sad story," Janet started to say, then looked at Tony.

"He never did go to college," Tony said. "He got tied up for a while here in the investigation after the trip, and there were a lot of people in town who thought that he had done something to Rebecca. In the end, he decided to join the army instead. Fought in Desert Storm, and was badly wounded. He got a Purple Heart and some kind of commendation." He looked at Janet. "He still lives around here somewhere, I think?"

"I think he's out with his parents," she answered, "but I think he has some real problems. He was pretty badly wounded in Iraq." The table grew silent, and Maggie asked if anyone wanted any more coffee.

"Oh, my goodness," Kristen blurted out. "Here we've been talking about hikers and I didn't even mention how much I enjoyed this dessert. Maggie, it was delicious!"

Dan agreed. "It sure was. Thanks for including me. And I'm

sorry to have brought my work with me here!"

"Hey, I'm glad you did," Cal said. "It makes me look better by comparison."

Janet was still mulling over the story about Rebecca Ritter. "Wasn't there another boy involved as well?"

"I remember this part," Maggie said firmly. "That guy used to live just a few doors down from us. Bryan Lafferty. I can remember being warned about him when I was in high school. He was a stalker or something."

"That's the name," Janet agreed. "And I guess he was up there fishing about the same time as the two were on their trip? But I don't think they ever found any connection at all to her disappearance."

"Didn't he show up one night in her bedroom, while she was sleeping?" Maggie asked. "I remember that because it seemed so terrifying to me. He was a couple of years older than I was, and I had nightmares for years about it."

"Oh, that's right," Janet agreed. "Her parents got a restraining order."

"I remember that," Tony added. "They were both in my class at that time. At one point we had to transfer him out to another class so they wouldn't be together."

"Ugh." Kristen made a face as she thought about this. "So she still had to see him every day at school? That must have been awful."

Tony waggled his head back and forth. "You know, he wasn't a bad kid. I know that sounds weird, but he wasn't really a bad kid." He looked around at the women at the table, who were all frowning at him. "I'm not saying he was completely normal, but he seemed pretty harmless to me. Smart kid, but really bored—and he wasn't interested in school much. But he didn't strike me as dangerous."

"Is this the same Bryan Lafferty that lives out off Big Hill Road?" Cal asked. When Tony nodded, Cal continued. "That guy's got problems ..." The rest of the group looked at Cal expectantly.

Cal considered for a moment, then said, "Sorry, I'm talking out of school …" and then, looking at Tony with a grin, he added, "If I can use that expression!"

"I think it is very appropriate," said Janet tartly. "And I hope that whatever you find up there in the mountains has nothing to do with Rebecca Ritter."

Tony nodded slowly. "Yeah, that would be very sad. She was a nice kid."

"Well, I guess we'll have a better idea tomorrow," Dan noted, looking at his watch. "Six o'clock start, right, Cal?"

Cal nodded. "Yeah. Man, I hope they bring lots of coffee."

Kristen suggested that it was time for her to leave, especially since Dan and Cal had to start so early the next morning. And with that the party broke up with a long series of thank yous and hugs and handshakes. Maggie was glowing with the praise for her food, and Cal was checking his watch to make sure it really was eleven o'clock.

Dan carefully managed his exit so that he would walk out the door at the same time as Kristen did, and he walked with her to her car. "That was really nice," he said to her.

"It sure was," Kristen agreed, smiling at him under the streetlights. She unlocked her car and opened the door.

"You know," Dan struggled on. "I don't think that I can invite you on a romantic backpacking trip yet …" he paused, to see how she was taking this.

Kristen was smiling, a note of caution in her eyes.

"But maybe I could at least invite you to a movie or something?" he finished up, feeling clumsy.

Kristen laughed. "A movie or something would be fun," she said. And then, before he could react, she leaned up and kissed him, ever so briefly, on his cheek.

Dan was stunned, and before he could say anything, she had

slipped behind the wheel of her car and closed the door. She rolled down the window and looked up at him.

"So I'll give you a call when we get back from our trip …" he said to her through the open window.

"That will be nice, Dan." Kristen was still smiling. "Now go home and get some rest."

"That's a really good idea," he answered. "See you soon."

And as he drove off in his car, he realized that it was going to be a lot harder to sleep tonight than he had expected.

chapter 5

The next day started badly for Dan. He had not slept well. He never did when he had to use an alarm to get up. He tossed and turned all night, losing track of the number of times he had checked the clock and to see how much longer he had to sleep. He finally stopped trying about 4:30. He got up, showered and dressed, made the bed, and lay there reading until it was time for him to leave.

The alarm, now forgotten, went off at 5:15 and startled him out of his book. Had he been asleep? He wasn't sure. He put the book down on the small table next to his bed, and pulled the chain to turn off the bedside lamp. It was still dark outside, and he felt his way through the house without turning on any more lights. At the front door he pulled on a jacket, grabbed the pack with his gear, and walked out to his truck.

The moon was in its last quarter, giving him plenty of light to see to walk, but not enough to see how dirty the truck really was. He needed to wash it, but that wasn't going to happen for a few days. The door handle surprised him by how cold it was. He hoped that the inside of the truck still held a little warmth from last evening, but he was sadly disappointed. It would take most of the drive to the trailhead to warm up again.

At the trailhead, he pulled his truck into the parking lot and left it where it might get a bit of shade in the afternoon. In the dim light of dawn, he could see Luis Aguilera was getting the horses ready. Quiet and competent, Luis was quickly loading up the packs and gear onto the pack mules. He shook Dan's hand, took his pack from him, and pointed to one of the saddle horses. "The black one is yours," he said softly. "That's Old Tom."

Cal Healey came out of the restroom, picked up a coffee cup from a picnic table, and walked over to Dan. "Good morning," he said quietly. "How did you sleep?"

"Not well," admitted Dan, looking around the parking lot at the SAR vehicle, which was now dark. "Who is coming with us today?"

"A couple of young kids," Cal answered. "Do you know Blake Vanden?" Dan shook his head. "His mom is the bank manager in Arnold," Cal explained. "Nice kid … a little too much energy. And Katie Pederson? She's new, but she's good. They're both in the restroom now, but we should be good to go in a minute."

As Dan watched, the two young people came into view and started walking toward them. Almost the same height, the two were strikingly different. Katie strode confidently with the ease of someone who had spent a lot of time playing sports. Her body, while not curvaceous, was tightly packed and powerful. Some people might have called her a bit overweight, but Dan guessed that most of the body was muscle, not fat. Blake's thin features and skinny body gave him a gangly walk, as if the feet were connected not with muscles but with strings. Even in the dim light, Dan could sense the energy that seemed to keep him in motion.

Katie's short, curly blond hair contrasted with Blake's close-cut dark hair and thin, trimmed beard and moustache. The two were smiling and chatting as they walked over.

Luis called Dan over to fit him on Old Tom. He stood ready to help Dan up into the saddle, but Dan managed to get up without needing any help. "This horse is a little tricky," Luis warned him. "If you kick him, you have to kick him way in the back or he'll crow hop." Luis lengthened the stirrups for Dan's long legs and nodded with satisfaction. "Is that good?"

"Seems fine, Luis. Thanks." Dan was still pondering the warning. He had occasionally ridden horses in his career, but he was far from feeling completely comfortable on them. In fact, he had never really been a fan of horses on the trails, and if it weren't for the need to cover a lot of ground on this trip, he would have preferred to go on foot.

On his left, Cal needed some help getting on his horse. The Sheriff's bad knee made it hard for him to get his left leg into the stirrup, but Luis gave him a quick boost. Cal gave a grunt as he adjusted himself on the saddle.

"You going to be okay on that horse, old timer?" Dan asked him with a sympathetic grin.

"As long as I don't have to get on and off him very often, I'll be fine," Cal replied. "Especially early in the morning." He sat in the saddle, slowly rubbing his knee.

Luis quickly had the rest of the team ready to go, and as the gray of dawn eased out of the sky, they followed Luis slowly down across the creek and up the trail toward the backcountry. It would be seven hours before they made camp that night.

The Emigrant Wilderness lies immediately north of Yosemite National Park. It is an impressive mass of granite, and only in a few places is that granite covered by trees. The ridges generally run parallel from northeast to southwest, and the trail today led them up and over three of them.

They climbed a dusty trail through a dense forest from the trailhead on the west side up to the top of the first ridge. Here they suddenly broke out of the forest and into the sun, and a vista extended toward the white granite of the far Sierra crest. Below them the first canyon showed far more granite than trees.

But the trail then descended into Pine Valley, dropping down through volcanic outcroppings into a narrow canyon that had enough soil to support a forest again. Long before the fresh white granite of the Sierra Nevada was pushed up from below, a series of massive volcanic eruptions had covered this area. The peaks in the area around Sonora Pass are almost completely volcanic in nature, and the rocks along the trail above Pine Valley show that the volcanism reached far beyond Sonora Pass.

Once in Pine Valley, the soil thinned out, and so did the trees, leaving more granite exposed. They crossed the creek, now just a trickle in the late season, and climbed briefly to Grouse Lake. Dan had always felt that this was the true beginning of the Emigrant Wilderness—it was the limit of most day-hikers, and from now on there would only be backpackers on the trail. The north side of the lake was worn down by years of horses being tied up there, and it gave the lake a feeling that was much more like a city park than a wilderness.

But from Grouse Lake the trail climbed up a steep notch between two solid granite masses. Here the trail was a beautifully crafted series of steps and ramps, stone fitted together over long stretches of the climb—a stone staircase made by craftsmen fifty years ago. At the top, the trail passed between two huge boulders, and Dan looked back over his shoulder. The view back down the trail reminded Dan of the gates of Hell: the narrow trail leading through the rocks and disappearing into the depths of the canyon below.

Once through the notch, the trail led up through Groundhog Meadow, which was dry this time of year, and then up a short climb over the next ridge. From the top of the crest the next few miles of the trail came into view, leading down into Louse Canyon and the Cherry Creek drainage. Here the trees were few and far between, clinging to the cracks and fissures in the huge granite plates that had been swept clean by glaciers ten thousand years ago. Dan could see the channel of the creek, a huge scar full of boulders along the bottom of the canyon. But the creek was almost bone dry. Only a small trickle showed black against some of the rocks at the very bottom of the channel, more of a shadow than a stream.

The hard granite of Emigrant Wilderness doesn't hold moisture. The snows of the winter melt quickly and turn the streams into roaring torrents. But by mid-summer it's almost a desert. The snow has melted and the water disappears as if it had been washed out of a gigantic granite bathtub. Only the lakes remain—the rivers that were swollen monsters during the snowmelt now creep through the rocks and crevices like small rodents, hiding from sight.

Luis led the horses down the switchbacks into the second deep canyon, and they paused at the bottom for a snack, allowing the horses to drink a little water from the creek. Cal groaned mightily as he was helped off his horse, and took a few minutes to slowly limp around the horses, stretching and slowly bending his knee.

Katie wandered off to find a place to pee, and Blake immediately headed in the other direction to do the same. Cal pointed up the trail to a rock cairn they had passed only minutes ago. "What's that cairn for?" he asked.

"Resasco Lake," Luis answered, then quickly glanced at Dan. "Sorry," he said. Luis clearly felt that he had spoken out of turn in front of the ranger.

Dan chuckled. "For what?" Then he spoke to Cal. "It also takes you to Hyatt Lake, if you go up on the ridge and then follow it down the canyon." He remembered the newlyweds who must have hiked through here yesterday. "I just issued a permit to a couple yesterday for that trip." He wondered how they were doing.

Blake and Katie returned to the group, and Luis led them up the canyon on the north side of the creek. From the trail they could see that during the spring, this creek would be a massive rapid, tearing into the rocks and trees on either side. But now it was barely audible as a trickle, and then only in a few places.

A few miles further up the creek, Luis turned the group off the main trail at another cairn, and they climbed up over a saddle and down into the next canyon. This one was almost solid granite, and the heat from the sun was now warm on their faces. Any hint of a worn trail disappeared, and Luis led them from one cairn to the next across granite slabs that stretched for hundreds of yards. They followed what was now a dry creek bed down the canyon, picking their way between rocks, trees, and granite slabs.

In less than half an hour they came to two huge cairns, piled fully three or four feet high with stones collected from around the area.

Cal, riding in front of Dan, turned around and pointed to the cairns. "Somebody had a little too much time on their hands, huh?" he grinned.

Dan smiled. "Actually, for the back country this is a kind of Grand Central Station," he answered. "This is a big intersection in this part of the park." He pointed west and said, "These aren't maintained trails, only use-trails. But here you've got the trail from Resasco Lake coming down there, and," he gestured in the other direction, "on the other side there's a trail up to Pingree. And we're going south and around the corner to Big Lake. So it all meets right here."

"How do you know which one is which?" Cal asked.

"You pay attention," Dan answered. "It's not really that hard. But we don't call this a trail. For us it's a route—which means there's a way to get there, but we don't maintain it, and we don't sign it. There are routes all over this area that you can take."

Luis led them down the canyon, still following the creek until they came to a narrow section that threaded its way between large boulders. Above them to the east loomed a granite dome, and as they emerged from the boulders the route led them out onto an enormous granite slab that stretched into the distance for hundreds of yards.

Only a few tiny trees dotted the surface of the slab.

They rode in silence for a few minutes, but Katie could not contain herself. "What is this place?" she cried. "This is absolutely amazing!"

"All of this drains down into Cherry Lake," Dan said. "It's just one huge granite bowl, and we'll cross this for about a mile."

The hooves of the horses clattered on the stone, and a few minutes later, Luis pulled to a stop and turned to face them. "Everybody always wants to stop here," he said, waving to the granite that stretched in every direction.

"What do you call it?" Katie asked him.

Dan explained that there wasn't a name for the area, but that everyone who took this trail knew about it. "It's just one solid sheet of granite. If we just walked down that slope to the south, we would end up in Cherry Lake … about ten miles away. And up there, above all of that to the south—that's where Yosemite starts. That's Styx Pass."

Cal reacted with a start. "Isn't that where they found that mule Tony was telling us about last night?" he asked.

Dan agreed. "Yeah. That must have been a tough mule, huh? There is nothing here but rock."

There was no trail. Luis led them across the granite sheet for over a mile, and then down into Big Lake. After a short rest there, he insisted that they mount up again, so that they could get to Yellowhammer Lake to camp.

An hour later they arrived at the camp, where an old cattle ranch cabin and corral stood near meadows and the inlet to Yellowhammer Lake. Luis quickly took control of the horses, and the rest of the group began to unpack their equipment. After so many hours on the trail, they moved slowly and carefully, but still managed to get their camp set up within a few minutes.

Once Dan had his tent up and his gear inside, he went to offer help to Luis with the horses.

"No, that's okay," Luis said. "I have it under control. It's easier this way." So Dan stood by and watched Luis efficiently tie off the horses and settle them down.

At one point, as Luis carried a saddle across the small corral, he stopped and looked right at Dan. "You don't have a name for that place with all the rock?" Luis asked Dan.

"Nope," Dan shook his head. "Not on the maps, anyway."

"Because I do," Luis continued. "It's where you see the rock that's underneath everything. It's the bones, man. *Los huesos de la tierra'*—the bones of the Earth."

chapter 6

The two young SAR members quickly had the camp set up, and Dan was a little amused to see how they worked together. He was used to being out on his own, and having the extra help made the whole process seem to fly. The kids knew what they were doing, and it seemed like they enjoyed showing off a bit for Dan and Cal.

"That ought to do it," Blake said as he used a rock to hammer the last tent stake into place. "If you guys want to put your gear in the tent, we're good to go."

Katie pulled the rain fly taut, and stood up with her hands on her hips. She looked around the campsite, then back at Dan. "Do you want to get everything out of the packs now?" she asked. "Or wait until later?"

Dan checked his watch and looked at the sun. There were still many hours of daylight left, even if they had been on the trail most of the day. From behind him he heard Cal give a small groan.

Dan turned and looked at Cal, who was sitting on a log near the fire pit. "Are you okay?" he asked the Sheriff.

"Oh yeah, I'm peachy," Cal replied with sarcasm. "And I can see by the way you just looked at the sun that you're not planning to take the rest of the day off, are you?" While he talked he slowly flexed his left knee back and forth. "It's pretty nice right here, you know."

"Well," Dan considered. "It's only about a mile to where they saw these bones, and we could just go up and look around. That would give us a better idea of what we have to do tomorrow." He paused, waiting to see how Cal would take this, but the Sheriff showed no reaction. The two younger SAR team members waited expectantly. "And it would also let us give Luis a better idea of his schedule, as well."

Cal gave out an exaggerated sigh and shook his head. "That is a great idea," he grunted, with a complete lack of enthusiasm. He slowly rocked backwards on the log and stretched his torso first one direction, then the other. "And when you say a mile, I am assuming that mile is straight up the side of a cliff?"

Dan chuckled and walked over to his pack and opened up the top of his pack. From the top level of the pack he pulled out the stack of printouts from the Bartletts, stored in a plastic bag to keep them dry. With the photos in his hand he sat down next to Cal on the log. He knew that if he could get Cal interested in the problem of navigation, it would help motivate him to get up off the log.

Katie Pederson walked around the fire pit and stood over the two men, unfolding a large topo map and orienting it to their current position. Blake took a position next to Katie, where he could look at her map and still see the photos held by Dan below. He pointed to the old cattle camp and said, "So here is where we are: Yellowhammer camp."

Dan stared at the photos with his notes on them. "Yeah, and we're going to have to go up the canyon a bit first … maybe a couple hundred yards … and then find this ramp of granite that slopes up to the right …"

"Yeah," Blake agreed eagerly. "You can see that here on the map, too. It goes up for maybe a few hundred feet?"

"And then there should be a little plateau, towards the cliff from there?" Dan asked him.

Katie and Blake nodded. "Yep—you can see that here, too."

Blake craned his head to look up the canyon, then took a few steps to his right to get a clearer view. "Well, you can't really see it from here," he said, "but it should be right up there." He pointed with his hand up above them.

Dan paused, looking sideways at Cal. Cal met his gaze, and shrugged.

"Shit. I guess we ought to go see about that, huh?" Cal said.

Dan got up, smiling to himself. "Yeah, I guess we'd better do that," he said.

While Katie folded up the map, Blake struck out smartly along the use-trail out of the cattle camp and up the canyon. The trail wandered through open granite and meadow, occasionally through a few thin stands of trees. In the granite sections there were few cairns to guide them, and Blake just continued to follow a general heading up the canyon and along the foot of the cliff. Almost imperceptibly, the slope of the granite began to steepen, and within a few hundred feet they were on the granite ramp, and slowly climbing out of the canyon floor. The scraggly forest blocked their view to the south and west, but the cliff above them was now fully visible.

Blake strode ahead, steadily climbing up the ramp, with Katie only a few steps behind. Dan, sensitive to Cal's stiff knee, held back a bit to keep pace with the Sheriff. And when he heard Cal stop for a breath, Dan pulled out the photos and called out to the two young SAR members.

"Do you see the plateau yet?" he asked them. Dan could see where it must be from where he stood, but he hoped that by asking them the question, he would encourage them to stop and respond. And they did.

Blake turned around and pointed up the slope. "It looks like it's right there," he said. But he also noticed how far back Dan and Cal were, and took the opportunity to look around below him. "This is amazing country!" he said. He took a sip from his water hose, and made a quiet comment to Katie, who was only a few feet below him.

Dan turned to see if Cal was ready to move on. The Sheriff gave him a nod and started hiking up the granite again. "You know," Cal said, "those two kids are too fucking young to be out here with us."

Dan laughed out loud. "Yeah," he agreed. "But only because they make us look bad." He was still smiling as his breaths got deeper with the effort of climbing up the slope.

"That's plenty of reason for me," Cal replied. "We're going to have to do something about this later."

"The only problem with that," Dan said, "is that we're going to have to catch them first."

They did finally catch up with Blake and Katie, but only after the younger two had arrived at the small flat plateau above the granite ramp. A few trees had taken root in the shallow soil of the flat area. Dan wondered if it had ever been a tiny pond at one point, or if it was simply a flatter slope that had filled in with soil washed down from above. From the massive boulders pushing through the ground he knew that it could not have been a very deep pond.

Blake and Katie were seated on one of the larger boulders, and they had clearly caught their breath by the time Dan and Cal arrived. Dan sat down on a nearby rock and pulled out the photos again. Blake was quickly on his feet so that he could look over Dan's shoulder and study the scene. Cal sat down heavily next to Katie and took a huge breath, trying to get his heart rate back under control. And then took another.

"So now we work our way back along this ledge here," Blake said, comparing the landscape to what he could see in the photos. He grew silent as his eyes followed the granite up to the top of the cliffs above him.

"How far up did they say they climbed?" Cal asked.

"We still have a ways to go," Dan answered. "They said that there were some deer trails through some of that manzanita that they followed for a while …" He, too, grew silent as he tried to see a path through the imposing cliffs above.

"Are we sure we're in the right place so far?" Katie asked.

"Yeah, I think so," said Dan. "So let's just take it one step at a time. Next stop is that ledge that runs up there. I can't see how far it goes, but once we get up there, we can check again."

Blake once again led the way, but this time the going was much harder, and the four were quickly strung out along the route. Instead of walking for fifty or a hundred feet, they were now moving in much shorter pitches, sometimes only five or ten feet before taking a breath and looking around. As they moved, each one looked for a better path up the cliff, trying to avoid the densest bushes and the steepest rock faces. The heat from the granite radiated back against them, and all four were gasping for breath.

Dan lost sight of Blake working ahead of him on the slope, whacking through the manzanita that grew wherever there was a tiny bit of soil for its roots to grab. He could see Katie above him, moving slowly through the bushes. And behind him, Cal struggled up the side of the cliff, swearing under his breath at the way the sharp branches of manzanita scratched at his legs. Dan could see sweat dripping down the Sheriff's reddened face.

"This sucks," Cal said.

"At least we're not doing it with packs," responded Katie from above. "That would be really hard work …" She had paused to take a breath and was standing out on a boulder that allowed her to enjoy the view.

They heard Blake's voice from above them. "Okay, I think we need to look at those photos again," he called out. "Is there some kind of a landmark up here that I'm supposed to be looking for?"

Dan could see Blake's head sticking up out of the bushes above him. "Well, I think you may be past the ledge they went up. What do you see up there?" he asked.

"Not much," admitted Blake. "This is pretty rough up here. And I don't see where to go from here … It's really steep."

Katie had stopped below him, in the middle of a large clump of manzanita. To go further she would have to push through it with brute force, and Dan could see that she was thinking over that decision.

"Wait a second, Katie," he called out to her. "Let's take a look at these maps and see where we are." She looked relieved when she heard his suggestion and walked back toward him.

Dan pushed through one last stretch of manzanita and joined Katie in a small clearing on the side of the mountain. He pulled out his package of photos and thumbed through the prints. The photos taken from Yellowhammer camp clearly showed where they had to go, but it was impossible to see that from where they were now on the cliff. He handed the first few photos to Katie and pulled out two photos taken on the cliff.

Dan stared at the photos, hoping to see some identifiable landmark in either one. The first photo showed a powerfully shaped obelisk of granite standing out above the manzanita. Dan handed that photo to Katie and said, "Here, try to find that rock."

Dan took the other photos and studied them. There was a stunted tree in this one that leaned into the cliff, its crown formed much like the rock around it by the wind and elements on the face of the granite. Dan scanned the cliff above and below, hoping to recognize the tree somewhere nearby.

Katie was holding her photo up in front of her face, comparing it to the landscape in front of her. "Hmmm, I'm not seeing what I want to see," she said.

"What am I looking for?" Blake yelled down to them.

"A rock. Or a tree," Katie responded, knowing that it wasn't helping.

"Yeah, thanks," said Blake. "That's helpful."

Dan continued to scan the cliff. He reached out and took the photo from Katie and held it out in front of himself … lining it up with a section of cliff above them.

Katie looked at the photo and followed Dan's eyes towards the cliff. "I don't see it," she said.

From somewhere below them they heard Cal Healey's exasperated voice. "Ah, shit!"

"What's wrong, Cal?" Dan asked. "Are you okay?"

"I'm fine," Cal said with a tone of pure disgust.

"So what's up?" Dan asked, still not looking down towards where the Sheriff was standing below them.

"Well … you guys are up. Too far up," Cal answered. "Because I've got bones down here, a lot of bones." After a pause he added, "A boot. A hiking boot with bones coming out of it."

chapter 7

Dan could hear Cal's slightly raspy voice from somewhere below him, and he tried to lean out from the slope to see where the Sheriff might be. The clouds of manzanita bushes covered most of the rock, so that it looked like a turbulent sea of pale grey-green leaves. He couldn't see Cal.

Behind him, Dan could hear Katie moving. Suddenly he heard her slip, and as he turned he felt her hand grabbing his shoulder from above. He reached out his arms toward her, holding them stiffly to support her, with that awkward movement that men use to avoid touching women inappropriately.

Katie's feet continued to slip on the gravel, and she grabbed Dan's left arm with both of her hands. She slowly sat down against the slope, her feet coming to rest on top of Dan's, her breasts pressing into his arm.

"Are you okay?" he asked.

"Oh yeah. Just great," Katie responded with a sarcastic grin. "Just a little embarrassed."

Dan stepped carefully to the side, to allow Katie room to stand up. She was still holding onto his arm as she pulled herself to her feet. "Can you see where he is?" she asked.

Dan shook his head. "It sounds like he is over there," he said, pointing to the west. "But I can't see how to get there from here."

The only possible path they could follow was the one they had taken up the slope, and so Dan slowly began to work his way back down it. Katie paused for a few minutes to check her arms and legs for scratches, then crept down after him.

"Over here, guys!" Cal's voice called to them. "Instead of climbing up the rocks, just follow the ledge below you." And then, with a tiny note of satisfaction in his voice, he added, "I figured that's what a couple of older backpackers would have done … you guys were being way too energetic."

Dan remembered the ledge now. He had struggled to get up the faint dirt- and gravel-covered deer track that led him away from it. Now he stood above it, wondering just exactly how much traction he would have as he eased down to the ledge.

Not enough, as it turned out. His right foot slipped out from under him, and by the time he had regained control, he was sitting on the ground, his legs out in front of him, and he had come down hard on his right hand.

"Are you okay?" This time it was Katie's turn to ask the question.

Dan tried to rub the gravel out of the palm of his right hand while he took stock of his aches and pains. His right wrist felt sore, but he didn't think it was broken. And his butt was bruised where it had come down hard on the ledge. "I'm fine," he said disgustedly, and then rose, slowly and painfully, to his feet. "Just a little embarrassed."

"Well, you made me feel better," Katie said with a smile. "Now I'm not the only one to have slipped up here." Above them, they heard Blake crash through the bushes and then swear loudly.

"Are you having fun up there?" Cal called out to him. "I hope you people don't kill yourselves. Because I'm not going to carry you out of here."

To Katie under his breath, Dan muttered, "With his knees, he'd be lucky to get himself out of here if he had to hike."

Dan offered his hand to Katie, who managed to get down to the ledge without slipping. Dan now saw why he hadn't followed it the first time. A large manzanita had grown out, nearly blocking it completely. He pushed on through the bush, scraping his legs as he did so. In another few steps the ledge opened up again, and he could see Cal kneeling on the ground ahead of him.

Cal turned and held up his hand, covered with a plastic glove, to slow Dan down. "There is a lot of stuff here," he said. "Be careful where you walk."

Dan eased up behind Cal and felt Katie close behind. He could see the boot now. Old and weathered, it still had its laces tied in a double knot, he noticed. From the top of the boot a thin white bone extended up to end in a knob where it would have joined the knee. The sole was surprisingly new-looking: the waffle pattern was very distinct.

And it was small. A small boot, from a small person. Dan noted a sad, hollow feeling in his gut.

Cal was still bent over the ground, slowly marking each bone as he found it. The granite ledge had widened here, and there was a hard surface of very fine decomposed granite that covered most of it. Only on the downhill side did the rough granite show through. It was as if there was a small pool of gravel that had formed behind that ridge. That was where Cal had knelt.

Dan pulled out a package of small plastic tags that he handed to Cal. "Put one of these on each bone, so that we can ID them."

Cal glanced up briefly, then took the tags from Dan while returning to his study of the dirt. One by one he started placing a tag near each small white bone.

Dan felt Katie ease around behind him, and then work her way to his left, onto the granite. "I am going to creep out over here and work my way further along the ledge," she said. "Can you give me some of those tags, too?"

Dan handed her a package of the tags. From behind him he could hear Blake pushing by the manzanita. Blake swore again, this time more quietly. He announced his arrival with a deep sigh to the group.

"I've got a camera here, so I am going to start taking pictures," Dan said. He turned to Blake. "Why don't you take a look directly uphill here, and see if you can find anything," he said, taking advantage of the young man's energy

Blake stared at the wall of manzanita above him, then glanced back at Dan. When Dan made no comment, Blake worked his hands into the manzanita and began to look through the bushes at the ground below.

"Hey, guys," Katie called out from her position further out on the ledge. "I think this is where … most of the bones are … I can see ribs … and the pelvis." She was now a bit above them, as the ledge rose steeply up to the tree that the Bartletts had used as a landmark. Dan now recognized it, even though it hadn't been so obvious from only a few yards up the slope.

Dan turned to Blake and suggested that he go up to help Katie. "Let's not move anything yet," Dan called out to them. "Let's just see what we can find, and I'll photograph it all. It's going to take some time to do that. And tomorrow we'll come back and collect everything."

He pulled out his camera and began taking photos. Cal often pointed to one bone or the other, helping Dan set the shot. The two men worked almost wordlessly for fifteen or twenty minutes. Dan slowly worked his way past Cal so that he wasn't shooting the photos into the sun. The two men could hear Katie and Blake, further up on the ledge, talking quietly between themselves, but could rarely make out the topic of the conversation.

Cal held his hands wide in a gesture of surrender. "I think that's all we've got here," he said. "Quite a few bones, but all very small.

Maybe mostly from a foot or something?" He looked up at Dan with raised eyebrows.

Dan nodded. His eyes followed the ledge up to his left, and he tried to imagine what had happened. "If Katie's got most of the big stuff up there, then this might have fallen down as the body decomposed," he said.

Katie heard him talking and spoke up. "Dan, we have most of the body here by this tree. We've got arms and ribcage, pelvis, vertebrae … some of this stuff is covered with manzanita leaves or duff from the tree, but we're just clearing it off carefully, and leaving the bones in place."

"Thanks, Katie," Dan replied. "Any obvious trauma?"

Katie thought about this for a moment. "A broken arm, maybe? I guess that could be fatal out here … if you couldn't get back to the trailhead. But this was a female, I know that."

Dan and Cal glanced at each other. "Really? You can tell from the bones?" Dan asked.

"Not exactly," Katie admitted. "But I can tell that there are scraps of clothing on the torso. And it looks to me like some of those are parts of a bra. I don't know what else it could be. And jean cut-offs, I think."

Blake spoke up. "We don't see the skull, Dan. The ribs are here, and the scapulae … but the skull may be further down the cliff."

Dan looked up, and Blake began an explanation. "The body looks like it was pretty much here," he said, waving his arms to show where it would have been. "But the feet look like they fell off further down the ledge. That's where Cal found them. And the head might have gone down the cliff on the other side of this tree."

"Can you get down there?" Cal asked. "Have you looked for it?"

Blake paused for a minute while he examined the scene. With his left arm he held onto the trunk of the twisted juniper tree, and swung the rest of his body around it to look down the cliff from there.

"It's pretty damn steep!" he said. "I'm guessing that it's another seventy-five feet or so to the next ledge." He paused again. "And I can't see anything on that ledge, either. There's one small spot closer up that's covered in crap from the tree. Might be there. Or it might be another couple hundred feet down… and just about anywhere at that point."

"Okay," Dan said. "Don't do anything stupid up there … just get back down, and we'll look tomorrow. Does it look like it might be easier to work our way up from below?" he asked Blake.

"Yeah, maybe. Let me plug in the GPS for this tree, and that will give us something to work off tomorrow."

A few minutes later they had all assembled on the ledge.

"So tomorrow we'll get up early, come up here, and collect all that we can," Dan said. "Let's just leave things as they are for tonight. And maybe mark the route a little on the way down, so we don't lose any time looking for it?"

"I'll take care of that," Blake said.

Katie pulled a roll of plastic tape out of her backpack. "I'll help. Let's use this. It's easier to see than a cairn … and easier to use." The two of them edged past Cal and Dan and started to walk back down toward camp.

Cal glanced at Dan and smiled. "I've got a fishing rod in that pack down there. Wanna join me? I figure there ought to be some fish around here somewhere …"

"Yeah, maybe," Dan replied. "I'm just going to take a few more pictures here first. I'll be down in a few minutes."

"Well, with my old knees you'll probably pass me on the way down anyway," Cal said. "See you when we get there."

Dan watched Cal ease his way along the ledge, and then past the manzanita. He would wait here for a few minutes, not so much to take pictures, but to think.

He could feel the slight afternoon breeze cooling him off, evaporating the sweat that had soaked his shirt on the climb up. The breeze caught his attention, and he looked out over the huge stony expanse of Cherry Creek Canyon. He could see a few trees moving slightly in the breeze, but aside from that there was no other motion.

The smooth rock extended for miles, and Dan considered that it was possible they were the only group hiking in the whole canyon. He looked up the steep slope above them. He could see no way to get up that cliff if you were wearing a pack. You would need ropes and experience to get up something like that. He wondered about the woman who wore the boot. What had happened? Had she been attacked by an animal? Or had she been climbing up? Or fallen down?

And where was the other boot?

chapter 8

As Dan looked back down over the canyon, he could see a slender thread of smoke rising up from Yellowhammer camp. That would be Luis, starting up the fire and getting things ready for dinner. The shadows were lengthening as the sun lowered in the west, and the granite was taking on a softer, more golden tone.

He was in no hurry to get back to camp. As he picked his way down through the granite ledges and manzanita bushes, he couldn't help thinking about what he had seen on the cliff above him. It was an isolated spot, and if the Bartletts hadn't been wandering around without any clear idea of where they were going, those bones could have stayed there for another hundred years without anyone noticing them.

But Dan wasn't thinking about the bones, per se. He was thinking about the person. The woman, he corrected himself. It was a woman who somehow found herself in a very remote section of the wilderness. And died. Did she die quickly, or slowly? He didn't like to think of her on that ledge, suffering, so far from anyone else, as she faced death.

He slowed his pace as he worked down the long granite ramp. There was nothing in camp that required his attention, and he wasn't in the mood for much conversation. Above the canyon to his left, hanging over the crest of the Sierra, was a large pale moon, three-quarters full as it rose into the sky. The sight was so beautiful that he stopped just to enjoy it for a few minutes. He thought of trying to capture it in a photograph, but decided that it would almost certainly fall short of the reality. He turned and continued on towards camp.

As he got closer to camp he could smell the sharp tang of wood smoke in the air. When he backpacked, Dan never made a fire. He cooked over a tiny but much more efficient gas stove, and he didn't like the profusion of fire rings that now dotted every possible campsite in the wilderness.

But Luis came from a different culture, a different sensibility, and Dan knew that. For Luis, a camp without a fire was a sad and lonely place. Right now, the last thing Dan wanted to do was make this camp any sadder or lonelier.

Luis was tending the fire, and he had a pot of water perched between some rocks. To the side Dan could see that he had most of the fixings for dinner laid out on one of the rough tables that had been built at the campsite. There was no sign of any of the others.

"Where is everyone?" Dan asked.

Luis tossed one more piece of wood on the fire, and then straightened up to answer Dan. "Cal is fishing at the lake. I told him I have a pan for those fish, if he catches them. And Katie said she was going to the creek to wash herself." He waved his right hand toward the meadows where the creek flowed slowly before entering the lake.

"And Blake?" Dan asked.

"I think he is in the tent," Luis responded, nodding towards a bright yellow tent on the edge of the clearing. Then he looked at Dan. "Everybody was very quiet when they came here," he said. "And a little bit sad."

"Yeah," Dan replied. "We found a body up there. It's been there quite a while, but still …"

Dan felt Luis' eyes staring at him, until the tall ranger felt a little uncomfortable with the silence. "I guess I'm feeling that way too," he added.

Luis nodded and turned toward the food. *"Qué pena,"* he said, shaking his head sadly.

Dan went to peer over Luis' shoulder to see what might be on the menu.

"I'm making you some fajitas," Luis said. He pointed with his knife to the array of ingredients on the table. "With some peppers and some meat … and onions." He glanced at Dan. "It's gonna be good, and make everybody feel better," he added with a quick nod.

Dan smiled. "It looks terrific, Luis. I can hardly wait. I'm going to go down to the lake and see if I can find Cal. What time is this all going to be ready?"

"I don't know … maybe half an hour," said Luis. "But don't worry. Whenever you want. It's gonna be good all night long."

Dan smiled and walked past the old wooden buildings of Yellowhammer camp, toward the lake. The sun was just dropping behind the ridge to the west, so his path along the creek went from shade to sun, and back again. Just above the lake he found a place to cross over the creek, stepping from the bank onto a log, and then getting his left foot slightly wet as he stepped onto the moist sand on the far side. He shook the leg quickly and tried to keep as much of the water as possible from seeping into his boot.

From there the trail led up over a series of boulders overlooking the lake. From the top of the first little climb Dan could see down the narrow lake, the water glistening in the late afternoon sun. On either side, rounded lumps of granite extended down into the water, leaving no room for soil or a beach.

Dan spotted Cal a hundred yards down the lake on the left-hand side, standing on a particularly low granite finger that stuck out into the lake. As Dan watched, Cal reeled in his lure, took a brief glance at it on the end of his rod, and then casually flipped it back out into the water again. He waited a few seconds, then slowly began the retrieve.

It took Dan another fifteen minutes to clamber over the rocks and around the cliffs to get to Cal. If Dan had been walking east and west, he could have followed a single tongue of rock for hundreds of yards, in line with the glaciation that had scored the landscape. But in this direction, the trail wound around one block, over another, and led back to the lake, only to climb again over the next block.

At least twice Dan was sure that the next finger of rock would be the one where Cal was fishing, only to be disappointed. When he finally arrived, he was well above Cal, and stepped carefully down the granite to join the Sheriff.

"Catch anything?" he asked.

"A couple," Cal said quietly. He didn't seem excited about it.

Dan's eyes searched the shoreline, looking for a stringer of fish. "Rainbows?"

"Yeah," Cal replied again, without looking at Dan. His eyes were focused on the lake where his line disappeared into the water.

"Are you keeping any?" Dan asked.

Cal didn't answer. He reeled in the lure and lifted it out of the water. He shook the rod tip once, to clear off a tiny bit of algae on the lure, then cast it out again. He gave a long sigh. "Nope, I'm not," he said quietly, slowly shaking his head.

Dan looked at Cal, waiting for him to continue. Dan's eyes drifted over the deep blue surface of the lake, where it reflected the High Sierra sky. Where the shadows of the granite fell, the water was almost black, like obsidian.

With a grunt, Cal reacted to a tug on the line, and his rod bowed with the pull of a fish. He reeled in vigorously, and a bright trout leaped into the air forty feet out into the lake.

"Nice fish," said Dan.

Cal nodded, and continued to reel the fish in. "Yeah," he agreed. "This is about like the other two ..." The fish flashed bright gold in the water, now just under the rock in front of Cal. Taking the rod in his right hand, he hoisted the glittering fish out of the water. The rod bent into an arc as the trout flapped and fluttered on the end of the line. Cal deftly reached out his left hand and grabbed the trout, then tucked the rod under his right arm. Within seconds, he had freed the hook and tossed the fish back into the water.

Cal paused, turning to look at Dan. "Do you want a try?" he asked the ranger.

Dan thought briefly before shaking his head. "Nah, not today. Thanks. Besides, I'm more of a fly-fishing guy." He reconsidered his answer. "But that's not the reason. I'm just not in the mood today…"

Cal nodded. "Yep, I figured you were a fly fisherman." He flicked the lure back out into the water.

"Luis says that dinner will be ready in a few minutes," Dan said gently. He didn't want Cal to stop fishing if he didn't want to do so. "But there's no hurry." He watched Cal slowly reel in again. When the lure came out of the water, Cal tossed another cast out into the lake. To Dan it seemed like a kind of therapy. Toss the lure out, reel it in, over and over. The fish, if hooked, were more a distraction than a reward.

Cal reeled the lure in one last time and turned to face Dan. "I guess we better go, then," he said. "I'm not really in the mood today either."

Dan waved Cal forward, inviting him to lead the way along the twisting, torturous trail back to the camp. "I once pulled a treble hook out of a kid's keister up by Disaster Creek," he said by way of explanation. "So I always let the guy with the fish hooks go first."

The two men walked silently through the granite, weaving their way along the rocks. When they reached the head of the lake, Cal stopped for a moment to study the creek and how to cross it. He waved his hand upstream. "I crossed up there on the way in," he said. "And I got my feet wet. Do you have a better plan?"

Dan pointed to his own footprint, deep in the sand in front of them. It had now filled with water. "That's where I crossed. I'm not sure it's much better."

Cal strode forward, stepping firmly into the soft sand and stepping awkwardly onto the log. "It may not be better, but it's shorter," he said.

Dan paused at the creek, looking for a drier spot for his first step. Cal turned and watched as Dan tried a different place, with the same result. Now both of Dan's feet were wet. He sighed disgustedly and shook his foot, then looked at Cal.

"You know what I don't get?" Cal asked him, his voice tense. His eyes caught Dan's and held them. "The other shoe. Where the hell's the other boot? There is one boot with most of the foot in it. And most of those bones I found up there were small, like from the other foot. So where is the other boot?"

Dan shook his head. "I don't know, Cal. We'll just have to look for it tomorrow." Cal turned and continued on towards camp. They walked the rest of the way in silence.

They arrived in camp to the sound of the food sizzling on the grill, and delicious smells wafting through the air.

"Hey!" Luis called. "Where's the fish?"

"No fish tonight, Luis," Cal replied with a thin smile. "I think they wanted us to eat your food instead."

Katie was at the fire, wielding a fork to move things around on the grill. Her short blond curls looked as if they had been freshly washed, and her spirits seemed to have revived as well.

Blake was by his tent, slipping on his shoes to join them. As Dan watched, the young man stretched, then wiggled and rolled his head around a few times. He shrugged his shoulders once, and then got up and walked over to the fire.

Luis stepped in and started serving the food, heaping each plate with warm tortillas, brightly colored peppers, and strips of beef.

Within minutes they were all sitting on logs around the fire. The only noises to be heard were the small crackles from the fire, and the satisfied sounds of hungry people eating.

Katie broke the silence. "Luis, this is incredible." The others grunted in agreement.

Luis grinned. "We eat like this every night at my house," he said proudly.

"Yeah, but you don't invite us," Blake said with a grin.

With the food, the conversation came back to life, and Blake, Katie and Luis bantered back and forth through many fajitas.

Dan sat a bit further from the fire, on a flat rock that had been dragged there, many years ago, to serve as another seat. He was content to sit back from the fire and enjoy the food and camaraderie of the young people. Only later in the evening did he stop to think that Cal had been uncharacteristically silent. True, he had demolished fajita after fajita, but now the Sheriff sat on a log on the smoky side of the fire, across from the rest of the group. From time to time he waved his hand in front of his face to clear the smoke. But often he just sat and stared.

At first Dan thought that he was staring into the fire, but now he realized that Cal was not staring at the fire. He was staring across the fire, toward Katie. Katie was leaning back, with her feet propped up on the rocks that formed the fire pit.

Cal was staring at the soles of Katie's boots.

chapter 9

Dan woke up before sunrise. The camp was lit by the soft gray light of dawn. He could hear a few birds in the trees, letting each other know that they had made it through the night. And somewhere nearby a squirrel or chipmunk was scampering around. Dan could hear the quick scratches it made on a tree or log. He wondered if it was worth getting up to make sure that none of their packs were getting nibbled, then decided it really wasn't worth the trouble.

Next to him in the tent, Cal was snoring lightly. Dan checked his watch: 6:15. He looked out through the bug screen, trying to see if the sun was hitting any of the ridges higher above the canyon, but from where he was, he couldn't tell. And he didn't want to get up quite yet—not because he wasn't ready, but because he knew it would wake Cal. And it had been a hard night for Cal. Dan had felt him toss and turn most of the night.

He checked for his clothes in the tent. Everything he planned to wear was alongside his sleeping bag on the right-hand side of the tent. On a cold morning, Dan would climb into those clothes without taking off his t-shirt and shorts that he wore to sleep in. But by the feel of the air on his face, he could tell this wasn't going to be necessary today. It was already above fifty degrees, and would only get warmer once the sun hit the camp.

Now Dan could hear movement in one of the other tents, and then the high-pitched noise of a zipper on nylon. That was probably

Luis.

Slowly, as quietly as he could, Dan eased his arms out of his sleeping bag and pulled his clothes up towards the head of the bag. He unzipped the bag slowly and slid up as far as he could, then slipped off his shorts into the bag.

Cal's eyes opened, briefly giving Dan a stare that looked like a scowl, then took a quick glance around outside the tent. Cal's arm came up out of his bag, and he looked at his watch, then scowled at Dan again, and rolled over to go back to sleep.

Dan quickly dressed and got out of the tent just in time to see Luis climbing out of his. The two exchanged silent greetings and got to work. By the time the rest of crew was up and dressed, Dan and Luis had breakfast ready, and Dan had a plan for the day. He explained that they would spend the morning doing a final search and then collecting all the items they had marked, including bones, fabric, and any other items at the site.

"Are we going to try and get back to the trailhead tonight?" Blake asked.

"I don't think so," Dan said. "Sorry to disappoint you, but I think we probably still have to explore above and below that site some more. We don't know how that woman got there, but I think it makes sense to look and see if we can find anything that might tell us more about what happened."

Cal looked at Dan with a bemused expression. "That's a pretty good climb going up from there," he said. "It might be easier just to hike around, and then rappel down that from above."

Dan nodded. "I thought about that." He looked at the two younger SAR team members. "Do either of you have any climbing experience, other than what they gave you in training?"

Katie's eyes opened wide as she responded. "I've done some climbing. Mainly indoors, but I love it!"

Dan wasn't sure that climbing in a gym was the best preparation for big granite. He looked at Blake, who shrugged. "I've always thought it was easier to go down than up," Blake said drily.

"Okay, let's get up there and see how it looks," Dan said. "If we think we can do it, I'd like to climb up from the body as far as we can … just to see what else we find. And maybe, Blake, you can rappel down from there with the same idea." Blake nodded. "But first we have to take care of collecting everything we've found so far."

"Luis, we may want to move tonight," Dan told the packer. "But I'm not quite sure where yet. Let's just leave everything set up. If we decide to move, we'll help you pack it up. We might as well let you have this morning off."

Tidying up camp with five people all pitching in was quick work. Within a few minutes they were ready to head back up to the bones. Dan noticed that Katie was wearing shorts today. They were a bit shorter than most people wore these days, and they fit her well. Her tanned, muscular legs still bore a few scratches from yesterday's struggles through the manzanita.

She caught him looking at her legs, and he smiled with embarrassment. "That manzanita scratched you up a bit," he said. She gave a short laugh and looked down at her legs. "Yeah, I guess I won't be wearing a short skirt to the disco tonight."

At the mention of a dance, Cal gave a groan and slowly rose off the log to join them. "Let's get going before I get any sorer," he said.

It was still early, but the warmth of the sun on the granite quickly got rid of any chill. Within minutes Dan was aware that he was sweating as he followed Blake and Katie up the smooth ramp. This time there was no time wasted in finding the bones. Blake led them there without hesitation.

While Cal slowly kneeled and began to collect the bones from the clearing below the ledge, Blake and Katie took their places up above and began collecting and labeling what they found up there.

Dan continued to photograph as much as he could.

Cal finished first, and he placed the collection of little bags in the shade under a manzanita bush and stood up beside Dan. There was no point in trying to help Katie and Blake, as there was no room on the ledge for more people.

"I've been thinking about that boot," Cal said to Dan.

Dan was looking west, where a smooth section of granite extended around the edge of the mountain. He could feel the sun warm the back of his shirt. "I know you have," Dan said. "I think you were dreaming about it last night."

"It just strikes me as odd that one boot is here," Cal said, "with the rest of the bones, and all tightly tied, double knot and all. And so where is the other one? I mean, I am pretty sure that these bones are the other foot." He pointed to his packages on the ground.

Dan shook his head. "Who knows? Maybe an animal found it, or took it. Once we get this part wrapped up we can spend a little more time looking for it."

"Well, I'm going to look for it now," Cal said. "Unless you need me for something, I'm going to look down here through this manzanita. Besides, I'm not going to be the one who is climbing anything today. Or rappelling, if I can help it."

Dan chuckled. "Fair enough. I'll go see how these guys are doing on the ledge."

When Dan had climbed the twenty feet up onto the ledge, he could see that Katie was very carefully picking out fabric and bones from the duff around the roots of the tree. Blake was leaning out over the granite on the far side of the tree, his face intent on what was below.

"How are you guys doing?" Dan asked.

Katie nodded toward a large bag near Dan's feet. "I think we've got everything in there except this part right here," she said, pointing at her feet with a plastic glove. She wiped her forehead with the back of her wrist.

"Do you need some help?" Dan asked.

"There really isn't room here for someone to help," Katie answered, her fingers going back to work. "That's why Blake is up there."

"What do you see, Blake?" Dan called to him.

"There's a kind of a pocket, a little place just a few feet down from here," Blake answered. "I'd like to check that out. And after that, it's a long way down to anyplace else. It's all pretty slick granite. It would probably be better to come at it from below, if we can get through the talus down there."

"Do you need a rope to get down there?" Dan asked.

Blake studied the rock carefully. "Maybe not," he said thoughtfully.

"Blake, I don't want to have to rescue you, or recover your body," Dan said. "Don't do anything stupid."

Blake turned his head to look back at Dan. The sun was bright on his face, and Dan could barely see Blake's eyes under the dark shadow of the bill of his cap. Blake's trimmed thin beard and moustache showed the effects of a couple of days without shaving. Dan couldn't read the young man's face.

"We've got all day up here," Dan reminded him. "Let's do it right."

Katie interrupted to ask Blake to help her move some of the more delicate fabric. Dan watched as they carefully transferred it into one of the waiting bags. He smiled. He wasn't sure that Katie really needed to ask for Blake's help, but he understood perfectly why she had done so. Blake was now firmly back on the ledge, in both body and mind.

"I think that's about it, Dan," Katie said.

"Okay," Dan replied. "How many bags do you have?"

"I counted everything we did yesterday and today," Katie

answered. "I think we have something like 195 or 196? And there are around 200 bones in a human body. We've got most of them."

For the second time on the trip, Dan was impressed with Katie's approach and knowledge.

"If you can back yourself down and get out of the way," Katie continued, "we'll carry this all down to where Cal is, and then you can take a look."

Dan was anxious to do exactly that, and once the two SAR team members had come off the ledge, he quickly climbed up and scouted the situation. The ledge was narrow, only eighteen inches wide in places, and the outside edge had worn to a rounded shape. Only the tree had kept this body from falling even further down the slope.

As he looked up from beneath the tree, the branches made it hard to see, but what he did see was impressive: a solid wall of granite that slowly curved up out of sight. Somewhere up above was the top of the ridge, and beyond that the lakes, and beyond that a trail back to the trailhead. But all he could see above was white granite and a deep blue sky. It was hard to tell how far up it went. He guessed it was almost certainly more than one hundred and fifty feet.

Was it climbable?

Below him Dan saw the slope of the granite ease up, and become less steep, but that was at least one hundred feet below the tree. At the foot of the slope was a pile of talus: jumbled rocks, hard broken edges of granite that had shattered as they fell from above. He could see that it would be awkward, but not impossible, to work through those rocks to get to the bottom of the slope.

Dan wrapped an arm around the tree and leaned out over the cliff. Now he could see how the ledge he was on had broken off, leaving only a small section fifteen feet below that was filled with detritus from the tree. And then the slope continued down to the talus below.

He clambered back down to the others and explained his plan.

While Dan and Katie went back to camp to get more climbing gear, Cal would belay Blake down from the tree to investigate the ledge. And when they were done, they would go down and explore the talus from the bottom, while Katie and Dan tried to climb the cliff above. They would take it slow, and easy, and nobody was to do anything that might be dangerous.

Cal snorted. "You think you are going to be able to climb that cliff?" he said to Dan. "That seems dangerous to me!"

"We'll stay within our limits," Dan replied. "There are a couple of obvious cracks to start. We'll keep it to short pitches, lots of protection. But I want to see if there is anything up there. And we're here. We might as well take a look."

chapter 10

Dan stood on the ledge, looking up through the branches of the tree at the face they were going to climb. He had tied into the rope, and now turned and said quietly to Katie, "On belay?"

"Belay on," Katie replied with a nod.

Dan took a deep breath and reached up with his hands. "Climbing." He found two good holds, and placed his right foot on a small nub well above the ledge. "Here we go," he said, and lifted himself upwards. The branches of the juniper shoved against his back, and he could feel the small needles falling down inside the neck of his shirt. The thickest branch was now just above his left shoulder, and he eased himself slightly to the right to go around it.

Two more pushes and he was above the heaviest part of the tree, looking down through its branches at Katie on the ledge. He was breathing hard now, and his left foot was not stable. There were enough needles on the rock to make him distrust that placement. He tightened his grip and called out to Katie. "You doing okay?"

"I'm fine," she said happily. "How about you?"

Dan was afraid his voice showed some of the strain of the climb. "Well, I am doing okay …" He peered upwards, scouting out a route on the rock. "There's enough tree crap on this rock to make me nervous." Dan was always surprised at how little you could see when you were actually climbing. With his face so close to the rock, he really couldn't tell where he was headed, other than up.

"Put in some protection," Katie answered. "That way I won't have to catch you."

With a grunt, Dan made one more move and found himself in much better shape. He was now in full sun above the tree, and a crack led him up and to the right nicely. He fitted a small block into the crack, clipped his rope into the carabiner, and worked upwards another six feet. He leaned back and peered up the rock face. The next twenty feet looked easy, and he worked his way up along the crack in the rock, adding a few blocks, then stopped to take another rest.

Above him, Dan could see another small juniper, this one only six or eight feet tall, that was clinging to the rock with massive roots. The cliff in between was free of cracks, but Dan could see a few small bumps, enough give him hope for the climb. It was only another fifteen or twenty feet.

He told Katie of his plan and then started up. The granite was warm against his stomach, and he could feel himself sweating heavily. He knew it wasn't only from the heat, but from nerves. His right hand found a strong handhold, and he used it hang from and take some of the tension off his legs. That wasn't good technique, and he knew it. And he didn't care. The rock seemed to curve just a bit here, so that it pushed against his stomach as he climbed. He hoped it wouldn't tear the buttons off his shirt.

Two more moves with his feet, and now his left hand could feel the rough bark of the juniper roots. Dan stopped to look at it, trying to see where he could best sit to belay Katie as she climbed up after him. The tree hugged the cliff, and Dan would have to wrap himself around it, one leg on the uphill side of the tree. If his leg would fit.

It would have to.

He laced a line around the trunk of the tree, only four inches in diameter but certainly more than thirty years old, and slowly eased himself into position so that he could belay Katie. The rough bark of the tree bit into his leg, but the position was very secure, and in a few moments Dan was ready to call out.

"Off belay!" Dan readjusted the rope one more time and then worked it around his body to get ready for Katie's climb. "Taking in," Dan called as he pulled up the slack in the rope. He was surprised at how much rope there was. He thought he had climbed close to seventy-five feet. As he took in the rope, he looked back down the cliff. It was more like sixty feet. And below that, Dan could see the long slope of the granite leading down into the talus field far below.

The rope pulled tight. "That's me!" Katie called.

"On belay, climb when ready!" Dan called. He could see the branches of the jostling as Katie's head began to poke through. Within a few minutes she quickly climbed the cliff, moving swiftly from one spot to another. Dan could see the concentration in her face as she scanned the rock … and the confidence and joy she was taking in the climb. Her body moved in a graceful rhythm as she quickly joined him by the juniper.

"That was great!" she said with a smile as she looked across at him. "Do you want to lead again?"

Dan gave a rueful smile. "I think you're doing a lot better than I did," he admitted. "Why don't I just stay here and belay you, and you can keep on going?"

Katie didn't need a second invitation. She turned her head up to scan the cliff and said, quietly, "Cool." In the time it took her to say the word, she had planned out her route and was moving up the cliff past Dan.

He adjusted the rope in his hands and then turned to watch her climb. Her tan arms reached easily for the next hold, tested it, then latched on. Her legs followed suit, and Dan couldn't help but admire her form. While not a beautiful woman in the traditional sense, Katie was in her element here, and she radiated health and beauty. And her tight shorts showed her tanned, muscular legs and derriere off perfectly.

Not for the first time, Dan wondered if there had been women like this when he was her age. Did he just not notice them when he was younger? Or were the women of his generation somehow different, and less obvious than Katie?

Before he could come to an answer, she called out. "Big move coming up, give me a little more slack."

Dan eased the rope out another eighteen inches and replied, "You got it!"

Like a snake the rope slithered up the cliff after Katie. Then it stopped. "Hey, Dan?" Katie called out. "I think I am kind of at the top here. Why don't you come up and see?" And a few minutes later, "Belay on!"

Dan struggled out of his perch on the juniper and faced the cliff. He remembered how easy Katie had made it look, and he was determined to match her. Within the first three moves on the cliff, he had slowed down and was sweating again. He had to admit it. She was a much better climber than he was now—than he had ever been.

With Katie belaying him securely from above, Dan followed her lead and worked his way up the cliff. He saw where she had needed a bit more rope, as she faced a long stretch to reach a horizontal crack in the rock. And above that, he could see her sitting calmly on a ledge, slowly reeling in the rope.

The good news was that Dan was taller than Katie. What for her had been a long stretch was not uncomfortable for him, and he pulled himself up beside her.

She smiled at him and said, "You made that last move look easy."

Dan grinned. "Being taller has its advantages. But you made the rest of it look a lot easier than I did!"

Katie beamed. "Oh, I love doing this!"

Dan sat down next to her and looked around. The cliff seemed to become less steep above them, and from their perch they had a perfect view of the slope below, all the way down to the talus at the bottom. They could see the top of the tree where they had found the bones … and the smooth granite below.

Katie reached into her pack and pulled out a bottle of water, offering it to Dan.

"You first," he said. "I want to look around a bit." He pulled out a pair of small binoculars and began scanning the slope below.

"Do you see anything?" she asked.

"Not really," he answered. With a start he said, "Oh … well, I see Cal and Blake down there." He put the binoculars down and pointed. Below them on the talus, two figures could be seen slowly picking their way through the mass of broken granite.

Katie wiped off the mouth of the water bottle on her sleeve and handed it to Dan. "I think we're having more fun than they are," she said. "That talus is a mess."

The water bottle was warm in his hand. Dan sipped slowly, allowing the warm water to fill his mouth before he swallowed it. "Do you see anything up here?" he asked Katie.

The blond curls fluttered in the breeze as she shook her head. "This is too steep. If there ever was anything on this cliff, it's down there now," she said.

Dan called Cal on the radio, and the two men below reported that they had no news either. While he talked to Cal, Katie was scanning the rock above them.

"So we should still rope up for this part," Katie said to him. "I mean, it's not going to be hard to climb, but if one of us slips …."

Dan smiled. "Absolutely. There's no such thing as a little fall on a cliff like this … because you would go all the way to the bottom."

Katie turned and looked down, then looked at Dan. "Or at least as far as that juniper," she said solemnly.

They organized the ropes and Katie led the way up the cliff, again climbing smoothly and quickly. The slope of the cliff led upwards, but also became less steep, and she was soon out of sight as the cliff curved away from the vertical. Dan focused on the line as he payed it out through his hands. The smooth, hard texture of the rope was slick and dry.

A few minutes later it was Dan's turn to climb. Now he and Katie were making full use of the climbing commands, because they could not see each other at all. Dan stood up to start climbing, and realized that once he joined Katie above, he would not be able to see the foot of the cliff anymore. The bulging granite slope would make that impossible.

"Give me five minutes!" he yelled to Katie. He turned back toward the talus below and pulled out his binoculars. There was no point in hurrying, and this might be his last chance to scan the rocks below. In the binoculars Dan could see Cal waving his arms toward Blake, as the two men carefully picked their way through the rugged rocks. It didn't look like they were having any success. Dan picked up the radio and confirmed this with Cal.

"Nothing yet," Cal told him. "This is pretty tough walking in here."

Dan slowly scanned the area below. The rough jumble of talus seemed impenetrable, and it would take the two men hours to cover it carefully. He wasn't going to be able to help them much from this far away, he realized, even with the binoculars. Anything down there would be in the cracks, between the rocks, not lying on top where he could see it from up here.

He pulled his gaze from the binoculars and looked around. He was on the face of a stunning slab of white granite, with views that went on for miles. Toward the west he could see the smog of the Central Valley clouding the horizon, but in the other directions the blue of the sky was hard to believe, almost edging on purple. Everywhere he looked, it was blue sky and white granite. A few green trees sprinkled in where there was enough soil for something to grow—and sometimes even where there seemed to be no soil at all.

He glanced down one last time at the talus. Cal and Blake were now at the face of the cliff. If something had fallen from above, that was where it would have landed. Cal had his hands on his hips, and Blake was sitting on a block of stone. Dan's eyes followed the line of talus across the slope to the west, where it finally met a small line of trees.

His eyes caught something odd. He blinked them and looked again. Something red, or orange? He lifted the binoculars up and tried to find the spot—much farther west than he was expecting. He scanned back and forth.

There it was. Just at the base of the cliff. A spot of dark orange, and something shiny as well?

As he stared through the glasses, his right hand brought the radio to his lips. "Hey Cal, I think I might see something from up here. Over."

"What's that?" Cal's answer came back.

"Try moving west along the bottom of the cliff." Dan traced the path with the glasses, then with his naked eyes. "Maybe fifty yards further west. There's something orange, with some metal. I think maybe it's a backpack."

Cal's voice on the radio sounded resigned. "So, over there?" he asked, waving his arm so that Dan could see it.

"Yeah," Dan replied. He took one more look through the binoculars. "I'm almost sure that's a backpack."

Dan climbed up to Katie while Cal and Blake clambered over the rugged granite talus. When he arrived, he asked her, "So if our young woman ended up where she did … where did she start?"

Katie looked down over the edge of the rock, hoping to see the tree where they had found the body. "I can't really tell, but I think we climbed pretty much straight up." She stopped and looked around, scanning the top of the cliff.

Twenty yards away, perched on the edge of the precipice, was an erratic, a small boulder that had been left on the granite by glacial action millennia ago. Katie walked over to it and sat down. "Do you have anything that we could toss over the edge to see where it lands?" she asked Dan.

Dan thought about this. "I don't want to throw anything over the cliff that we can't find later. And I don't see how we'll be able to tell where it lands from here." He turned to look at Katie. She was staring up at him, with her hand shading her eyes against the glare of the bright sun.

"What if we tied a bag on the end of the rope, and asked the guys to tell us where it pointed?" she said. "It wouldn't go all the way down, but it would sure tell us what the general direction was."

Once they had filled a bright red stuff bag with Dan's fleece jacket and tied it to the end of the rope, they called Cal on the radio. The Sheriff confirmed that Blake had found the backpack. "It looks like it might be from our hiker," Cal said. "We're still looking for anything that might have fallen out of it. We found a pot. I don't know what else …"

Dan walked back to where they had originally topped out on the cliff, and gave the bag and line a healthy heave down the slope.

"Yeah, I can see that," Cal said. "I think you're pretty good there. You may be just a little too far out this way—to the west. I think you'd miss that tree and end up down here where we are."

Dan coiled the rope back up and went over to the erratic Katie had used as a seat. He gave the bag another toss and called Cal again.

"Yeah, that looks pretty good. I think the bag is just about straight up from the tree now," Cal called in.

"How are things going down there?" Dan asked him.

"We're putting together a real collection down here," Cal replied. "There's stuff scattered all over the rocks."

"That's to be expected," Dan said. "Animals will get into a pack in a few minutes."

"Yeah … but this pack wasn't closed," Cal replied. "The main flap on the pack wasn't tied up. This thing was open when it fell down the cliff." Cal paused, then added. "And we could use some help, if you guys want to come down here and get to work."

Dan looked at Katie. She shrugged her shoulders and nodded at him.

"Okay, Cal," Dan said into the radio. "We're on our way down."

He looked at Katie. "Do you want to just rappel down here? Or hike around?"

Katie peered over the edge to evaluate the situation. "A rappel would be faster. We can just tie into that rock." Dan nodded.

Katie quickly took care of the rope work, had Dan inspect it, and then prepared to lower herself down the cliff. Before she did, she stopped to say to Dan, "You know, this rock is where she sat."

Dan looked at her questioningly. "What do you mean?"

"I mean the girl down there," Katie answered him. "I bet she sat on this rock."

She let Dan think this over and started to rappel down the granite.

chapter 11

Dan sat on the rock and watched her slowly disappear over the edge of the granite. He could see the rope slowly wiggle and twitch as Katie dropped down below, her feet easing down the cliff. Off to his right, he could make out Cal and Blake among the blocks of talus at the bottom of the cliff far below. From so high above, he could barely see them moving, tiny spots of color in the sea of white rocks.

Katie got to the end of her rappel and called out to him. But Dan had other thoughts. "I think I am going to hike down from here—go over by Red Can Lake," he yelled down to her. "Are you okay with that?"

"Sure," she called out from below. "And once I get the rope down here, take the sling with you!"

Dan watched as the rope began to slide through the sling, then pick up speed as it slithered down to Katie. He worked the sling free of the rock, stuffed it in his backpack, and set out to find the route that the Bartletts had ultimately used to climb up to Leighton Lake.

He walked the ridge above the lake. Below him to the right he could see Yellowhammer Lake, and the stand of trees that must be their camp. To his left, on the other side of the ridge, the cool water of Leighton Lake lapped against the solid granite of the mountain.

Leighton was not a deep lake, and it was filled with small barren islands of rock. Here you could see how the glaciers had cleaned the rock and left a shallow, bumpy basin of granite. When the basin filled with water, the lake was formed, like a bathtub with only a thin film of water in it. In places it looked to Dan as if you could walk across the shallows to the other side.

But when Dan tried to hike along the ridge to Red Can Lake, he was disappointed to see that the outlet stream stood between him and the rest of his route. A deep fissure in the granite allowed a small trickle of water to cascade over the edge and down toward Cherry Creek Canyon and Yellowhammer Lake. Dan was forced to carefully climb down and across the fissure.

It was harder than it looked, and at one point he was seriously considering letting go of the rock and simply falling down into the deep water of the outlet pool. The water would have been icy cold, and he really didn't like the idea of getting everything wet. After a moment to compose himself, he managed to hang on, and a few minutes later was on the other side of the outlet, breathing hard and feeling a little relieved.

From the other side of the outlet, Dan could see the eastern part of Leighton Lake; from there the trail would lead across to Red Can Lake and then to the canyon below. But as he studied the terrain, he noticed another set of cairns, quite far apart, that seemed to lead down directly from the outlet down into the canyon. The granite was steep, but it looked perfectly possible, and would cut at least forty-five minutes off his hike back to camp.

He started out down the smooth slope, determined to turn around if things got too dicey. But sure enough, the cairns showed a steep but consistent gradient down into the canyon. He realized that this was the route that the Bartletts were hoping to find, but never did.

He placed each foot carefully, making sure he had good traction with each step. His toes began to pinch in the steady steep drop of the route, but Dan loved this kind of hiking. The afternoon sun was brilliant, and it was reflected by the granite on all sides. Climbing up this same route would be a very warm adventure, he was sure.

Only twenty minutes later Dan found himself at Five Acre Lake in a small bench just above the canyon floor. This was where the Bartletts had camped one night, after they had found the body. Dan quickly found their campsite in a small clearing on the south shore of the lake. From here to Yellowhammer would only be a hike of half an hour or less.

And there wasn't any hurry. He stopped to drink some water and looked up at the cliff above him. He could just see the ramp he had descended, and the outlet of Leighton Lake far above. Off to the west the cliff became far steeper, and just at the horizon Dan could see the area where they had found the body. From here he could see how steep the rock really was.

He pulled out his binoculars and looked to see if he could see any trace of Katie on the cliff. He could see roughly where she would have descended, but after searching for a few minutes he concluded that by now she would have reached the bottom, and probably gone back to help Cal, or back to camp. He took another drink and noticed that he didn't have much water left. He decided to go back to camp and check in with Luis before seeing how Cal and Blake were doing in their search.

Somehow the sun seemed warmer the nearer he got to camp. The bottom of the canyon collected the heat, and the dust from the trail rose around him as he walked through the trees. Dan realized that he was getting dehydrated.

The camp looked abandoned when he arrived. The horses were still in the corral, flicking their tails at the flies that landed on them, but Luis was nowhere to be seen, and a thin haze of dust made the heat palpable.

Dan walked to the shed where Luis had set up the kitchen and helped himself to a bottle of water. In the shade of the shed the temperature was noticeably cooler, and Dan let himself enjoy the sensation, savoring the water as it cooled his throat.

A noise outside caught his attention and he turned to see Luis arriving with a full container of water from the lake. In a quiet voice Luis asked him how things were going.

"I think we're doing okay," Dan said. "I'll go help Cal and Blake finish up over in the talus, and maybe we can leave here tomorrow," he explained.

Luis nodded his head toward one of the tents. "Katie is resting in there right now," he said quietly. "She just came here about half an hour ago."

"I'm here, I'm awake!" Katie called out from the tent. "Is that you, Dan?"

Dan laughed. "Yeah, it's me. I just came to fill up on some water. I was thinking of going over and helping Cal and Blake …"

"I'll help," Katie offered. "I just needed a few minutes of rest after that time on the rock. It's amazing how much that takes out of you."

"Take your time," Dan advised. "I'm going to lie down for five minutes and rest my back, and then we can go."

He climbed into his tent, put his hands behind his head and let his body flatten out on the sleeping bag. A groan escaped his lips as he felt his spine slowly straighten out, making a few pops and crackles as it did so. "Oh, man … I am getting too old for this stuff," he muttered.

"You're not too old," Luis replied, almost reprimanding him. "You are stronger than many of my friends in their twenties!"

Katie chuckled. "You're never too old for the mountains, Dan. You just have to adjust how you do it."

Dan stared at the ceiling of his tent. "Well, I could use a nice cold attitude adjustment right now," he said. "A beer, for example!"

"Geez! We're out there in the sun working our tails off, and you guys are resting in here drinking beer!" Cal's voice broke into the conversation. "Luis? I've been played for a sucker!"

"Just got back here ourselves, Cal," Dan explained. "And if you have any beer, we'd be delighted to share it with you!"

"Luis!" Cal called out. "What did you do with that beer I asked you to pack?"

Luis shook his head, grinning. "No, you didn't give me any beer, Mr. Healey. But I have lots of water here if you want a drink."

Dan grinned. "Thank you, Luis. You just made me feel a lot younger! See, Cal? He calls you Mr. Healey because you're so much older than the rest of us …"

"No!" objected Luis, laughing. "He is Mr. Healey because he is the Sheriff!"

"Exactly," Cal agreed. "And I don't mind being called Mr. Healey. It sure beats some of the things that people call you, Dan!"

Dan chuckled, still staring at the inside of his tent. "So how did you guys make out over there?" he asked Cal.

"Who knows?" Cal added with a sigh. "We found a lot of stuff that we can take back to the department and have them take a look at … the backpack, a cook kit, some rope, and a bunch of stuff that was probably inside the pack. It was scattered all over the talus field. But I think we got most of it. I don't know if there is more out there. The last hour or so, we just didn't find anything else."

"So should we go through what you found, and see if it makes any sense?" Katie asked.

"I don't think so," Cal replied. "I think we should get this back to town, and let the pros handle it. We've just put it all into bags and we'll get it packed back out of here. At that point, it's somebody else's problem."

"Where's Blake?" Dan asked.

Cal pointed to the cliff with his chin. "Back up there, trying to figure out why we've found the body, but no head. He's convinced he can find it."

Dan climbed out of his tent and joined Cal in the shade of the shed. "Do you think we're ready to pack up and head out tomorrow?"

"Unless you can think of something else we need to do up here," Cal replied.

"Got it!" they heard Blake's voice call out from above. "I got the skull! It's up here, in some bushes below the ledge."

Dan gave a sad smile and shook his head. "Looks like we're about done," he said. "I mean, I can think of a lot of things that I'd like to do up here, but not on this trip."

And besides, he thought, I'd like to get back into town to make a phone call.

chapter 12

The next day they packed up early and were on the trail right after breakfast. It was still cold enough that Dan wore his fleece on the trail, something he rarely did this time of year while hiking. But sitting on top of a horse was a lot less work than hiking.

The waters of Big Lake were ruffled lightly in the breeze, reflecting the white granite ridges like an impressionist painting. And the immense expanse of granite on the far side of the lake was a lot cooler in the morning sun than it had been on their way in.

They stopped for lunch at Grouse Lake, where they met a group on horseback from the pack station. Both groups kept their distance from each other, as if spending time with other riders would take something away from the wilderness experience. Dan didn't much feel like sharing stories with them anyway.

By mid-afternoon they were back at the trailhead, where they were met by an ambulance. Dan let Katie and Blake manage that part of the process, while he and Cal helped Luis load up the horses into the trailer.

The ambulance slowly drove away. There was no hurry, and there were no flashing lights. Cal noticed him watching the ambulance drive off.

"I'll give you a call once we ID the body," he said to Dan quietly. Dan nodded. "Yeah, thanks. And then I guess I'll have a bunch of paperwork to fill out."

Cal agreed. "I'd offer to help, but I know how much you enjoy that stuff," he said dryly.

"Well," Dan said, "I am going to have to wait to hear from the coroner before I can write the whole thing up …"

Luis got in his pickup and eased the horse trailers forward, slowly pulling them around the parking lot. He stopped to wave goodbye to Dan and Cal, then pulled out onto the road.

Cal nodded toward Blake and Katie, once again returning from the restroom. "Those kids did pretty well, huh?" he said.

"They did great," Dan agreed. "And Katie is a terrific climber. Very impressive."

Cal patted Dan on the shoulder and walked toward his truck. He paused at the door and turned to face Dan and the two young SAR crew. "Thanks, guys, it was a pleasure!" he called out.

Katie and Blake climbed into their truck and quickly pulled out of the parking lot. Cal let them go and then rolled down his window as he rolled past Dan.

"You know, we never did find that other boot," he said.

"I know," Dan answered. "I guess I'll put that in the report."

Cal drove off, and Dan climbed into his truck. He was pleased to see that he had calculated his parking space correctly, and the truck was neatly in the shade of one of the taller trees. The cab was cool and comfortable.

He pulled out onto the road and began the drive up to the highway. He flicked on the radio, hoping for some music, but there was nothing but static. Deep in the canyon, no signal penetrated.

He turned the radio off again, rolled down the window, and rested his arm on the door of the truck. There was no hurry to get back, and he took his time, enjoying the smells of the forest as he drove, and thinking about what he would say to Kristen when he called her tonight.

Maybe he should call her as soon as he got home, and invite

her for dinner tonight. But that might seem a little too eager or aggressive. It would be better to call her later, after dinner, and then make a date for the weekend.

A marmot scurried off its rock and down into a nearby crevice as Dan drove by.

Dan kept the truck at under twenty-five miles an hour, taking the turns even slower, and allowing his mind to wander a bit. At one point he noticed a car behind him, and he pulled over to let it go by. The driver honked and waved as she sped past.

Slowly the rest of the world came back to Dan. First one car, then another. Then there was the trash on the side of the road where someone had tossed it. An older couple walked along the side of the road, and Dan gave them a wide berth as he drove past.

He took the cut-off so that he wouldn't have to drive by the ranger station. He knew that if he drove by, he would have to stop, and then he would have to explain to Doris what they had found. Then she would expect him to call Steve Matson, and Steve would probably want to talk to him about it in person.

And the rest of the day would be gone.

Instead, he took the cut-off and went straight home. When he got there, he found his mail on the dining room table, where his next-door neighbors always left it. He glanced at it, just to make sure there was nothing worthy of his attention. Other than a few bills, there wasn't.

He opened the fridge, pulled out a cold beer, and sat at the kitchen table to drink it, thumbing through a magazine as he did so. After ten minutes he got into the shower and let the hot water wash over him. He decided that he would call Kristen now, anyway. Maybe she could meet him for dinner.

He toweled off and pulled on a pair of pants. He found Kristen's number, punched it into the phone, and waited. It rang three times, then her answering machine came on. Leave a message and she would call back.

Dan left his number and went back to look at his mail again. Still nothing important there. He tossed the junk mail into the trash, then put on a shirt and went out onto his porch.

"Is everything okay, Dan?" his elderly neighbor called out to him.

"It's great," Dan answered. "Thanks for keeping an eye on the place."

"No problem! Did you have a good trip?"

The phone rang and Dan nodded quickly, then slipped inside to answer it.

It wasn't Kristen; it was Cal Healey.

"Hey, I checked with the coroner." Cal came right to the point. "He must have been having a slow day. Anyway, he's sure that we found Rebecca Ritter. He says the dental records are still in his files, and it checks out. First thing he checked."

"That's the girl that went missing years ago?" Dan confirmed.

"Yep," Cal answered. "He doesn't have a cause of death or anything, but I have a feeling that a lot of people are going to be interested in this."

Dan thanked him and hung up the phone. He knew Cal was right. Just from what he had heard at the dinner party a few nights ago, this was going to be big news in Tuolumne County.

He sat down and read the magazine cover to cover. At one point he looked at the clock on the wall, and noticed it was 7:45. He pulled a frozen pizza out and heated it up, opening another beer to drink with it. At ten o'clock he was asleep on the sofa, the phone on the table next to him.

He woke up hours later and checked his watch. It read 1:15. He got off the sofa, brushed his teeth, slipped off his clothes, and climbed into bed. As he fell asleep, he wondered why Kristen hadn't called. And why she was out so late.

chapter 13

The next morning Dan luxuriated in the knowledge that he could follow his usual routine. He got up early, as he usually did, and made his way into the kitchen.

He pulled out his huge bin of bulk granola. The crunchy cereal made a reassuring sound as he poured some into a bowl. He grabbed a handful of walnuts to toss on top of the granola and poured himself a large glass of orange juice.

Before he added milk to the cereal, he went out onto his porch and collected the New York Times newspaper that his neighbor Ruth from down the street had left him last night. It didn't bother him that the news in the paper was a day or two old. What he wanted was the crossword puzzle.

He sat down at the table, opened the paper to the crossword, picked up a spoon, and started to eat. Between mouthfuls he began to fill in the squares, starting as he always did with the upper left-hand corner of the puzzle, and never adding an answer that was not connected to what he had already filled in.

He rarely finished the puzzle before the granola, and this morning was no exception. Most days he would leave the puzzle to be filled in when he came home that evening, but today he had plenty of time.

Except for one clue, the puzzle was done well before eight o'clock. Where the first name of a current pop singer crossed with an

Arabic coffee urn, Dan left the square blank. There were at least six letters that might work, but he couldn't be sure which was correct.

He opened the paper and began to read some of the news articles, passing over those about political issues or crime, and focusing on stories about distant corners of the globe. The phone rang, and Dan found himself talking to Steve Matson.

"Dan, what do we know?" Steve asked him.

"Not much," admitted Dan. "We took a Search and Rescue team to Yellowhammer Lake and went there and found the remains. They were human remains, and we also found a backpack and a few other things. And last night Cal Healey called me to tell me that they had been identified from dental records as Rebecca Ritter."

"I got a call this morning from the Sheriff," Steve said. "But here's the deal, Dan. If this is a suspicious death, then we turn it over to the FBI. It happened on federal lands, and it's their jurisdiction. If it's an accident, we don't need to bother them. So what do we know?"

"I don't know," Dan answered. "Can you give me a day or two to work through the files with the Sheriff? They've already got a case file on this from when she disappeared."

Steve thought this over. "So you'd be back at work on Sunday on your regular schedule?"

Dan agreed. "And I'll review everything they've got down in Sonora, and get you a report by the end of day tomorrow."

"Sounds good," Steve agreed. "Don't overthink this. Remember, if it is suspicious, we turn it over to the FBI. We don't have the staff or the expertise for something like this."

"Got it," Dan said.

Dan hung up the phone and went to clean off the kitchen table, putting his dishes in the sink. He'd wash them tonight. Right now he wanted a shower.

He was toweling his hair dry after the shower when the phone rang again. This time it was Cal Healey.

"I've got a box full of files for you, Dan!" Cal sounded almost gleeful about the prospect. "Do you want me to have them run up to your house, or do you want to come down and get them?"

"I'll come down there," Dan said. "I may just read through them down there, if you have an office for me?"

"Sure, we can find a spot for you," Cal answered. "Hey, I didn't wake you up or anything, did I?"

"Nope, sorry to disappoint you," Dan said. "But I'm up, showered and I'll be down there in twenty minutes."

When he arrived at the Sheriff's office, Dan was met by Cal with a large cardboard box full of manila folders. Cal let it drop, heavily, on the counter.

"It's all yours," he said with a grin.

Dan looked at the box. "So have you looked at any of this?"

"I read through a few things," Cal admitted.

"Got any ideas?" Dan asked him.

"Maybe, but I'll let you work through it and then we can talk it over," Cal answered. "I've got you set up in an office down the hall here."

Dan reached to pick up the box, but Cal beat him to it.

"I'll carry that for you," Cal said with a smile. "It's the very least we can do for you." He paused for moment, then added dryly, "The VERY least."

He showed Dan into an office. "If you want coffee or anything, just give a shout," he said, and left Dan to read the files.

Dan pulled out the files and stacked them in front of himself. The labels identified the folders by name. The story that Tony di Conti had told now came back to him, character by character. Todd Walters and Bryan Lafferty each had their own files, and they were by far the thickest.

Dan picked up Todd's file and started to read.

Todd had been questioned numerous times, and his story was very consistent. The two young people had left Crabtree trailhead later than planned, and hiked up to Chewing Gum Lake. They camped there the first night, and Rebecca had seemed grumpy, or worried. The next day they had hiked down to Y Meadow Lake, and then through Whitesides Meadow to the Wire Lakes. They camped at Middle Wire Lake the second night, and Todd had fished the Upper Lake that afternoon. Rebecca seemed in better spirits, and had spent the afternoon sunbathing on the rocks above the lake, and reading a book, writing in her diary.

That night they had dinner and stayed up, talking around the campfire.

The next morning, Rebecca got up very early and started cooking breakfast. By the time Todd was up, she had eaten and was packing up her pack. She then told Todd that she wasn't going back home, wasn't going to Berkeley. She was tired of living up to other people's expectations, and she was going to hike off and leave him behind. And he was not to follow her.

When Todd complained that he would have problems back in Sonora when he returned, she tore out a page from her diary and wrote a note on it for him. And then she left, hiking towards Long Lake.

Todd was stunned, and disappointed. He stayed around the lake for most of the morning, then decided to hike down to Woods Lake and camp there. That was when he found out that Rebecca had taken most of the food. He caught a few fish for dinner, and then hiked out the next day.

He'd gone straight home and told his parents about Rebecca, and they were the ones who brought him into the Sheriff's office, where he told the whole story.

One thing Todd wanted to make very clear: He and Rebecca were just friends. They were not sexually involved.

Dan scanned the rest of the pages in Todd's folder, then opened Bryan Lafferty's.

Even from the printed page, Dan could see that these interviews had been very different. Bryan was described as very uncooperative, and he had been very tight-lipped about what he would say.

According to his own words, Lafferty had gone fishing that week in the Emigrant Wilderness. He refused to say where he had been, on the grounds that he didn't want his secret fishing spots exposed. When the interviewing officer had pressed for more information, Lafferty had insisted on calling his parents, who called a lawyer.

The rest of the interview was held in the presence of Lafferty's attorney. It was a slow and painful process, as each question was resisted, reworded, or challenged. Dan flipped to the end of the file, where the officer had made a kind of summary.

Lafferty had started his hike the day after the other two, and had hiked in through Gianelli trailhead. He had followed more or less the same route, but had stopped to fish and had never seen Rebecca Ritter or Todd Walters. At Wire Lakes he had also gone south toward Woods Lake and then hiked out through Grouse Lake, and then climbed up through Camp and Bear Lakes to get back to Gianelli Trailhead. He got back into town two days after Todd Walters.

The Sheriff's office had requested permission and received it to search the backpacks of both Todd and Bryan. Bryan's had nothing that could be connected to Rebecca Ritter. Todd's backpack had a few things that Rebecca had left behind at the campsite when she left: a hair ribbon, a washcloth, and a pair of socks.

Dan put Bryan's folder down and looked through the rest of the files. One was marked Lori Marchand, and he picked it up.

Lori Marchand was a student at Sonora High, and apparently Rebecca Ritter's best friend. In her interview, she confirmed that Rebecca had felt a lot of pressure to please her parents. Lori described Rebecca as being depressed and angry about her future, and happiest when she was distracted from thinking about it. Dan couldn't help thinking that this was true of just about every teenager he'd ever known.

Lori Marchand's folder was not thick, and Dan finished up reading through it. Lori suggested that if the officer really wanted to know what was going on in Rebecca's head, that he should read her diary. According to Lori, Rebecca wrote every night in her diary, and had shown some of the pages to Lori.

And yes, Lori confirmed that the page Todd Walters had brought back from the wilderness looked like it came from Rebecca's diary. And it looked like something she would write.

Dan picked up the last folder. It was for Anson and Marjorie Ritter, Rebecca's parents.

This had not been a pleasant interview. The Ritters were vehement that Todd Walters had done something to their daughter. They bitterly resented the suggestion that their daughter had felt any pressure from them at all, and were furious that the Sheriff had not yet charged Todd in Rebecca's disappearance.

As Dan read the file, he could almost hear the anger and fear in the voices of Rebecca's parents. But there was little information here to help him. He did find it curious that they had refused to provide their daughter's diaries to the Sheriff's department. Instead, they had insisted that the Sheriff organize a search party.

Which brought Dan to the last folder. While not an official search party, Ranger Ralph Gephart had hiked the trail that Todd Walters had suggested and looked for any trace of Rebecca Ritter. He had found nothing. The US Forest Service had also posted notices on all trailheads, asking for information. And there had been a brief public relations campaign to ask people in the area to be on the lookout for Rebecca Ritter.

The last few pages were reports that the Sheriff had received over the years. Rebecca Ritter had been spotted in Minden, Nevada working at a casino. She had been seen in a gas station in Modesto, a convenience store in Bishop, and on Market Street in San Francisco. She had been reported living in Yuba City. The Sheriff's office had investigated each of these tips.

Rebecca Ritter had not been found.

chapter 14

Cal stuck his head in the door and asked Dan how he was doing.

"I don't know," Dan said. "I've read most of this stuff, but I still don't know what I think. I'd like to talk to some of these people again, to see if their story has changed. I know that the freshest information is the best, but I wonder if any of these people have changed their story—and if they have, it would be interesting to know why they might do that."

"Yeah, I thought about that, too," Cal said. "I've got some time over the next couple of days, if you're interested in my help."

"So where are these guys now?" Dan asked Cal, handing him the folders for Todd and Bryan.

Cal glanced at the names on the folders. "Todd Walters lives over in Tuolumne. It's kind of a sad story. He got badly wounded in Iraq, and he's in a wheelchair now. He's not in good shape."

"What do you mean?" Dan asked. "He's in a wheelchair. Of course he isn't in good shape."

"Yeah, but it's more than that," Cal responded. "When he was wounded, he came back to town as a real hero, and deservedly so. He pretty much saved a couple of the guys in his unit singlehandedly, and damn near died because of it. And he spent months in a hospital in Germany. The whole town here sent him flowers and gifts and things. But he's not a happy guy these days. He spends a lot of his time at the VFW hall, and we've picked him up a couple of times for

DUI. I think he's lost his license once or twice now."

"How does he get around?" Dan asked.

"Hell, I've driven him home a time or two," Cal answered. "He was married, but that fell apart, and he's living on his parents' property. He's got an RV in the back that's his. But he drives a souped up four-wheel drive that he's adapted for his wheelchair."

Dan thought that over. "Does he have a job?"

"No," Cal replied. "He tried to get a job as a substitute teacher at some point, but that really didn't work out. And when his wife left him, he really became pretty depressed. Like I said, a sad case."

"Why did she leave?" Dan asked.

"Oh, man, she had it rough," Cal answered. "He was a hurt and angry man, and he took it out on her and anyone else that got near him. We got pretty tired of showing up there to settle him down. The only good news in the story is that there weren't any kids in the house to watch the whole show."

"So do you think we should try to talk to him?" Dan asked.

"If he hasn't already had too much to drink, it would be worth a try," Cal answered. He looked at his watch. "I've got a car out front if you want me to drive."

Dan collected his box of files and followed Cal out to the car. The sun was already warm, and the seat of the car was hot to the touch. Dan held the box on his lap as they drove.

"You can put that in the back if you want," Cal told him. "I got rid of the body in the trunk."

"Yeah, thanks," Dan said. "But I want to be able to look through this stuff." He pulled out the second folder. "So what about Bryan Lafferty?" he asked.

"Small time druggie," Cal answered. "He went to the JC in Columbia, but dropped out. We busted him for marijuana at one point, and he spent a little time in jail on that one. I heard that he was working for a contractor over in Angel's Camp for a while, but that didn't work out. His mother died in a car crash while he was still at the JC, so he was on his own then. His dad had left years ago."

"So what's he doing now?" Dan asked.

"He lives off Big Hill Road, way off the grid," Cal answered. "There are parts of this county that are pretty much on their own, and Bryan lives in one of them. We don't go there unless we have to."

Dan vaguely knew the area, which backed up against the lower portion of the National Forest. It was dry country, and the land was steep, often covered in scrub. The roads were dirt, and not always maintained. It would be easy to disappear there.

"When his mother died, Bryan ended up with some money somehow," Cal continued. "He bought some property way off the grid and built a house out there. It's pretty rustic. I don't know if he has any permits to do what he's done out there, but nobody cares enough to find out. He rents out space to anyone who needs it, and he's got a bunch of old trailers and a camper shell for them to live in."

"Nice," Dan said sarcastically.

"Yeah, well, he stays out of town these days, and we don't worry too much about what happens out there," Cal said.

"Not married?" Dan asked.

Cal thought this over. "He's got a couple of boys, and I guess he was married. But she left a long time ago—ten years or more. He's raising the kids himself, and he's probably got a girlfriend out there. Seems like he can always find some cutie who needs a place to stay; one that needs a place to stay bad enough to want to sleep with him."

They drove in silence for a few minutes. Then Cal continued. "Those two boys are getting old enough to get into trouble," he said. "They must be thirteen and sixteen? Something like that. My kids see them in school."

"So where are we headed first?" Dan asked.

"I thought we'd go over to Todd's place, and see if he's home," Cal answered. "If he is, we can talk to him. If he's not, we can at least talk with his mom and dad, and see if they know where we can find him. They're old enough that they don't get out much, so they should be there."

The driveway to the Walters' home had been paved at one point, but over the years it had deteriorated into potholes, gravel, and dirt. Cal eased his car around the biggest holes and pulled up in front of an older double-wide home. The aluminum porch was decorated with faded plastic flowers. He and Dan waited for a minute or two, just to give the people inside a chance to notice them, and then got out of the car. Their steps sounded loud on the cheap metal stairs leading up to the front door.

Cal knocked and a wiry older woman answered the door. She was stooped from age, and it gave her face a hopeful look as she looked over her glasses at him.

"Mrs. Walters? We were wondering if Todd was home," Cal said. "We'd like to talk to him." The look on Mrs. Walters' face grew immediately less hopeful.

"I suppose this is about that Ritter girl," she said with disgust. "I heard that they found her body somewhere way up in the mountains."

Cal nodded. "Yeah, that's right," he answered her. "Do you know where Todd is?" Dan was astonished that the news could travel so fast in this small community.

"Well, he left here a while ago," Mrs. Walters said. "I'd guess he's down at the VFW hall with his friends. Some friends picked him up in a blue pickup truck."

"Okay, thanks," Cal said. "We'll go on down there to see if we can find him." He turned and the two men started to walk back to Cal's car.

But Todd Walters' mother wasn't through with them. "You don't have to bother him, you know," she said. "That girl took off on her own, and left Todd to do all the explaining. She didn't give a damn about what happened to him."

Cal and Dan were on the gravel path below the steps, but they stopped to turn and listen to the old woman.

"It ruined his life," she continued, "and her parents just made it worse. Todd was so upset that he never did go to college. That was his dream, to play baseball. But those people hounded him like crazy. That's why he went into the army. To shut them up."

Cal made a small noise in his throat, something that might be construed to mean that he understood what she was saying … without actually saying any words.

"They damn near killed our son," Mrs. Walters continued, now yelling. "Even though we were all in the same church together. They just slandered him right and left until Todd couldn't take it anymore. And instead of going to college, he just signed up and joined the army."

Her eyes were now full of tears as she spoke. "That girl ruined Todd's life, and the poor boy is in pain twenty-four hours a day. And now you want to bring all that up again with him."

"Well, we'd just like to ask him a few questions, because of what we found out there," Cal said. "Maybe this will clear everything up."

"It's too late for that," Mrs. Walters said. "Clearing things up won't help him now. That won't give him back the life he lost. It won't give him back his legs." She stared angrily at the two men. As they turned once more to go, she called out to them.

"What you really ought to do is go talk to that Lafferty kid," she said. "He's the one who was causing all the problems. That's who you ought to talk to."

"Thank you," Cal said. "We'll do that."

As they got in the car and drove away, Dan looked over at Cal. "That was ugly," he said.

"This whole story is ugly, Dan," Cal said. "And I don't think it's going to get any better once we talk to the other people. Just like the di Contis said, the whole town was in an uproar when this first happened, and it's all coming back. There's a lot of bitterness in these hills."

"And skeletons in the closet," Dan added.

Cal looked over at him. "I hope not," he said. "I hope the only skeleton we get is the one we already found up on the cliff."

chapter 15

When Cal drove right by the VFW hall without stopping, Dan turned and looked at him.

"He's not there," Cal explained. "His mother lied to us. Todd drives a big four-wheel drive SUV with oversized tires that's been outfitted for a disabled driver, and it wasn't at the house. It's pretty obvious when you see it. So nobody picked him up; there was no blue pickup truck. And he's not at the VFW hall."

"Where is he?" Dan asked.

"I don't know," Cal replied, "but it will be easier to find him when he's back home than trying to track him down all over the county or state. He drives that thing everywhere, including way up into the hills."

"So where are we headed now?" Dan asked.

"I thought we'd go out Big Hill Road and see how much shit we can stir up," Cal answered. "You can always track down Todd later today or tomorrow, but I don't think it's such a good idea for you to come out here on your own."

They slowly rolled through the old gold mining town of Columbia and picked up Big Hill Road behind it. As it twisted and turned, climbing up the side of the mountain, Cal dodged potholes and an occasional oncoming vehicle.

Dan found that he couldn't study the files in front of him on such a road. When he felt the first twinges of motion sickness, he put the files down and turned to Cal.

"Lafferty says that he was fishing in Emigrant Wilderness when all this happened, but he never saw Todd or Rebecca …"

"That's what he said," Cal agreed.

"How likely is it that a guy who was cited for stalking this girl would let her go off with somebody else, and then go hiking in the same area without trying to track them down?"

"We spent a lot of time asking those sorts of questions back then," Cal said. "But the kid was calm, and there was no way of disproving a single fact in his story. And he knew it."

"So if we've found new evidence, would that change things?" Dan asked Cal. "What do you think we ought to tell him about what we found?"

"I don't think we tell him anything," Cal answered. "Let him worry about that. His suspicions may be far worse than anything we can say."

Cal turned the squad car onto a dirt road that led off to the left, and the tire noise immediately became louder as they crunched on the gravel and dirt. Two miles in, Cal turned again, and this time the road climbed steeply over a ridge. On the far side of the ridge was a small valley, and an even worse road led down to a cluster of buildings and trash at the far end.

"I see what you mean," Dan said.

A chain decorated with a few scraps of cloth ran from one tree to another across the road. On the far side of the chain was a sunny stretch of flat ground that led fifty yards into the cluster of houses and trailers.

"This is new," Cal said, as he parked the car. "I guess we'll have to walk in from here."

"I'm not armed," Dan informed Cal.

"I don't think that's a problem," Cal said. "But I do want to give them a little warning before we show up." He honked the horn a couple of times and got out of the car.

The heat was fierce in the sunshine, and not for the first time, Dan found himself suffering from the weight of his uniform. As the two men approached the first house, a voice came out from inside.

"Well, look who's here!" it called out. "It's Deputy Dawg!" Dan noticed motion in the shadows of the doorway to the house in front.

"And he brought along an Eagle Scout as backup!" This was followed with a cackle of laughter. To his left, Dan noticed two men come out of one of the mobile homes and stand on the porch.

Bryan Lafferty waited until they got within ten feet of his steps before he came out on the porch. Dan studied him quickly: six feet tall, slim, with thinning blond hair and wire rim glasses. He was wearing khaki shorts and a torn t-shirt and sandals.

Lafferty's eyebrows shot up as he said with a big smile, "Unless you boys have a search warrant, I am going to have to ask you to leave."

"No warrant, Bryan," Cal answered. "We just want to ask you a couple of questions."

"No warrant, no questions," Bryan answered. "And don't invent some crazy ass story about hearing a scream and investigating. I know my rights here, and I've got ten witnesses that will back me up." He waved his hand at the small collection of inhabitants who had now appeared in different areas around the house.

"Bryan, we found Rebecca Ritter's body two days ago above Yellowhammer Lake," Cal said. "We'd like to try and figure out what happened to her."

Dan watched as the expression on Bryan Lafferty's face changed noticeably. Was it fear? Sadness? Shock? Dan couldn't be sure.

"Shit, I answered all that stuff years ago," Lafferty replied to Cal. But the tone of his voice was different. He was no longer challenging them.

"I know you did, Bryan," Cal answered. "But we're just

wondering if there is anything else you can tell us. Even the smallest detail might be important. Where did you go, what did you see …"

"Are you sure it's her?" Lafferty asked them.

"Yeah," Cal answered, nodding. "Confirmed with dental records."

"Shit." Bryan Lafferty leaned his arm up against one of the posts holding up the roof of his porch. He stared at Cal and Dan. "So what are your questions?"

"Would you just run through what you did that week, on your fishing trip?" Dan asked.

Lafferty looked at Cal and said, "Who's this?"

"Dan Courtwright," Cal answered. "He's the ranger who organized the search party."

"Dudley Do-right, huh?" Lafferty responded. "Well, I don't think I can tell you anything about this." He paused for a moment. "You've got it all there in the reports. I was fishing on a weeklong trip out of Gianelli. I caught a lot of fish, and I didn't see Rebecca or Walters. I don't remember exactly what I did each day, but I bet you've got that anyway."

"It says in the report that you more or less followed the same path that they did for the first few days," Dan said. "Did you see any other people on the trail?"

"I didn't meet anyone on the trail during the whole week," Lafferty answered testily. "And I'll bet it says that right there in your report. You might want to read it."

"Yeah, it probably does," Dan admitted. "And I have read it. But I also know that sometimes people remember other stuff as they think about it."

"I don't remember any other stuff," Lafferty said in response, hoping to end the conversation.

"I understand," Dan said, "but let me ask you one thing that I didn't see in these reports. Did they ever ask you if you had seen any trace of Rebecca or Todd Walters on the trail? I mean, you followed the same route for part of this hike. Did you see any trash they may have left behind, or did you get any sense how far they had hiked together?"

This brought a long pause from Bryan Lafferty. When he answered, it was with a tired and frustrated tone of voice. "I was fishing," he said. "I'm not a fucking Indian tracker, and I didn't put my ear to the ground to see if I could tell how far away the horses were. I went fishing, and I came back. And I never saw either of those two people while I was doing it."

He glared at Dan and Cal. "And I think that you guys have just about used up your get-out-of-jail-free card," he said. "If you want to ask any more questions, you can save yourselves a long and scenic drive out here. Call Barry Wong and tell him you want to talk to me."

"Yeah, okay, we'll do that," Cal agreed. Before he and Dan started to walk back to the car, he turned to Bryan Lafferty one last time. "If you do think of something, give me a call, will you?"

"Oh, yeah," Lafferty replied sarcastically. "You'll be the first person to know about it."

Back in the car, Dan noticed that Cal was driving faster back down the dirt road.

"The guy's kind of a jerk, huh?" he said to Cal.

Cal waited a few moments before he replied. "You know what pisses me off?" he asked Dan. "I bet somebody knows what happened out there, and it is really going to piss me off if we don't figure it out."

"Yeah, but there are unsolved cases all over the place," Dan said. "You guys must have your fair share."

"Agreed," Cal answered him. "But not like this one. And it really ticks me off that one of these guys might know something and isn't telling us."

Once back on the pavement of Big Hill Road, Cal seemed to have calmed down a bit. "Let's try one more person," he said to Dan. "Lori Marchand works at a café in Columbia. Let's stop in and see if she can tell us anything."

The crowds were thinning out on Main Street, and Cal and Dan walked into the café to find a lone family of four enjoying some ice cream at a table in the front. Lori Marchand was behind the counter in the back, cleaning up and getting things ready for the next day. Her dark brown hair was pulled back in a ponytail, and she wore just enough makeup to suggest that she had made an effort. But not so much that it looked like she really cared. A strand of hair, showing just a slight hint of grey, fell down the side of her face.

She greeted Cal with a smile and asked what brought him to Columbia. When he explained that he wanted to ask her a few questions, her face fell and she started scrubbing the counter.

"Is it about Rebecca?" she asked, without looking up again.

"Yeah," Cal answered. "I guess you heard?"

"I heard they found her body at the bottom of a cliff," Lori replied, still not looking up.

"Well, we were just wondering if you've thought about all of that," Cal said. "Do you have any idea what might have happened?"

Lori stopped scrubbing and fixed Cal with a stare. "Yes, I've thought about it. I've thought about it lots. And I'd pretty much finally forgotten about it until yesterday, when I heard that you'd found her body." Her gaze moved on to Dan. "And yeah, I have lots of ideas of what might have happened. And I have absolutely no idea of what really did happen." Dan found it hard to meet her eyes, and he glanced away. Lori continued, "So how can I help you?"

Cal eased slowly into the topic. "Well, we know you were good friends with Rebecca, so anything you can tell us would be helpful. I guess what we're really trying to figure out is if she really thought about killing herself. Did you ever hear her talk about that?"

Lori placed both hands on the counter in front on her and blew the strand of hair out of her face. "Look, I knew Rebecca, and we were friends. Maybe not best friends, but friends. Do I think she killed herself? I don't know. I doubt it. But if you want to know that, you should read her diaries. That's where she wrote about all this stuff. It seems to me that if she thought about that, she'd put it in her diary."

"Did she ever talk to you about it?" Dan asked her.

"No. Never. But she didn't talk to me about everything, either," Lori explained.

"Did she talk to you about her boyfriends?" Dan asked.

"She didn't really have boyfriends," Lori said. "She had admirers. Most of it was all pretty much one way. They loved her— or at least wanted her. And she played along. But she was never as interested as they were."

"Was she ever afraid of any of them?" Dan asked.

Lori gave a short, derisive snort. "She wrapped them around her little finger."

Dan and Cal glanced at each other. "Did that bother them? Do you think any of them could have wanted to hurt her?"

Lori stared at them for a moment, then looked down at the counter. When she raised her eyes again, they were filled with tears. "That's what I really don't know," she said. "That's what I think about. And I really don't know the answer." An awkward silence followed the remark.

Dan gave Lori his card and asked her to call him if she thought of anything else. "Yeah," she sniffed. "I'll do that."

The two men thanked her and walked back to the car. "Not a great day, was it?" Dan said to Cal as they drove back into Sonora.

"Tomorrow we'll get to the Walters' place earlier, and talk to him," Cal promised.

Dan drove home and allowed his mind to wander over the

files he had studied. He kept thinking there was something else, something he was missing. When he walked into his house it came to him. He had not heard back from Kristen. He checked his answering machine. There were no new messages.

Dan went into the kitchen and made himself a salad and a bowl of ramen noodles. He spread the files out in front of himself and read through them again. This time he forced himself to read every word.

He took a break for a bowl of chocolate almond fudge ice cream at 8:45, and stretched for a few minutes before sitting back down at the table. The phone still had not rung.

At 10:30 he closed up the folders and headed for bed. He did not have any more answers than he'd had this morning. And Kristen still had not returned his call.

chapter 16

The phone by his bed rang. Dan answered sleepily and was surprised to hear his boss, Steve Matson, on the line. He sat up in bed.

"What time are you planning on coming in today?" Steve asked.

Dan checked the clock by the bed: 7:43. "I can be there by eight, if you want," Dan replied. Which wasn't quite true, but he would be close.

"Anson and Marjorie Ritter are going to be in my office at 9:00 a.m.," Matson said. "They got the call from the coroner about you finding their daughter. They want to come in and talk to you about it."

Dan closed his eyes tightly, then opened them again. "Okay. I'll be there by 8:30."

"Make it 8:15," Matson insisted. "I'd like to hear about it before they get here."

"Okay, I'll see you then," Dan answered, then hung up the phone. There was time for a quick shower, but probably not much in the way of breakfast. He couldn't remember what he had in the kitchen, and there would be no time to stop at a café.

A few minutes later he was trotting out the front door and climbing into his truck. As he drove up Highway 108 he remembered the little donut shop in Sugar Pine. He checked his watch. He had a few minutes to spare.

He left the engine running as he ran inside. He was relieved to see that there was no one in line at the register. He ordered a few donuts … then reconsidered. He ordered a dozen donuts, and a cup of coffee.

Back in the truck he placed the box of donuts carefully on the seat beside him and drove up to Matson's office. As expected, Steve was seated at his desk in his office, deep in conversation on the phone. He waved Dan to a seat on the other side of his desk.

Dan placed the box of donuts on the desk in front of him, and Matson raised his eyebrows and smiled.

"Jerry, we don't know yet," Dan heard Steve tell the person on the phone. "I can't tell you because we don't know. And it may take us some time to figure it out."

Dan saw Matson hold the phone farther from his ear. Even from his position on the other side of the desk, Dan could hear a bit of what was coming from the other end of the line.

When the noise level dropped, Steve answered. "I am sitting across the desk from my guy right now," he explained into the phone. "But I can't talk to him about this because I'm talking to you instead. If you want me to find out more, you're going to have to hang up and let me talk to him."

Dan knew Steve Matson pretty well, and Steve was not someone who was easily angered. But Dan was not fooled by the calm in Steve's voice. He knew his boss was furious, so furious that he seemed almost completely calm. Just the tiny twitch on the left side of his mouth gave him away.

"Thank you," he heard Steve say. "I will call you back when I have some real information to report."

Dan could hear the phone click on the other end of the line, and saw Steve Matson carefully replace the receiver on the phone in his office. The two men sat in silence for a moment.

Steve slowly shook his head at Dan. "This thing's a fucking

avalanche," he said to Dan. "It started somewhere up near the top, where Anson Ritter called somebody in Washington and started yelling. And that person called someone below him, and every time that call got repeated, this got to be bigger and uglier."

Dan waited. He knew that Steve would try to protect him from some of the fallout. He was right.

"So I am not going to do that to you," Matson continued. He took a deep breath. "Do you know who Rebecca Ritter is?" Matson asked him.

"Well, I've heard that she was a young woman who disappeared about fifteen or twenty years ago on a backpacking trip," Dan replied. "And now that you mention it, I can assume that she is some relation to Anson Ritter?"

"His daughter," Matson confirmed. "He and his wife reported her missing sixteen years ago. She was never found. He is furious that we didn't take his concerns seriously the first time. And he wants somebody to pay for that." Steve paused for a moment. "Do we know how she died?" he asked.

"I don't have a report from the coroner," Dan explained. "But she was a couple hundred feet down a steep granite cliff. Right now, his best guess is that she died from injuries in the fall."

Steve nodded. "It would be nice if that were true," he said. "Because that way it wouldn't have mattered when we found her. When do we expect to hear more from the coroner?"

Dan shook his head. "I don't know. That's something you'll have to ask the coroner."

Steve glanced at his watch. "The Ritters are going to be here in about twenty minutes," he said. "Is there anything you think I should know before we go into that meeting?"

Dan thought about this for a second. "There were a couple of things that didn't make sense to us," Dan suggested. "And I haven't had any breakfast."

Steve chuckled. "Open the box and dig in! And tell me what didn't make sense."

Dan pulled open the top of the donut box and picked out a chocolate donut. He raised it in his hand as he spoke, as if to illustrate his point. "So all of the remains were on a ledge, up against a tree, on the cliff. We found shreds of clothing, a boot, and I think Katie said that she counted over 195 bones. That's pretty much a whole body."

He looked at Steve, who nodded to show that he was following the story.

"So one thing that bothered Cal Healey: if the bones were all there, where was the other boot? Because one boot was still on a foot, more or less. But we never did find the other boot."

"Okay," Steve said slowly. "But up there, an animal can drag something away pretty easily."

Dan nodded. "Yeah. But as far as we could tell, the bones of the other foot were still there."

"Hmmph," Steve grunted. He thought about this for a minute. "Okay, and what else?" he asked.

"We think we found her backpack as well," Dan continued. "I guess we'll ask her parents to identify that for us. And there were a few other things there with the backpack. But the pack wasn't near the body. It was at least a couple of hundred feet away, maybe more than that. Cal has the exact info. And much further down at the bottom of another part of the cliff. So I don't think she could have been wearing it when she fell."

He paused and let Steve consider this. While they waited, Dan took another bite of donut. One more bite and it would be gone.

Steve took a stab at an explanation. "So we don't know what happened, but maybe she stopped to rest on top of the cliff. For some reason, her pack fell down the cliff. She decides to climb down after it, because without it, she's in big trouble. And she falls."

"And the boot?" Dan asked, then popped the last bite of donut in his mouth.

Steve sat back in his chair. "I don't think we should get into the fine details with the Ritters," he said. "Let's focus on what we know. We know we found her body down a cliff. We found a pack nearby that we also think is hers. And we don't know how they got there, and we are investigating all of that."

A commotion in the outer office indicated that the Ritters had arrived. Steve checked his watch again. "Sounds like they are a few minutes early." He looked Dan. "Are you ready for this?" Dan wiped his mouth with a napkin and nodded. "I guess so."

There was a knock on the doorframe, and Matson waved his hand to invite the group into his office. Anson Ritter was smaller than Dan expected. Five feet six or seven, Dan guessed. He walked with just a hint of a stoop, and his wire rim glasses and thinning hair made him seem older than he probably was. His shoulders were bent, and he shook both of their hands with a small smile of irrepressible courtesy.

He paled in comparison to his wife Marjorie. She was a good two inches taller than Anson. Her thoroughly gray hair was combed straight down with severe bangs in front. But it was the line of her jaw that really caught Dan's attention. This was a woman who was used to getting her own way. She made no offer to shake either man's hand.

Steve Matson was first to speak. "I want to offer our condolences to you," he said. "I know this must be a very difficult time for you, and I am sorry." He gestured to encourage everyone in the office to sit down.

Dan noticed that Anson seemed to check with Marjorie for permission before they sat. When she fell firmly into a chair, he took a seat beside her. "I don't think you have any idea how we feel," Marjorie began, her voice steeped in bitterness.

"I'm sure that's true," Steve agreed with her.

Marjorie plunged on. "Sixteen years ago we reported that our daughter was missing. Neither you nor the Sheriff's office took that report seriously. You never mounted a serious search. And now you tell us that she has been lying at the bottom of a cliff for the past sixteen years."

"It appears that we have found your daughter's body," Steve replied. "It was in a very isolated part of the wilderness, far from any trail. In fact, it was found because of a couple of hikers who were well off trail, and a little bit lost."

"So why didn't you start looking for her sixteen years ago?" Marjorie insisted.

Steve Matson put his hands palms down on the desk in front of him, as if he were trying to calm the waters with the gesture. "Mrs. Ritter, I wasn't here sixteen years ago, and I can't address your concerns on that matter. I am sorry." Dan could feel the rage building in Marjorie Ritter, sitting to his left.

"I would like to ask you a favor," Matson continued. "The SAR team found a backpack near your daughter's remains. We think it might well be her backpack. Would you be willing to go to the Sheriff's office and help us identify it, and some of the equipment in it?"

Marjorie Ritter was implacable. "It doesn't really matter now, does it?" she asked combatively. "That isn't going to bring her back."

"No," Matson agreed. "It isn't going to bring her back. But it if is her backpack, it might help us understand exactly what happened sixteen years ago. And I think that might help everyone."

"Well, it's nice of you to be so concerned about it now," Marjorie replied acidly.

"We will do everything we can to resolve this," Matson said. "I know that is important to you." He waved his hand in Dan's direction. "This is Dan Courtwright, the ranger who formed the search party to find your daughter's remains." He looked straight at Dan. "Dan would be happy to meet you down at the Sheriff's office in Sonora so that you can help us identify her belongings, if you could." Dan nodded. The last thing he wanted to do was to prolong this conversation.

The Ritters looked at each other, and Marjorie stood up. Anson quickly followed. Marjorie Ritter turned to stare at Dan. "It would have been nice if you had done that sixteen years ago," she said.

"Sixteen years ago Dan was a student at Humboldt State," Steve explained quietly to her. "Dan, you'll head straight down to Sonora to meet the Ritters there?" Dan nodded.

The Ritters left without saying another word, leaving a vast silence in the office. "Hurry up and get down there to meet them," Steve said. "I'll call the Sheriff and let him know they are coming."

Dan hurried out to his truck. In the parking lot, he saw Anson Ritter opening the door for Marjorie on the couple's Cadillac.

Dan started the truck and pulled out on the highway, going west. Sixteen years ago he was at Humboldt State as an undergrad, long before his doctorate. And his marriage had dissolved about two and a half years later.

chapter 17

By the time the Ritters arrived at the Sheriff's Department, Cal and Dan were seated at a table in an interview room, and they had armed themselves with a few folders in front of them.

When Anson held the door open for Marjorie Ritter, Dan stood up to greet her, extending his hand to her, and Cal followed his lead. After very minimal courtesies, Dan took the lead in the conversation and again offered his condolences to the Ritters. He then moved directly on, and asked them if they would be willing to help with the investigation of her death.

"Of course!" Marjorie Ritter erupted. "That's why we're here!" Anson nodded his agreement.

"I can think of three areas where we could use your assistance," Dan continued. "The first one would be to take a look at the backpack and equipment we found with her body, and to help us identify that. It would be very helpful."

"Okay," Marjorie Ritter said slowly, reluctantly agreeing to this. It seemed to Dan was as if she was expecting some kind of trap.

"Thank you," Dan said. "We'll have you do that when we're finished here. The second thing you could do would be to review the statements you made sixteen years ago. There may be something that has come to mind since then, or something that you have noticed. It would be helpful if you could do that for us."

"I don't think there is anything to change," Marjorie said firmly.

"I told you at the time that Todd Walters had killed my daughter, and you wouldn't do a damn thing about it. I suppose that now you are going to tell me that you don't have enough evidence, even after you've finally found her body."

Dan waited until she was finished, then spoke very softly. He knew the next thing he said would be critical to the future of his relationship with the Ritters, and he chose to use her first name. "Marjorie, I wasn't here sixteen years ago, so I can't really answer for that. I can tell you that Cal and I found your daughter's body two days ago. And that we are going to do everything we can to find out how she died. That's why we need you to look at the statements you made back then. We want answers to what happened, and we are not going to stop until we get them."

Marjorie Ritter met this with stony silence. Dan allowed the pause to extend for quite a few seconds, until Anson Ritter finally broke the silence. "I think we can help with that, can't we, Marjorie?" He glanced at his wife for approval. Marjorie Ritter didn't respond to her husband, and Dan waited for her to lodge an objection. When she didn't, he pressed on.

"Finally, we know that Rebecca kept a diary," he continued. He could see Marjorie stiffen visibly at the mention of the diary. "I know that was mentioned to the Sheriff's office back when you first reported her missing. If you still have that, we would like to take a look at it."

"Absolutely not," Marjorie shook her head. "We are not going to allow this to become some kind of public circus. We've been through that once, and we will never go through that again."

Cal shifted in his chair, and Dan turned to look at him. "Mrs. Ritter, nobody is going to see that diary except Ranger Courtwright and me," he said, "but it is the only voice your daughter has now, and if it can tell us anything about what happened, I think you'd want us to hear that."

"Absolutely not," Marjorie replied. "A seventeen-year-old girl writes a lot of ridiculous things in a diary. Everybody knows that. And so does Todd Walters. And I am not going to have him, or his attorney, read through that diary and desecrate my daughter's memory with it. If you charge Todd Walters with murder, that's exactly what they will do."

A long silence followed this statement. Cal cleared his throat, then spoke again. "Mrs. Ritter, if we charge Todd Walters with the murder of your daughter, his attorney can probably subpoena Rebecca's diary anyway. And we can't stop that. But if her diary does have any clues to what happened, there's only one way we can find that out. And that is to study it." He glanced at Anson Ritter, who was staring at his wife. "Mrs. Ritter, I have a fifteen-year-old daughter myself. She goes to Sonora High School just like Rebecca did."

"And what?" Marjorie Ritter interrupted. "You think you know how I feel? You have no idea how I feel. Your daughter is still alive." The venom dripped from her voice. "Now why don't you do some police work and find out what happened to our daughter, and leave us in peace?"

Dan realized that Cal wasn't getting anywhere. "Marjorie, nobody can feel what you are feeling," he said. "We know that. But we are trying to do the very best investigation we can, even though this is sixteen years later. That really limits the kind of evidence and information we can collect. It makes every single item far more important than it would have been sixteen years ago."

He looked at Cal, who offered no help. The Ritters stared at him in silence. "Look," Dan continued, retreating. "We don't need to resolve this today. Why don't you take a look at what we found up in the mountains? Maybe it will help us—help you remember something that will help us."

"Can you at least tell us how she died?" Marjorie asked.

"We've just got the report from the coroner," Cal said, indicating a folder on the table in front of him. "There were multiple injuries, consistent with a fall; some broken bones, a fractured skull. The coroner thinks it is likely that she died because she fell down the cliff where we found her."

This was met with silence. The two officials waited for Marjorie to break the silence.

"So we don't know why she fell, or if she was pushed?" she asked.

"No, we don't," replied Cal Healey.

"That's why we think her diary might be helpful," Dan added.

"Why? So that you can prove she was depressed?" Marjorie accused them. "That would make your jobs very easy, wouldn't it? And if the people in this town assumed that her parents drove her to suicide, then your job would be over, wouldn't it?"

Under the table, Dan moved his hand to nudge Cal slightly on the leg. It was a motion that went undetected by the Ritters, but it stopped Cal before he could answer Marjorie's question.

"Marjorie, if you don't want us to investigate your daughter's death, I can understand that," Dan said. "I can only imagine what you are feeling, but I can see how the pain of the process would be very difficult for you. So if you really don't want to know what happened to your daughter, if you don't want us to find out, then you don't really have to help us at all. We will investigate her death as best we can, sixteen years later. That's all we can do."

Dan paused to glance at Cal, and then continued. "But when you came up to Mi-Wuk this morning, you said you wanted action, and I completely agreed with you. We are going to investigate this. But I have to ask you a question. What do you think people are going to say in this community, if you don't cooperate with us as we investigate your daughter's death?"

Marjorie looked at Anson Ritter and then abruptly stood up. "I think I'd like to see her things now," she said.

Cal Healey quickly opened the door and asked her to follow him as he led the way. For a moment, Anson Ritter stopped at the door and looked back at Dan. Dan thought Anson was going to say something to him, but instead the older man turned and followed his wife and Cal Healey down the hall.

As Cal entered the next room, he could hear Cal explaining the condition of the backpack and the other equipment they had found. Cal worked his way through each piece of evidence, asking Marjorie Ritter to identify it, confirm it, explain how Rebecca might have packed it. The conversation was very quiet and Marjorie Ritter was calm, even professional in her response.

The pack was an external pack frame, and showed heavy abrasion in two places where it had hit the granite cliff on the way down. Marjorie confirmed that her daughter would have had her sleeping bag tied on the outside of the bag, on the lower part of the frame. The cook kit was one that Marjorie had used as a Girl Scout herself, and had loaned to Rebecca for this trip. Each small item was studied, discussed, and explained.

As Cal continued to talk with Marjorie, Dan found himself watching Anson Ritter. Rebecca's father wasn't really listening to Cal or to his wife. At first Dan thought that he was simply bored, or lost in thought. But then he noticed Anson Ritter's right hand, which was resting on the edge of the table. Between his thumb and first finger he held a small piece of the hip belt from Rebecca's pack. Dan could see him slowly rubbing his thumb back and forth on the faded nylon. A tiny splash of water caught his eye, and he looked up at Anson Ritter. Dan could see tears slowly rolling down Anson Ritter's face.

The Ritters left the Sheriff's office without agreeing to share their daughter's diary.

chapter 18

The tension from the conversation with the Ritters left Dan and Cal both drained. Dan walked out into the parking lot behind the building, not because he wanted to get in his car and drive away, but because he needed space and fresh air. He made it as far as his truck and leaned back against the left front fender. Sunlight washed over him, and he took a deep breath and let it out slowly. Despite the heat, it felt good.

He looked up to see Cal walking towards him in the parking lot. "That was brutal," Cal said to him.

Dan nodded. "I understand some of what they are going through," he said, "but how do they expect us to figure this out? This was a long time ago, and we don't have much to go on."

"They don't care about that," Cal answered. "For them, this is all just about their pain. They don't want to know our problems; they just want the pain to go away. And I am not sure that we're going to be able to do anything to make that happen."

"So what do we do now?" Dan asked Cal.

"Do you want to see Todd Walters?" Cal asked. "I got a voicemail just now that says he's over at the VFW hall, having a beer."

Dan checked his watch. It said 10:48. He looked at Cal.

"Don't worry," Cal chuckled. "We don't have to drink with him. Come on, I'll drive."

As they walked from the bright sunlight in the parking lot, the darkness of the VFW Hall left them almost blind. The air conditioning didn't work very well, and Dan was still sweating from the heat in his truck. Dan removed his sunglasses and peered around the room. A bar at the far end of the room was surrounded by a few tables. At one table a man in a wheelchair sat with his back to the door. His companion, a clean-cut African-American, glanced up at Dan and Cal as they walked toward the bar.

Cal walked up to the table and greeted Todd Walters. Lean and angular, Todd's strong jaw dominated his face. His jet black hair contrasted with his pale clear skin. Dan thought that in another life, Todd might have had the good looks to work as a model. Todd's arms were thin and wiry, and seemed to have enormous energy. They moved from the wheels of his chair to the table, to the bottle of beer in front of him. His companion had a glass of something clear in front of him—either water or vodka, Dan couldn't tell which.

"So I guess you heard about us finding Rebecca Ritter?" Cal said, as a way of starting the conversation.

Todd Walters looked at the man seated next to him, and answered, "Yeah, I heard."

The other man at the table asked Todd, "Do you want me to leave? Or do you want me here?"

Todd took a swig from the beer bottle before he answered. "I don't care what you do," he said to the man. And then to Cal, he repeated, "Yeah, I heard that."

Dan watched the black man slowly stand up and walk over to the bar. He left his drink on the bar and walked toward the door, pulling out his cell phone as he did so.

Cal asked Todd if he remembered the trip well enough to go over the details again. "Oh, yeah," Todd said, nodding his head. "I remember it." He waited, looking expectantly for Cal or Dan to ask the next question.

Dan pulled out a chair from the table and sat down. "Look, I'm new here, so I am just going to ask you to run through what you remember," Dan said. "Just start from when you started hiking, and tell us what happened."

Todd held his beer bottle in his hand and slowly rocked it back and forth on the table. "She wasn't ready when I picked her up at her house," Todd began, still staring at the bottle. "And her pack wasn't ready either. So we spent a lot of time there, and then we had to stop at a store to buy some stuff for her. I don't remember what, but stuff for the trip. Chapstick, or something. So we started late."

Todd sat back in his chair and locked his hands on top of his head. He was staring at the ceiling as he continued. "We hiked in from Crabtree Cabin, and the first day was to Toejam. We camped there, and everything was fine."

Dan nodded. "Did you fish at Toejam Lake?"

"I guess so," Todd replied. "I mean, that's what I did on this trip: fish."

"And how did Rebecca seem?" Dan asked.

"She was fine," Todd answered. "She took too much stuff, so her pack was pretty heavy. She had a hard time keeping up. But she was fine. She was happy."

"So you camped at Toejam Lake the first night," Cal encouraged him.

"The next day we hiked through Whitesides Meadow to Wire Lakes," Todd continued. "We camped at Middle Wire, and I fished there. Rebecca took off that afternoon, said she wanted to go sunbathing, and I didn't see her until dinner."

When Todd paused, Dan waited. "Yeah, she seemed fine," Todd responded. "She seemed fine the whole trip until the next morning. Then she got up, got dressed, and told me she was taking off, and that I shouldn't follow her."

"And that's when she handed you the note?" Cal prompted him.

"Yeah, well, not exactly," Todd said. "She was going to leave, and I told that I was going to get a lot of heat about all this. So she said she'd write me a note that would explain it all. And that's what she did."

"And she took all her stuff?" Dan asked.

"She took most of the food," Todd said. "She said that I was fishing, so I could eat the fish I caught. And we were sharing a tent, but she was happy to sleep out under the stars." Todd took a swig of beer. "I was pretty damn hungry by the time I got back," he added.

Dan was trying to piece this together on a map in his mind. "So when she left camp, what direction was she headed?"

"We were on the west side of Middle Wire Lake," Todd answered. "She walked back down the trail toward Lower Wire, and that's all I know. I was going to follow her and try to talk her out of it, but she turned around and told me to mind my own business and leave her alone."

"So you don't know where she went from there?" Dan asked.

"No idea," Todd said curtly. The door opened and Todd's drinking companion walked back into the hall. Todd paused to look over his shoulder to see who had opened the door.

"There are trails that would take you to Kennedy Meadows, or Gianelli, or Crabtree trailhead," Dan said. "She could go just about anywhere from there. Even down to Woods Lake and down that way," he added as he met Cal's gaze. Woods Lake was an easy hike from Leighton Lake.

"So where did you go after that, Todd?" Cal asked.

Todd paused before answering. "I hiked out the top of Upper Wire Lake, down into Deer Lake, then back along the trail to Crabtree," he said.

Dan had hiked the route a few times. "That's a long day to the trailhead, or maybe two, right?" he asked Todd.

Todd nodded. "Yeah, maybe. But I decided to hang out for a

day or two and fish." He looked at Dan. "I mean, we'd planned on a weeklong trip, and I still wanted to do that. And she knew our route, so I thought maybe she would change her mind… so I stuck to it."

"In case she wanted to find you?" Cal asked.

"Yeah," Todd agreed. Todd's companion collected his drink from the bar and sat back down at the table.

"And you had no idea that she was going to do this?" Cal asked.

Todd just shook his head slowly. There was something odd about the way Todd's companion was sitting, almost too close to Todd.

"So who is this?" Dan asked, pointing to the man. With his eyes adapted to the dark, Dan could see that the black man was neatly dressed. Dan guessed that he was about forty years old, very neatly groomed. In this town, having your shoes polished was a statement of social class, and this man's shoes gleamed in the dim light of the bar.

The man stood up briskly and extended his hand. "Chester Fowler," he said, meeting Dan's hand with a firm handshake. He then turned to Cal and repeated the whole thing, including his name.

"So how do you know Todd?" Cal asked him.

"We served together," Fowler responded.

That explained the dress and manners of the man to Dan. They were remnants of military service.

"And do you live around here now?" Cal asked.

"Modesto," Fowler responded.

Todd Walters interrupted them. "If you guys are done now, I'd like to be left in peace?"

Dan glanced at Cal, who nodded toward the door. "Thanks for your help," Dan said. "We'll let you know if we have any more questions."

Todd was now ignoring them. As Cal and Dan opened the door into the bright sunlight, they heard Todd call out, "How about another round?" to the bartender.

Dan eased himself onto the blistering seat of the truck and looked at Cal. "We don't really know enough to say anything at all about this, do we?"

"We know pretty much nothing at all," Cal agreed. "And I don't think there's much more we can find out."

"What do you think I should tell Matson?" Dan asked. "He wants to know if we should refer this to the FBI or not …"

Cal snorted. "Hell, they aren't going to figure out anything more than we did," he said. "Why? Do you think they somehow are going to solve this thing? How are they going to do that?" He glanced at his watch. "It's lunchtime. Do you want to grab a bite to eat somewhere?"

Dan shook his head. "Thanks, but I think I want to get back to the office and start writing this up. If I am going to hand this over to Matson, I want to make sure that whoever gets it really gets it—that they understand our thinking on this."

"Do you think that will make a difference?" Cal asked. "I don't care how seriously they take it … there just isn't enough here to figure it out!"

"Not my problem," Dan replied. "I don't have to help them solve it; I just have to decide that it is something to be solved, and then turn it over to them."

"There is one thing that I'd like to see solved," Cal said.

"What's that?" Dan asked him.

"People who commit suicide usually tidy things up. They don't leave one boot off when they jump down the cliff," Cal said.

"Yeah … that's what I was thinking," Dan answered him. "And I was up on that cliff. I don't think anyone would fall off that by accident. Sure, people do stupid things, but Katie and I sat up there and wandered around. I don't think she would have suddenly fallen down the face of the cliff unless she had help."

"So that leaves only one other option," Cal said.

"Yeah," Dan said slowly. "I turn this over to the FBI."

chapter 19

Once he dropped Cal off at the Sheriff's station, Dan had second thoughts about going into the office. Instead, he turned off the highway and went home. He told himself it was quieter at home, and he would get more done. And that was true.

It would also make sure that if Kristen called, he would be there to take the call. Not that he thought she was going to call. He didn't know what had gone wrong, but if she were going to call him back, she would have done so by now. Unless there was something wrong with her voicemail?

Once inside the house, Dan checked the phone. No messages. He went into the kitchen to make a sandwich and thought about calling Kristen again. What would he say? That he thought he was falling in love with her, and she apparently didn't feel the same way about him?

After some thought, he came to a compromise with himself. He would eat lunch, finish up the report, and then leave Kristen a short message—just something to say that he was calling again, in case she didn't get the first one, and that he was still available for dinner sometime if she was interested. That's all, he decided.

He took the sandwich, a half-eaten bag of corn chips, and a glass of water out onto the back porch and sat down to eat. He realized he must have been dehydrated, because the water tasted wonderful to him.

As he reached into the bag of chips, his next-door neighbor called to him over the fence. "Got the day off today?" Walt asked him. In his seventies, Walt still spent most of his days working in his garden, and Dan wasn't surprised to see him there.

"Hi, Walt," Dan answered. "No, I've got to write a big report today. Thought it would be easier here than up at the office."

"Are you working on that Rebecca Ritter thing?" Walt asked. Dan wondered, yet again, if everyone in the county knew about it. "How did you hear about it?" he asked Walt.

"Oh, hell, everybody is talking about it," Walt said. "Ruth was down at the store this morning, and it's the only topic in town. She said there were at least three theories about what happened to her."

Dan nodded. "Probably more than that, Walt," he said. "But it's out of my hands. I'm just writing up what we found and turning it over to the Feds. They can figure out what they want to do with it."

"Well, at least you found her," Walt said. "This must be hard for her folks, but at least they know she's not living in some part of the country and not talking to them. I guess that's something."

While Walt turned his attention to his tomatoes, Dan finished up his lunch in silence. When he was done, he walked over to see how Walt was doing. "Nice-looking tomatoes," he said to Walt.

Walt leaned back on his haunches and took a breath. "It's been a pretty good year for them," he said. "I'll bring some over this afternoon, once Ruth decides how many she needs for tonight."

"Thanks," Dan said, "but I wasn't asking for some, you know."

Walt looked at him, shielding his eyes a bit from the sun. "I know. Do you want some?" Dan laughed. "Sure, that would be great, thanks," he said.

Walt turned back to his tomatoes. "I wonder what her parents are going to complain about now," he said. "It's got to be something."

Dan walked back into his house and started to write. The first part of his report was simple. He just catalogued all the files from the Sheriff's office and explained a little bit about each one. In addition to the folders on Todd Walters, Bryan Lafferty and the rest, there were also notes on all of the reported sightings of Rebecca Ritter over the years. It occurred to Dan that if someone had killed Rebecca, that person might find it helpful if there were reports that she was still alive.

He read through the files carefully, looking for any connections between the sightings and any of his potential suspects. Most of the sightings were from people who had seen the reports about the missing girl on the news. A few seemed as if they might have a connection with someone here in Sonora, and Dan considered giving them a call.

Then he remembered Steve Matson's directive: it was the FBI's case now, and he was turning it over to them. If they wanted to follow up with these people, they could. Dan put the folder back in the box.

The last sheet of paper was an inventory of evidence. There was very little on it. They had listed all of the backpacking equipment that Todd had in his pack when he returned. Dan scanned the list. It was amazing how backpacking had changed in these last fifteen years. Few of the older, heavier items that Todd had carried would be found on backpackers today. The kid must have been carrying a fifty-pound pack when he started out. Rebecca may have been carrying another forty-plus pounds, herself. No wonder Todd said that she had been unable to keep up with him that first day.

The last item on the list caught Dan's attention. It was described simply as "a note Todd Walters identified as being written on a page of Rebecca Ritter's diary." There was an evidence locker number on the item, so Dan assumed that it was still somewhere in the Sheriff's department. He would have to track that down and give it to the FBI as well.

He seemed to remember seeing the note. Sure enough, stapled

to the back of Todd's interview was a photocopy. Dan found it, now graying with age. "I am so sick of trying to live up to everybody's expectations, especially Mom and Dad's. I can't live this way anymore!" it said. Then, in much larger letters, big block letters that shouted, the note said, "I am going to live my own life!!!"

Dan studied the note. The handwriting was careful and clear. There was no date on the sheet, but the page number was forty-three. A little shorter than the size of a small paperback book, the sheet was torn along the left edge. It was, Dan thought, probably the last thing that Rebecca Ritter had written in her life. He placed the papers back in the folder and set to writing his notes on the trip to recover the body.

The phone rang, and startled Dan. He had been working for hours now, and he stretched quickly before reaching for the phone. "Hello?"

"Dan? It's Steve Matson." Steve paused for effect. "How are you doing with that report?"

Dan looked around at the piles of papers on his desk. "I'm getting there," he said. "I've got all the photos listed in order; and pretty much wrapped up all the various parts. Now I just have to write up my conclusions."

"Do you have some?" Steve asked.

Dan thought about this for a moment. "Yeah, I do," he answered. "There is a lot of stuff we don't know here, I'll admit that. But I am going to ask you to refer this to the FBI."

Steve greeted this news with little enthusiasm. "Okay," he said slowly. "And what exactly are we going to tell them?"

Dan scanned the papers on his desk again, looking for inspiration. "I guess we're going to tell them that there is no evidence that this young woman decided to commit suicide. I don't think the note was a suicide note. It talks about wanting to live her own life ... not about dying." Steve grunted an affirmation into the phone.

"And when she went down that cliff, one of her boots was not on. We found her right boot, but not her left. Her right boot was tied on tight, and was still connected to her foot. We never did find her left boot. People who commit suicide usually tidy things up more than that."

"Okay," Steve said. "So let's say that she didn't commit suicide. Could it have been an accident? Did she just fall?"

"Katie Pederson and I climbed up to where she must have been, at the top of the cliff," Dan said. "And by the way, Katie is quite a rock climber. She made me look old and gimpy."

"You are old and gimpy," Matson answered. "Almost as old and gimpy as I am. So what did you see up there?"

"This is not what I would consider a dangerous place," Dan said. "The rock is clean, smooth. There's an erratic boulder up there that Katie is sure was used by this kid as a chair. It's hard to imagine how someone falls down from up there. Sure, people do stupid things, but this kid knew the outdoors."

"So you think …" Steve prompted him.

"The most obvious and simplest explanation is that somebody pushed her," Dan said. "Or she jumped. I have no idea who did it." Then he corrected himself. "Actually, I think there are a couple of people who could have done it, but I have absolutely no proof."

"That's going to make the FBI really happy," Steve said sarcastically.

"Yeah, I know," Dan answered with a sigh. "But I think there are still some possible leads to follow up, and I just can't see letting this go. And I think her parents would be furious if we did that. I would be, too, in their shoes."

"They're furious already," Steve admitted. He remembered all too well the meeting in his office. "So you'll write it up and have it ready by tomorrow?"

Dan's phoned beeped, to let him know that he had another call.

"Yes," he promised.

"About what time?" Matson asked.

Dan was trying to see who was calling him, while still talking to Steve. "I can get it there first thing in the morning," he said.

"Good," Matson answered. "That way I can read through it before I send it out. Can you give it to me on a thumb drive, so I can make changes if I need to?"

Dan realized that he was not going to be able to answer the other call in time. The message screen on his phone just said "Unidentified number."

"Yeah, I'll email it to you, and then drop off a printed version with the box of files," he told his boss.

By the time he hung up, the other caller was gone. Dan punched into his voice mail to see if there was a message.

"You have one new message," his phone announced. "Here is your first message:"

Dan waited expectantly. "Dan?" a female voice asked, and then silence. Whoever called him had either hung up or lost the connection. Dan listened for twenty seconds, until the voicemail system cut in and said, "End of message."

Dan looked at the phone, then at the pile of papers in front of him. He carefully placed the phone on the desk next to him and got back to writing on the computer.

chapter 20

It was a long night. Dan worked in big chunks of time, writing an outline on paper, then filling in the larger blocks of text on his computer. At least three times he stood up and paced around the room, allowing his mind to work through the details of the report. Twice he cut large sections of text and moved them to another part of the report. And once he moved the section back again.

He first organized it all chronologically, and wrote it out. But it was some time after he had stopped to eat a bowl of ramen noodles that Dan went back to the outline and organized it all by his two primary suspects: Todd Walters and Bryan Lafferty. That made sense for a while.

In the end, he settled on a compromise solution. He began with an explanation of who Rebecca Ritter was, and why she was hiking in the wilderness. That allowed him to introduce both suspects. And then once he explained that she had not returned from the trip, he could talk about both of the suspects in detail in a middle section.

He wrapped up the report with the discovery of her body near Leighton Lake, and the anomalies with the missing boot, the odd "suicide" note, and the recent interviews with Todd, Bryan, and Lori.

It was well after dark by the time he finished. He checked the printer for paper, pushed the "print" icon, and sat back, listening to his printer methodically print out page after page of report.

Dan looked around the room and noticed the phone again. He picked it up and with no further thought dialed Kristen's number. As he listened to the phone ring, he decided that he would just leave a simple message to reiterate his invitation to get together soon for dinner or maybe a movie.

"Hello, this is Kristen," the live voice startled Dan.

"Kristen. Hi. This is Dan," he managed to sputter out. Now what? He hoped Kristen hadn't noticed how unsettled he was.

"Hi, Dan. I am sorry. I guess tonight didn't work out?" Kristen asked him.

Now Dan was at a loss. "No … I mean … I am sorry. I had to write up a big report tonight …"

Kristen paused just a moment—long enough for Dan to think that he had said something wrong. "That's okay," she said. "I understand …"

From the way she said it, Dan wasn't sure that she did understand. This wasn't going at all the way he had hoped.

"Well, we've got to turn the case over to the FBI now, and so I had to write all that up …" Dan explained. "It was just a lot of work …"

"Well …" Kristen allowed the word to linger. "I guess we'll have to wait until I get back. That is, if you still want to have dinner."

"Oh, no …" Dan quickly assured her. "I would love to have dinner with you. When do you get back? Where are you going?" he asked.

"Huckleberry Lake? I'm going there for five days?" Kristen was now asking a question with every sentence. "Didn't you get my message?"

How could this conversation be going so wrong?

"No … oh, that was you!" Somehow, Dan did not seem to be able to get the words out right. "I mean, I got a message from someone, but it was garbled. I couldn't tell who it was, or what they said. Sorry." This last bit he mumbled.

Kristen sighed. "Well, that explains a lot." She started from the beginning. Dan detected a hint of frustration in her voice. "I left you a message this afternoon to say that I would love to meet you for dinner tonight. I guess it's too late for that now. And tomorrow I have to leave. I've been asked to cook for a group at Huckleberry Lake for five days." She paused. "So I guess it will have to wait until I get back …"

"Shoot …" Dan said. "I'm sorry. I was buried with this report, and I needed to get it done by tomorrow morning. We're turning the case over to the FBI …"

Kristen sounded more contrite. "Well, I'm sure it's important."

Dan realized that Kristen didn't know anything about the case. "I guess you haven't heard, although you must be the only one in Tuolumne County," he said. "We found Rebecca Ritter's remains up by Leighton Lake."

"Oh … no, I hadn't heard." Kristen's voice was subdued. "So that's what you found? What we talked about at dinner at Cal and Maggie's house? And she was … well … what do they say? Foul play?"

"We're not sure," Dan admitted, "but we think it is worth having the FBI look into it."

This was followed by a long silence. Kristen was first to speak. "I guess we'll just have to plan dinner another time," she said.

"When do you get back in town?" Dan asked, trying to move the conversation into happier territory.

"I'll be back late Thursday," Kristen said.

"Do you want to try to plan something for Thursday?" Dan asked.

"I don't know," Kristen sounded guarded. "I may have to go somewhere that night … maybe we should just talk when I get back in town."

Dan reluctantly agreed. Their farewells were cordial, but Dan couldn't help thinking that the conversation had been a step in the wrong direction. And what could have been an evening with Kristen had been spent working on his computer for Steve Matson.

He hung up the phone and looked at the report. First thing in the morning, he would drop it off at Steve's house and be done with it. That would give him the rest of the day off. That sounded pretty good right now.

chapter 21

Saturday morning dawned bright and cheerful. Dan was up with the sun, and he took his breakfast out onto his back porch to eat. It was just warm enough for him to eat there in his bathrobe and slippers without feeling cold.

The two squirrels that lived in the big pine at the back of his property were scampering happily up and down the trunk, occasionally pausing to look at Dan and chatter a warning. First one, then the other would race along, then stop, then race off again.

A blue jay landed on the porch railing and looked expectantly at Dan. Dan didn't bother trying to frighten it away. He never fed any of the animals in his backyard, but he didn't see any reason to chase them out, either.

He finished up his bowl of granola and drank the huge glass of grapefruit juice. The tang of the slightly bitter juice caught his attention, and he sat up straighter and stretched his back. He twisted his right shoulder and was gratified to hear and feel a light pop in his spine. The blue jay took flight at the sound and motion.

Dan stood up and collected his breakfast things and took them into the kitchen. Twenty minutes later he was showered and dressed. He picked up the report on Rebecca Ritter, added it to the files from the Sheriff's office, and walked out the door to his truck.

When he got to Steve Matson's place, Steve opened the door before Dan could ring the bell. Steve invited him in and led Dan into the kitchen, where Dan put the box on the counter. On top was his report. Steve thumbed through the report and asked Dan a few cursory questions, which Dan answered.

Steve then dropped the report on the counter and looked in the box of files. One by one he pulled them out and leafed through them, his glasses sliding further down his nose as he did. Satisfied that he had what he needed, he put the last file down, used a finger to push his glasses up into place again, and turned to Dan.

"This is going to piss the FBI off," he said with a tight-lipped smile.

"It's your call, Steve," Dan cautioned him. "You asked me to write up what I found, and what I thought. So that's what I did. And then I made a recommendation."

Steve nodded. "I know," he said. "I am not complaining. But this just isn't a simple case. And the guys at the FBI are going to hate it."

Dan thought this over. "If you don't want to give it to them, I could spend some more time on it," he offered. "At least some of the next steps are pretty obvious, I think."

"Nope," Steve said firmly. "We don't have the time or the budget for that. And it's their job. And if they don't like it, we'll just to tell them that we feel their pain."

"That should be fun," Dan said.

Steve looked up at him. "Monday morning, in my office," he said. "They're sending somebody up to meet with us and pick up the files. Agent Frank Oliver. Ten o'clock. And I'd like you to be there."

For some reason, Dan checked his watch. "Sure, I'll be there."

"Good," Matson said. "And I know you've only had one day off this week, but can you get back to your normal schedule tomorrow? I don't want to leave Doris up there alone."

"No, I expected that," Dan said. "I can get a few things done today around town …"

"Thanks, Dan." Steve stood up and walked him to the door. "I'll make it up to you in the fall."

"Not a problem," Dan assured him. "I know you're good for it."

Steve smiled. "We may not have any money, but I can usually get you some time!" he said.

Dan spent the rest of the day in his truck. He picked up some socks and underwear in Sonora and bought gas for the truck. He stopped in Jamestown to get a hamburger for lunch, and he paid his utility bill. He bought groceries and then took them home to put them away. And all the time, he was working through the details of the report he had just written, looking for something he had missed, some way to answer some of the questions that still remained.

In fact, he had been so deep in thought at the grocery store that he didn't recognize Janet di Conti until she said hello to him in front of the meat counter. Even then, it took a second for him to surface and place her face.

"You've been a busy guy," Janet said to him. She turned away for a minute to order some sausage and pork chops.

"I guess everybody in town knows the story, huh?" Dan asked.

"It's really very sad," Janet replied. "It must be so hard on her parents to have this come up all over again."

"It is," Dan agreed. "It's hard on a lot of people."

"I guess it's good that they are finally getting some closure," Janet said. "Are you going to the funeral?"

"I don't know anything about it," Dan replied.

"It's Monday afternoon at the church," Janet told him. "I think they're expecting a big crowd. I know a lot of the teachers are going to be there."

"I don't know," Dan said. "I may have to work …"

"I would think that you could take time off work to go to a funeral," Janet said gently. "Especially since you were the one who found her."

"Well, I didn't really …" Dan thought better of explaining that in more detail. "I'll ask about the funeral," he said.

"We'll see you there, I'm sure," Janet said as she began to roll her cart toward the produce section.

Not for the first time, Dan had second thoughts about living in such a small community. There were no secrets here. And everybody's business was everybody else's business.

Once home, Dan put away the groceries and sat down at his computer. At first he just scanned the news, then started surfing the web, following one link after another. It was a mindless activity, and he fully realized that he was simply escaping into the web, allowing his mind to wander.

He checked his email, hoping to find something of interest there. As he scanned the list in his inbox, his heart gave a tiny leap. There was an email from Kristen. He opened it up.

"Dan," it said. "Sorry things didn't work out for dinner last night. Hope we'll have better luck next time. Kristen."

Dan sat back in his chair, arms folded across his chest. He did not want to mishandle this the way he had bungled the phone call.

After a few minutes, he began to type.

"Kristen,

Thank you for writing. I think we should try to make our own luck next time … I would love to have dinner with you … And I promise to try to make my own luck …"

He wrote, he deleted, and he wrote again. Whatever made him think that he was going to be able to write something more successfully than he had managed the phone call? Finally, he wrote her:

"Kristen,

Thanks for the note, and thanks even more for trying to work out something last night. Now it's my turn. I would love to have dinner with you Thursday night, after you get back in town. And if that doesn't work out, then Friday night. And if that doesn't work out … some other night. Just let me know when.

Dan"

He read it one more time and then pushed the "send" button. She wouldn't get it for five more days. But when she did, she would know that he had written back immediately. And maybe she would get back in time for dinner on Thursday.

Dan opened his calendar and blocked out Thursday night. Then he did the same for Friday night, and Saturday. He didn't want to take any chances this time.

Sunday would have been a quiet day at the Pinecrest Ranger Station except for one phone call. Amid the hikers and campers who came to ask for directions, get their permits, or tell their stories, Doris took a phone call. She wrote down a few notes as she spoke, and then explained that she was going to transfer the call to a ranger.

She looked over and made eye contact with Dan. With a slight inclination of her head, she indicated that Dan might want to take this call in the other office.

He walked into the other office just as Doris was saying, "I am transferring you now …"

Dan picked up the phone. The caller was a man, calm and serious. "I think you might have a problem up here near Cedar Ridge," he said.

"Okay, what's that?" Dan asked.

The man explained that he lived right on the edge of the development, which backed up to the National Forest. And over the past few weeks he had noticed a lot of people walking down through the empty lot at the end of the street, and down into the National Forest.

Dan tried to remember if there was a trailhead there. He didn't think so.

The man continued: The people were almost always alone, and they were often carrying things on the way in. And they were almost never carrying things on the way out. Most of the visits were right around evening, when it was already getting dark. He didn't know where they parked, but it must have been somewhere farther away.

Dan began to get the picture. He asked for the man's address, and promised to stop by and check things out. The man wanted to know when. Dan told him that he would stop by tomorrow evening, if that would work.

The man explained that he would be out in the afternoon, but Dan could stop by after about four o'clock. And he wanted to make very sure that Dan didn't use his name, or cause him any trouble. Dan assured him that he would keep that information confidential.

When he walked back out into the main office, Doris was facing a room full of people who were anxious to be helped. Dan pitched in immediately, and it wasn't until he was driving home that he thought any more about the phone call.

But that would have to wait until after he met with the FBI in the morning.

chapter 22

Frank Oliver was not exactly what Dan expected. Sure, he was nearly as tall as Dan, and his broad shoulders filled out his dark suit with no room to spare. But he was older, in his mid-fifties, Dan guessed. And there was something odd about his head—it was slightly too small for his body.

Dan shook his hand and welcomed him to the office. Frank Oliver met Dan's eyes briefly and then immediately glanced around the office. "Is there somewhere I can set up shop here?" he asked Dan.

There was something about his hair that was not quite right. At first Dan suspected that it was a toupee, but after a few minutes he decided that it had been dyed deep black in an attempt to maintain that FBI look of power and confidence.

Dan decided that it hadn't worked. And the oil that held the hair in a tight embrace over Oliver's forehead just added to the failure. And the long, wrinkled face of the FBI agent reminded Dan in some ways of a small camel.

Dan led him into a spare office and gave him the cardboard box with all the files. "Make yourself at home," Dan said. "Do you want me to hang around to answer any questions? Or do you just want some time to study all this?"

Oliver looked at the box of files for a few seconds. "Why don't you give me some time with the files … and then I'll let you know if I have questions …"

It was said not as a question—more like an order.

Dan nodded. "Sounds good," he said. "Let me know if you need anything, and I'll stick around until you're ready for me." But Oliver didn't bother to respond. He had already sat down at the table and was pulling out the files.

Dan stood by awkwardly for a moment or two, then walked out the door. He didn't know if he should leave the door open or closed, but he decided that if Frank Oliver wanted the door closed, he could close it himself.

For the next hour Dan busied himself in the office. He wrapped up two small accident reports that had been due the previous week, checked the weather report, and reviewed the stack of wilderness permits to see how many people were in which areas of the forest. It was going to be a busy week in the back country, and that was before the usual party at Bear Lake on the weekend.

He called Doris up at the Summit Station and asked her how things were going. She assured him things were fine, then had to hang up to respond to some visitors who had arrived.

A few minutes later Dan wandered into the kitchen, carefully took a chocolate cake donut from the box there and cut it in half, then sat down to eat one half. He wondered what Kristen was doing now—probably tidying up after breakfast in camp. And then she would probably be reading a book until lunch. Or going on a walk around camp? He thought he remembered that she would be at Huckleberry Lake, and could imagine the morning sun on the water of the lake.

Dan looked at the other half of the donut and forced himself to put it back in the box and get up to go talk to Sara at the front desk. She was a bright young woman who had started a year ago, and always had time for a chat with Dan. He was still chatting with her twenty minutes later when Frank Oliver appeared. Oliver stood in the doorway and waited.

"You've got some questions for me?" he asked Oliver. Frank Oliver nodded, turned without saying a word, and walked back into the office he was using. Dan exchanged a glance with Sara and followed him.

Frank Oliver motioned to Dan to shut the door, and Dan closed it behind himself and turned to face Oliver.

The FBI agent pulled out a file and started to scan it. Under his right hand was a yellow legal pad, and Dan could see that it was full of notes. Oliver checked the pad quickly, turned a page in the file folder, and said, "So why are you turning this over to us?" He did not look up from this file.

Dan was still standing, and looking down at the top of Oliver's head he could see a fine, pale line in the part in his hair. Yep, dye job.

Dan pulled out a chair and sat down. "Pretty suspicious circumstances," he said. "People don't take one shoe off and then commit suicide. And it's hard to imagine she just fell down the mountain. She knew her way around this country …"

Frank Oliver's eyes continued to move back and forth between his notes and the files he was shuffling in front of himself. When Dan's voiced drifted to a stop he looked up and stared at Dan. It was a long wait until the agent spoke.

"That's it?" he asked. Dan realized that he had yet to see a smile on Frank Oliver's long face.

"This was a bright, healthy young woman," Dan said. "She was an experienced hiker, and there was no reason for her to go over the edge of that cliff. And we found her body: all but the one boot that was missing. She must have taken it off …"

"And you have no witnesses or other evidence …" It was a statement, not a question, that interrupted Dan.

"We have a guy who was stalking her …" Dan replied. "And the last person to see her alive was her boyfriend … so we have two legitimate suspects."

"Except that they weren't very serious about the romance," Oliver reminded him. "So that would leave the boyfriend out. And you have absolutely nothing to tie this guy ..." he paused to check his notes ... "Lafferty to anything within twenty miles of the place."

"Her pack wasn't closed up when she fell," Dan said. "We found it untied at the bottom of the cliff. She must have taken it off. You don't carry a backpack around that isn't closed up. Stuff falls out."

Frank Oliver stared at his notes a minute longer. "So she stops to take off her backpack," he began, "and something, maybe the whole backpack, rolls away and falls down the cliff. She decides to go after it. She walks around until she finds what she thinks is a way down the cliff. And she falls down and dies."

He looked up at Dan with a tired expression on his face. "And the boot?" Dan asked.

"On her foot," Oliver replied. "It may be not tied tightly. Some animal takes it away after she's dead."

Dan's jaw tightened, but he nodded to show that he understood Oliver's skepticism. "I can't think of an animal that would take the boot off and not touch the rest of her," Dan said, "except maybe another person. And if it was another person ..." He left the words dangling.

Frank Oliver stacked the files up neatly on the table in front of himself and looked at Dan, still not smiling. "And so your theory is what?" he asked.

Dan took a deep breath and let it out slowly. "She's sitting there, her pack is open and her boot is off her foot. Somebody comes up behind her and pushes her over the cliff."

Frank Oliver opened his hands, palms up, on the table. "Motive?"

"She and the boyfriend have a fight," Dan said. "Or the stalker, Lafferty, is jealous of the time she is spending with the other guy and shoves her."

"So why is the pack not where she fell?" Oliver asked.

Dan thought this over. "Whoever pushed her took the pack and went through it. And then tossed it down the cliff later."

It was Frank Oliver's turn to let out a slow breath. "So she stops to mess with her boot," he suggested. "She opens the pack. A bear sees or smells her, or the food in the pack, and rushes at her. She falls down the cliff. The bear pokes around in the pack, and drags it around on the cliff. It finally falls down later … away from the body."

A flash of embarrassment shot through Dan as mulled this over. "I don't think a bear would do that, rush a person like that," he said. "And we didn't find any claw or teeth marks on the pack."

Oliver looked straight at Dan. "If the pack were open, would a bear need to tear into it to get at the food?" he asked. "Have you checked the records of bear attacks here in that time period?"

Dan shook his head and admitted that he hadn't. "But if I had to choose between a bear and a person attacking her, I would not put my money on the bear being the attacker."

"Right," Oliver said, "and I don't disagree. But there is nothing here that proves anything. There is no case. And after sixteen years, we aren't going to be able to prove anything. There's no point to this." He put his pen down on the pad and sat back in his chair.

Dan wasn't ready to give in. "We don't know that," he said. "There were sightings of Rebecca Ritter for years after this. What if one of them were faked by someone who knew her murderer? That would indicate that someone was trying to cover up. That they knew she was murdered."

"That would be interesting," Oliver admitted, "but it wouldn't really change anything, would it? Because we still don't have enough evidence to convict a raccoon."

Dan could feel a flash of anger rise on his neck. "So you think that she was probably pushed by someone, probably murdered, and you're not going to do anything about it?" he asked.

Frank Oliver stacked the files into the box while he spoke. "I am going to take these back to my office, and open the case officially. And when I have time to do so, I will make inquiries." He folded the top of the box shut, then looked up at Dan. "And I will do that because I know who Anson Ritter is, and I don't want him calling my boss about this. But not because I think there is any chance in hell that we'll ever resolve this, or bring someone to trial."

Dan slowly exhaled through puffed-out cheeks.

Frank Oliver picked up the box of files and stood up. "If you find anything that might be real evidence here, you just give me a call," he said. And with that he walked out of the office.

chapter 23

The First Church of the Covenant of Christ was larger and grander than what Dan was expecting. He'd never driven down the side road to see it before, and he was surprised to see not just the church, but the massive parking lot that surrounded it.

Admittedly, that parking lot was only one-third full, but it was still early. Dan never liked to arrive at the last minute for a funeral. He parked his truck at the west side of the lot, hoping that the pines there would offer some shade later in the afternoon.

He was in no hurry to get out of the truck, and took a moment to tidy up the cab from the usual bits of trash that had accumulated over the past few days. As he did so he heard a car pull into the space next to him, and was delighted to see Janet di Conti in the passenger's seat.

He smiled at Janet through the window and got out of the truck. Tony di Conti greeted him over the roof of the car, and the three of them walked together into the church.

"I wasn't sure who I'd see here today," he said to the di Contis.

"Oh, there are going to be a lot of people here today, Dan," Janet assured him. "You might get a shorter list if you tried to count the people who are not going to be here."

Once inside the church, Tony insisted on sitting in the center section of the pews, near the back, along the right aisle. "I always want to make sure I can leave if I have to," he explained to Dan.

"You never have to," Janet remarked. "You just want to, sometimes."

Dan looked around the cavernous interior of the church. Huge beams supported a massive A-frame roof that towered over the pews, and a modern polished metal cross hung behind the altar. An ornate white casket lay in front of the congregation, and a few people were now clustered around it. Dan was able to identify Rebecca Ritter's parents among them.

"Shall we pay our respects?" Janet asked Tony.

"I guess we should," Tony replied. And then to Dan, "Do you want to join us?"

Dan shook his head. "No, thanks. I am not sure that the Ritters would be completely happy to see me here, and I don't want to intrude."

He watched as Tony and Janet walked up to the front of the church and spoke to the Ritters. The pews were filling up now as people began to arrive in earnest. Dan hadn't been in a church since he attended a wedding three years ago, and he found himself wondering how people chose where to sit at a funeral. Some clearly had a preference for one side or the other of the aisle.

He saw Cal Healey walk in with his wife and sit on the left side of the church, halfway to the altar. Cal nodded to him, but didn't stop to talk. His wife Maggie was soon involved in a conversation with a family sitting in the pew behind them.

Dan glanced behind him at the back of the church. A few people were standing back there, perhaps waiting for someone else to arrive before they sat down. In the far left corner of the last row, Dan was pretty sure that the man in dark glasses was Bryan Lafferty. As he stared at him, the man in dark glasses turned his face at Dan, then slowly turned away again. Janet and Tony joined him back in the pew.

"Is that guy over there in the sunglasses Bryan Lafferty?" he asked them.

Tony took a long look as he sat down. "Yep, I think it is. I guess the restraining order doesn't matter anymore, does it?"

A large group of people entered the church all at once, and after composing themselves, slowly walked down the aisle to sit in the second row.

Janet nodded toward them as they walked by. Once they had passed, she whispered, "I bet those are the cousins from Modesto. I had one of them in my class years ago. Each one of them came to live with the Ritters for a year." She sighed softly. "She was not a great student …"

"That's right," Tony agreed. "I never understood what that was about … I guess her parents didn't want Rebecca to grow up as an only child, so they brought in some cousins to live with them …" He paused for a minute. The three women in the group were now taking turns hugging Rebecca Ritter's parents. "But I guess that makes these three girls the heirs now, right?"

Janet looked at him with a scowl. "What?" he asked her innocently. "The Ritters have a lot of money, and now it will go to those three girls, won't it?"

"I don't know what their plans are," Janet said quietly. "And neither do you." Tony shrugged and looked at Dan with raised eyebrows.

A voice interrupted them from behind. "Hi, Mr. di Conti," Lori Marchand said. "Hi, Mrs. di Conti."

The couple greeted Lori by standing up, and Janet gave her a hug. They shared a few quick courtesies before Janet started to introduce Dan.

"Oh, we've met," Lori said quickly, and held out her hand.

"Nice to see you again," Dan said, shaking her hand and finding it warm, soft, and very moist.

"Do you mind if I join you?" Lori asked them, looking at Janet, who quickly moved over to make room for her on the pew.

From the motions at the front of the church, it was clear that the service was about to start. A minister in a very white polyester robe came out, and Dan settled back in the pew thoughtfully. Behind him he could hear people sitting down and adjusting themselves for what was to come.

There was something surreal about the proceedings, Dan thought. Perhaps it came from the fact that Rebecca had died so long ago that most of the people in the church had said their farewells to her long ago. The memories that were shared during the ceremonies had a veiled, distant feeling to them. They lacked the raw emotion that so often rose up during a funeral. Even the hymns had a slightly clearer sound, as voices sang without worries of deep sorrow.

When the guests were invited to share their thoughts, Dan could see Lori fidgeting in her seat. He suspected that she was trying to decide whether to speak or not. In the end, the minister began to move along with the ceremony, and Lori sat further back in the pew, and wiped her eyes with a tissue.

The minister finished with a kind prayer for both Rebecca and all who knew her, and then went down to speak with the Ritters, who were quickly surrounded by family and friends.

Dan felt a tap on his shoulder, and turned to see Frank Oliver in the pew behind him. "How's it going, Dan?" he asked. Dan shrugged. What was Oliver doing here? Dan quietly introduced the di Contis and Lori to Frank Oliver, then turned to look at Bryan Lafferty. But Lafferty was no longer sitting in the pew in the back. It was empty.

He turned back around to hear Oliver saying to Lori, "So you were a friend of Rebecca's?" Lori nodded. "Did you know her well?" Oliver asked.

Janet interrupted to say protectively that "Lori and Rebecca were good friends, but that was a long time ago, wasn't it?"

Oliver nodded in agreement. "Can you tell me a little bit more about her?" he asked Lori. Lori Marchand thought this over for a moment. "She was very smart," she said, "and beautiful. And she loved the mountains very much …"

Frank Oliver smiled indulgently at Lori. "I am sure she did," he said. "Did she have any serious relationships? Boyfriends?" Dan shot a look at the FBI agent. This wasn't what Dan considered appropriate procedure here, but he wasn't the expert.

Lori was struggling to answer, saying that Rebecca had dated some, but didn't really have a steady boyfriend.

Frank Oliver listened carefully, then leaned in towards Lori. "Are you saying that she wasn't sexually active?" he asked. Lori pulled her head back from him and stared, shocked. With a deadly whisper she said, "This is a funeral! And that is not a respectful question!"

She looked at Janet and Tony, who joined in the chorus. "Completely inappropriate!" Tony stressed.

Frank Oliver nodded to them, nodded to Dan, and eased his way out of the pew. "Sorry," he said. "I am just trying to get to the bottom of this thing. Sorry," he repeated.

The other three turned to look at Dan, who held his arms out to his sides. "He's with the FBI. I don't know what's going on …" he said. "All I know is that that guy is now in charge, and I am not working on it at all."

Frank Oliver was now walking out of the church, and Cal Healey stopped to say hello. Dan gave a sigh. He chatted with Cal briefly and then turned to follow Cal out of the church and get into his truck.

It was still in full sun when he got there. It would be a hot drive to the cemetery. Dan waited for most of the other cars to join the funeral procession before he joined them. He could feel the sweat inside his shirt as he sat in the heat. His truck was not going fast enough for the air conditioning to really take effect.

When it became unbearable, he rolled down both windows and drove with the hot air blowing gently through the cab. Up ahead he could see the cars pulling off the highway and turning down the road to the cemetery. He pulled to a stop at the rear of the line of cars and started walking across the grass to the gravesite.

The crowd had dwindled to about half its size from those who were in the church. Dan wryly considered that the ones who had not come to the cemetery were the smart ones. He sat down on one of the white plastic chairs and looked around. Lori and the di Contis were sitting farther forward, and Dan was now among those in the very back.

He couldn't quite hear what was being said at the ceremony, but he didn't mind. It allowed his mind to wander. But his thoughts didn't lead him to think about Rebecca Ritter's life or her family. Instead, he went back to the slab of granite above Yellowhammer Lake, and what might have happened there.

Somebody must know more about that. But there was no guarantee that Dan would ever find that person.

When he arrived back at the Summit Ranger Station, the parking lot was nearly full, and he felt a twinge of guilt. He knew that Doris would be harried. Inside, he saw her at one end of the counter, helping a group of five or six young people with their wilderness permit. Sara was there as well, at the other end of the counter, talking with another group.

They both looked up as Dan walked in. He felt a silent reproach as he came quickly through the gate and joined them behind the counter.

"Who's next?" he asked, looking up at the group of people at the counter. Within minutes he was deep in discussion with an older couple who wanted advice on day hikes in the area.

The rest of the afternoon was a steady stream of visitors, and

Dan didn't really have a chance to take a breath. At first Doris and Sara were almost chilly to him, but as the afternoon wore on, they slowly allowed him to work his way into their good graces again. First Doris smiled at one of his jokes, then Sara turned to ask him a question about a region that she didn't know so well.

When the phone rang about 3:30, Sara answered it, but quickly turned it over to Dan. "Something about some people out behind Cedar Ridge," she whispered as she handed him the phone.

"I thought you were going to do something about these guys!" the caller began. "I called you and you said you'd look into it. And I guess that means that you are going to ignore things and hope that they go away!"

Dan waited for a moment for the caller to finish his rant, and then answered. "I understand your concern," he said. "We're a little short-handed here today. Is there someone there now that you can see?"

"Hell, no, I can't see them!" the caller answered. "They come in the middle of the night, or early in the morning. I guess they know that you guys only work nine to five, and so they're safe as long as they don't work office hours!"

Dan could see that Doris was glancing over to check on him. "I understand," he said. "I will try to get out there either tonight or tomorrow morning." Dan knew that he would need to at least drive by so that the man could see his truck at some point in the next twenty-four hours. But it would be better to stop and visit with him. He took down the address and promised to stop by.

chapter 24

That evening after work Dan drove by Cedar Ridge. He wasn't really familiar with the streets in the area, and it took him a few minutes of driving up one hill and down the other before he found the address of the man who had called him.

This wasn't a subdivision as much as it was a collection of mountain cabins. Dark wood and A-frames were the preferred style, and some of them had cute names as well. All of them had a welcome sign somewhere on the front.

Dan parked his truck in front of the house and walked up the steps to knock on the door. This one was called "Woodstock" and had an elliptical trainer on the front porch. The welcome mat had a dog's head on it. The place seemed pretty quiet, and there was no answer to Dan's knock. He waited a few extra minutes, and looked around from the front porch. The rest of the street was quiet, and there was only one car, sitting in the driveway three houses down the road.

From the porch, Dan could see the end of the street, and the National Forest land that would lie beyond it. He walked down the steps of the porch, grabbed a bottle of water from his truck, and walked out along the road until the pavement ended. There was a steel gate across the road, but Dan could see where the old fire road continued beyond it into the forest.

He took one more look around, then walked around the gate and started down the double-track dirt road. The left side of the road was clearly more worn, and Dan could see both footprints and mountain bike tracks in the rocks and dirt.

The air was cooler now, and the sun streamed through the trees in bars of light. The tension eased out of the tall ranger as he walked down the road. It felt good to stretch his legs, and to feel the forest wrap around him again. He walked for a few minutes as the road quickly deteriorated into a broken track between bushes and young trees, twice blocked by big berms of dirt intended to deter 4WD vehicles.

On the right-hand side the forest stretched uphill to the east, while the left-hand side became a steeper and steeper downhill slope. After something less than half a mile, the dirt road veered off to the right and uphill.

Dan noticed that there were traces of a footpath that broke off from the road and went steeply down through the open forest. He stopped to look around and saw nobody. The end of the paved road was now well beyond his sight, and the sense of freedom and solitude that he loved so well seeped into his shoulders.

He took a deep breath and carefully began to ease down the steep trail, leading with his left foot on the slippery surface of dirt, rock and gravel that led downhill. After ten feet of very steep terrain the trail flattened out a bit, and Dan was able to walk normally as it led downhill through the second growth firs. His toes pinched down into the front of his boots as he walked the steep trail. Below him Dan could see a thicket of alders and brush, and the trail that led down and around it to the right.

"Hey, Eagle Scout!" a voice rang out from behind Dan. "I'd be careful down there!" Dan stopped and turned around. Bryan Lafferty was a hundred feet behind him on the trail. He was carrying a rifle with a scope in both hands.

"I'm serious!" Lafferty continued. "There's lions and tigers and bears, and all kinds of shit down there. Snakes, too."

Dan stared at Lafferty and eased himself slightly downhill, edging closer to a large fir tree along the trail. He didn't like the way this felt. "Are you threatening me?" Dan asked him.

Lafferty cackled with laughter. "Not threatening, warning," he replied. "There's bad shit down that trail." He paused for a moment. "I just wouldn't want you to get hurt." He still held the rifle in his arms. Dan could see Lafferty's right hand near the trigger.

"I'm not really worried about bears or lions," Dan said. He was still shifting his feet, slowly easing down the trail towards the big fir.

"Yeah, well, there's other shit, too," Lafferty said. "And you really don't want to find out about it." All of the humor had gone out of his voice, and there was no smile on his face.

"I'm going to ask you to put the rifle down, Bryan," Dan said.

"What, you think I'm going to shoot you?" Lafferty asked, feigning incredulity.

"I am a federal officer, and I am directing you to put the rifle down," Dan repeated. But while he tried to make his voice sound forceful, he was also trying to sense how far away the fir tree was. It was still too far away. This was not a good situation to be in, and he didn't have an easy way out.

"Hell," Lafferty replied, "if I wanted to shoot you I would have shot you by now. And you wouldn't be able to get behind that tree in time, either!"

Dan watched as Lafferty waited just a second too long before allowing the rifle to slip out of his right hand, so that he was holding it only by the barrel with his left hand.

"See?" Lafferty held up his right hand and waved it. "I'm putting down the gun!" He leaned over and allowed the rifle to slowly slip until the butt touched the ground, then laid it down at his feet. "Is that good enough for you?"

"Now step away from the gun, please," Dan directed him.

Bryan Lafferty gave a small sigh of derision and backed up the trail a few feet. He held his hands up in front of himself and waved them slightly. "See? No gun!"

Dan slowly began to walk back up the trail toward the man. There was a smaller tree twenty feet up the trail on the right, he realized, and that one might serve as cover if Lafferty tried to grab the gun and fire at him. And then he was past that tree, with only thirty feet to go. Bryan Lafferty still stood above him on the trail, hands now resting on his hips.

Dan was conscious that his breathing was hard as he hiked up the trail, and he didn't like the idea that Lafferty would see that. But it was too late now. He reached the rifle and picked it up, carefully bending his knees so that he could keep Lafferty in his sight.

"Nice job, Scoutmaster," Lafferty grinned at him. "So do you know how to use that thing? Or are you more a bow and arrow kind of guy?"

Dan checked the chamber of the gun, noted that it was empty, and looked at Lafferty. "What are you doing out here, Bryan?" he asked. He didn't find the man at all amusing.

"Trying to keep you from getting killed," Lafferty answered him with a grin. Then, when he saw Dan's stern face, he softened his tone. "Hey, I'm serious. There are trip wires and shit down there that will make for a really bad day."

"Yeah? And how do you know about that?" Dan asked him.

"I live here," Lafferty replied. "I hike all over these hills. I could show you all sorts of stuff that you don't know about. And some of it could kill you."

"So who put it here?" Dan asked him.

"Hey, I don't know." Lafferty was once again waving his hands innocently in the air. "I don't necessarily see the people, I just see the stuff."

He pointed down the trail behind Dan. "See that log down there at the bottom of the trail?" He paused for Dan to turn and find the log. "Well, that log wasn't there ten days ago. Now it's right next to the trail. And there's a piece of bark from the log right on the trail. My guess is that there's something underneath it that isn't going to make you happy if you step on it."

Dan got a brief chill thinking about this. He had been only twenty feet short of the log when Lafferty had called out to him. He looked at Bryan Lafferty again.

"Don't believe me?" Lafferty asked him. Lafferty's eyes searched Dan's face. "Here, give me that gun and let's see what happens." He held his hands out for the rifle.

Dan scanned the hill behind Lafferty and held on to the gun. "Are you carrying any other weapons?" he asked.

"You gonna pat me down, Scoutmaster?" Lafferty chuckled. His hands went into his pockets and came out with a Swiss army knife. "I promise not to stab you with this one."

Dan looked hard at Bryan Lafferty, his eyes not only taking in the face, but the clothing and body of the man. "Why don't you just turn around once for me," he suggested.

Lafferty held the knife dangling from the fingers of his right hand as he slowly turned around. "Nice ass, huh?" he asked Dan.

"Yeah, perfect," Dan replied. Then, pointing to a couple of cobble-sized rocks in the cut of the trail above them, he added, "How about if we use these?"

Bryan Lafferty chuckled. "Okay, sure. Let's see what happens, Scoutmaster."

He pried two of the rocks out of the dirt and walked down the trail, with Dan following behind. As they got near the bottom of the hill, Lafferty slowed down, then turned to look at Dan. "You ready?" he asked. Dan nodded.

Bryan Lafferty bent slightly at the knees and gently lofted the rock in his right hand up into the air. It arced high above the trail, and then fell down just to the left of the strip of bark on the trail, hitting with a solid thump.

"Shit," Lafferty said with disgust. He shifted the second rock into his right hand and paused. "Think I can hit it this time?" he asked Dan, over his shoulder. Without waiting for an answer, he lofted the second rock towards its target. This one fell true.

A roar exploded out of the ground and pieces of bark and dirt showered down in front of them.

Bryan Lafferty turned around with a grin. "Told ya, Scout Boy. I knew it wasn't an accident that log was there."

Dan's eyes scanned the forest around them, looking for any motion or sign of life. A gentle breeze blew through the trees, but there was no other motion. The deafening roar was already history, and the forest was silent.

Dan pointed up the trail with his chin. "Let's get out of here," he said to Lafferty. "Sure," Bryan responded. "You still want me to go first?"

Dan nodded.

"You just like checking out my ass," Lafferty said over his shoulder, and started back up the trail.

When they got to where they had first met, Lafferty turned to look at Dan. "Are you going to let me go home from here, or are you going to make me hike all the way back out to your car?" he asked.

Dan stopped to look around again. "Which way is home?" he asked.

Lafferty pointed off to the right. "See that big fir? Well, about two miles straight down from there is my place." He paused. "Wanna walk it and see?"

For the first time, Dan permitted himself a small smile. "No, thanks. I think I want to go back to my place."

Bryan Lafferty stood in front of Dan and gave a sigh. "So are you going to keep the gun, or do I get to take that with me?"

Dan thought this over for a moment, then handed the rifle to Lafferty. Bryan's eyebrows went up high and he looked at Dan. "Hey, thanks, Scout." His head nodded slightly in recognition of Dan's gesture.

Dan responded with a nod. "Thanks for the warning about the trail," he said to Lafferty.

The two men stood in awkward silence for a minute, then Lafferty said, "Right. I guess I'll go first, huh?"

Dan couldn't help but chuckle. "Yeah," he said. "That's right …"

When Dan returned to his truck the sun had set, and it was getting dark enough that there were a few lights on in some of the cabins. Dan checked, but there was still no light on in the "Woodstock" house. He went up to the porch and knocked anyway, but he didn't get an answer.

He walked back to the truck, wondering if someone in one of the cabins had heard the explosion. Maybe they had even placed the trap. Dan looked around. The street was silent. He realized that if someone here had set the trap, they would probably be in a cabin where the lights were off, not on.

And there were lots of those.

He got into his truck and drove away. He needed to write a report on what had just happened, and he also wanted to call Cal and talk to him about it. But he didn't. He just drove home.

It was only when he took out his keys to unlock his front door that he realized his hands were shaking

The next day Dan was a little late in getting to the Summit Ranger Station. He hadn't slept well the night before, and then somehow he was distracted by a story in the three-day-old newspaper that his next door neighbor had left for him. At one point he looked up at the clock, realized that he was running late, and started to fold up the paper. Then he stopped and made the decision to finish his reading. He arrived almost fifteen minutes late.

It was unusual enough that Doris gave him a curious look and asked if he was all right. Dan nodded but didn't give her any response more than that and went into the back office to start writing his report.

Which let her know that he was certainly not all right.

Dan struggled at first, trying to figure out where to start. He filled in the date and time of the incident report, and took care of all of the other required fields. He was still staring at the screen when Doris stuck her head in. But he didn't turn around to look at her, and she quietly withdrew as she heard someone open the front door.

Chronology.

That's what Dan decided. He would just start at the beginning and tell what happened in the order that it happened. But what really happened was that he was nearly killed last night. And it bothered him that whoever read this report was going to have to wait until the end to find that out. What he really wanted to write was simple: "I

DAMN NEAR GOT KILLED LAST NIGHT."

And how did it happen that Bryan Lafferty was there just at the right moment? How should he try to explain that?

The phone call. The first one, from a few days ago. That was where to start.

And then the second call, and Dan's decision to go check things out. And then a long explanation of visiting the house, and finding the trail. Was it too much detail? Did it sound dispassionate enough?

Dan focused on the facts, trying to present them evenly, fairly. He wrote down the facts about Bryan Lafferty: He was on the trail. He called out to Dan. He put down his rifle when requested. It was not loaded. It all seemed so calm and reasonable.

As he got to writing about the explosion, Dan realized that he really should get a team out there to collect as much evidence and information as possible. He should have done all of this last night. And he didn't really have a good excuse.

He finished up writing the report quickly, and emailed it to Steve Matson down at headquarters.

He picked up the phone and called Steve.

"Matson here," Steve answered.

"Hi Steve. It's Dan. I just sent you an email—an incident report, from out past Cedar Ridge last night."

"Okay …" Steve said slowly. "I have it here …" Dan waited for Steve to start reading through the report.

To Dan's relief, Steve's reaction was first of concern. "Are you all right? Did you get hurt at all? Anything at all?" And after making sure that Dan was, indeed, fine, Steve asked him to tell the story all over again.

As Dan did so, he tried to avoid looking at his computer screen. He realized that this was an opportunity to take a second shot at getting the story right. But with Steve he could add more of the innuendo that he didn't want to put into the written report.

Steve let him finish. Again, Steve asked Dan if he had been hurt in any way. Dan said he was fine. "Even your ears?" Steve asked. "Fine," Dan assured him.

And then Steve started asking questions. Not surprisingly, they were many of the questions that Dan had asked himself. And Dan still didn't have any of the answers.

"Okay," Steve said. "First thing we have to do is to get a crime scene team out there right away, so I am calling the Tuolumne County Sheriff. And I think it would be a good idea if you went with them. Agreed?"

"Sure," Dan said.

"And the second thing is that I want you stay back and make sure that you let them do all the work. Stay back, and stay safe. Because we don't know what else might be out there," Steve continued. "Agreed?"

Dan found himself nodding into the phone. "Yeah, that's fine," he said.

"I'll have them give you a call when they are ready to go," Steve said. "And I am going to suggest it be right away."

Dan hung up the phone and sat back in his chair. From out in the front office, he could hear Doris talking about Disaster Creek and the beautiful trail alongside it. She was right. It was beautiful. But Dan couldn't seem to get himself to care about that right now.

He carefully shut down his email program and clicked to open a web browser to scan the latest news. There were lots of stories about actresses and distant wars, big sports scores and the latest economic news. But nothing about an explosion in the Stanislaus National Forest, of course. Dan wondered if there would be something about it in the news tomorrow.

The phone rang and he let Doris answer it. She stuck her head in the office a moment later. "It's Cal Healey for you," she said.

Dan picked up the phone. "So let me get this straight," Dan

heard Cal saying. "You get a tip about a possible dope grower up behind Cedar Ridge, and you decide the best thing to do is to go up there alone, unarmed, and just start poking around?"

"Hi, Cal," Dan said.

"Is that what they teach you in ranger school?" Cal asked, before continuing, "because generally we consider that a bad idea. Then again, I don't have a Ph.D., so maybe you know something I don't about that whole deal ..."

Dan couldn't help but smile at Cal's rebuke. "Yeah, okay, it was stupid."

"You think so? Really?" Cal asked. "Yeah, so do I. But I have good news for you. Because some of us here are going to go up and take a look around for you. Of course, we're not Ph.D.s or anything, but we do know how to do it in a way that won't get our heads blown off. And we're going to let you watch, so that you can learn a few things. Does that sound good to you?"

"When do you want me there?" Dan asked.

"We're going to leave here in about fifteen minutes," Cal said.

"Okay, I'll do the same," Dan answered.

"Fine—but Dan?" Cal paused.

"Yeah?" Dan knew that Cal was playing with him a little bit, but he was willing to go along with the game.

"If you get there before we do, would you do me a favor?" Cal asked. "Would you just sit there in your truck until we arrive?"

"Yeah, okay," Dan assured him.

"Because I don't want to have to explain to anybody that you were stupid twice," Cal finished.

"See you there," Dan said, and hung up the phone.

He walked out into the main office and spoke to Doris. "I'm running out to Cedar Ridge to meet the Sheriff's Department," he said.

"What's going on?" Doris asked, her face in a worried frown.

Dan shook his head. "Just some problems with somebody maybe growing non-native plants," he said dryly.

A look of disgust flickered across Doris' face. "Well, be careful," she warned him.

Dan stopped at the door and looked back at her and smiled. "Yep," he said, "I am going to be careful," and walked out the door.

By the time he got to the cabins at Cedar Ridge, the place looked like a Hollywood set: flashing lights, crime scene tape, and more vehicles than Dan had seen in quite a while.

He pulled up behind the first Sheriff's car and climbed out of his truck. He could see a group of officers down by the end of the road, where the trail started. He looked around at the houses on the street. On one porch, an elderly couple stood, arms crossed, staring at the commotion. None of the other houses seemed to be occupied.

Cal Healey walked over to meet him with a smile and a handshake. "Are you okay?" Cal asked. The gray eyes of the Sheriff stared intently into Dan's.

"I'm fine," Dan nodded.

Cal mouthed something silently. Dan frowned. "What?"

"I said, 'How's your hearing?'" Cal laughed. "Come on. Why don't you show us what happened last night." Dan stepped forward to start down the trail, but Cal put a hand on his chest and stopped him.

"Nope," Cal said. "You are going to show us, but you are not going to lead us. As you may have noticed, we are wearing big thick flak jackets and helmets. And we are going to be careful here. Like you weren't last night."

Dan stopped and waved a few of the officers ahead. "Okay, gentlemen, right this way. It's a mile or so down into this canyon …"

Dan was impressed with the way the men spread out silently and began to work their way down into the canyon, guns at the ready. It was quite a contrast with Dan's cheerful hike of the night before. This was all business, deadly business.

As they got close to the spot where Dan had been warned by Bryan Lafferty, the group stopped, and fanned out over a larger segment of the hillside. Cal pointed to a spot on the trail and said, "So you are going to sit here and watch." Dan gave him an annoyed look, but nodded.

Cal directed his team, splitting them up into four groups, then sat down with Dan. "I'll keep you company here, so you don't get bored."

"You guys sure look good in all that equipment," Dan said dryly.

Cal looked at Dan for a moment, considering this. "You know, it's funny," he said. "The stuff not only looks good on us, but it also keeps us alive. You ought to check it out sometime, instead of depending on Bryan Lafferty."

"So how long are you going to keep working that one?" Dan asked Cal.

Cal grinned. "I think we're about done with it, as long as you promise to use a little common sense next time."

It took more than three hours for the team to complete their work. While Cal occasionally got an update on the radio, it made for a long morning for Dan. By eleven-thirty their conversation had stopped entirely, and the only sounds were grumbles coming from Cal's stomach.

By noon the team had reassembled back with Cal and Dan. The results were not nearly as exciting as he thought they might be.

"About one hundred pot plants down in the meadow down there," one of the officers explained. "It looks like a pretty small-time operation."

"Did you find any more booby-traps?" Cal asked.

"There was a trip wire down on the other end, where an old

logging road comes in," said the officer, "but it didn't work. It was broken. It was connected to this." He held up a shotgun shell in a plastic evidence bag and handed it over to Cal.

"The shot has been removed," Cal said, staring at the shell through the plastic.

"Yeah," the officer replied. "It would still make a hell of a bang, but I don't think it would be a very effective weapon. More like a warning."

Cal looked expectantly at another officer, who had been working down by the explosion Dan had triggered. "Could have been the same kind of thing," the officer said, nodding. "I found a shell casing in the dirt… nothing to aim it. And the way it was set up, it probably would have gone off about five or six feet in front of whoever stepped on that log."

Cal turned to the group as a whole. "Did we find anything we can use to follow up on this?" he asked the group.

"I have a couple of plastic bags from Ace Hardware in Stockton," one of the men responded. "So I guess that's where they bought the plastic pipe and stuff … but there isn't a campsite that we could find. This is small potatoes, Cal."

"Good …" Cal said slowly. He didn't sound convinced. "Anything else?"

"A few clothes, a couple of bottles and some other trash. We might get some prints or DNA off of that," the officer continued. "Although I bet the DA won't pay for that. There's no point in finding out that it belongs to some illegal alien with no record and no DNA in the database."

"Bryan Lafferty's DNA is in the database," Cal said. He turned to Dan. "No reason for you to hang around here, unless you just want to watch," Cal said. "We'll wrap things up, but that may take a while."

Dan agreed. "Fine," he said. "What are you going to do with all the stuff down there?" He waved his arms toward the canyon and meadow.

"We'll collect everything we can use for evidence," Cal said. "Normally, we'd try to put this whole area under surveillance and catch the guy when he comes back … but I think we've pretty much blown that option. Whoever was growing this stuff is long gone by now. And it isn't worth it for some guy growing a hundred plants."

Cal pulled out his radio and tried to contact Cal Fire. He glanced up at Dan. "If I can get a team here from CDF, and if we can get permission from the Forest Service, we'll burn the rest of the pot … I don't want to leave it down here unguarded, and I sure don't want to try and guard it, either."

Dan nodded. "If you get CDF here, I'm sure we can let you burn the stuff. It rained a bit a few days ago. Make sure they manage it, though?"

"We do crime, they do fire," Cal grinned. "It's a good system. And you …?"

Dan smiled. "I go back to the office and get some work done," he said. "Let me know if you need anything."

"We need lunch," Cal said, "but I think I've got that covered."

chapter 26

As he walked back up the trail to his truck, Dan had to recognize that he felt a little disappointed. After some introspection, he realized with a start that he had hoped for a more extensive pot plantation—a really big one. He hadn't found a major drug deal so much as a small-time operator, maybe even a local kid.

And maybe he hadn't come so close to death after all.

He wondered if Bryan Lafferty was really behind the pot plants. He met the criteria of a small-time grower. But despite his reservations about Lafferty, Dan had never got the impression that Bryan was trying to protect the pot plants. It had seemed as if Bryan was more interested in keeping Dan safe.

Which was a good thing, after all.

He stopped in Twain Harte to pick up a sandwich at the store, then decided that he would eat it quickly in the truck on his way back to the Summit Ranger Station. So for most of the drive he was carefully trying not to get any mustard on his shirt. It kept his mind off other things.

He was successful: when he arrived at the ranger station, his shirt was still spotless. Admittedly, there were a few potato chip crumbs in his lap, but those would fall out when he got out of the truck, especially after he brushed them off.

Doris was waiting for him when he walked in. "Somebody left a package for you," she said, "and there is no return address." She paused and looked at him expectantly to get his reaction.

"Okay," he nodded. Dan resisted giving Doris the response she wanted.

Doris looked at him severely. "Dan, I heard what happened yesterday," she said. Dan gave her a little smile. "It wasn't that big a deal," he said. "I spent the morning down there with the Sheriff, and it looks like it's just a small-time grower …"

Doris stared at him. "And getting blown up is no big deal? Dan, who are you trying to kid? Somebody tried to kill you!"

Dan sat down in his chair and turned on the computer. "Yeah, that was scary," he said. "But nobody knew I was going down there … so I don't think it was anything personal." Dan realized that the man who had called on the phone, the one who had complained, knew perfectly well that Dan would go down there. That was something to think about. But he would have to consider that later. "So it wasn't somebody trying to kill me. It was someone trying to scare away anyone who came down there. I was just the lucky one."

"And now a package arrives with no return address, and you aren't worried that it's a bomb, too?" she asked.

Dan looked up at her calmly. "How did it get here? Did someone deliver it?"

Doris nodded, pleased that Dan was finally paying attention to the matter at hand. "He was an older man, older than me," she said. Doris was in her early sixties, but didn't like to admit it. She began to tick off her fingers as she worked through her description. "He was short, with grey hair that was combed back over his head. No beard or moustache. Glasses—bifocals, I think." She paused, looking at her fingers. She grabbed her ring finger and said, "Okay. He was wearing slacks and a nice shirt. Definitely not a camper or anything."

Dan grinned. "That's pretty good, Doris. Height and weight?"

Doris paused. "Well, taller than me, shorter than you, but that doesn't help much."

Doris was just over five feet tall, and Dan was six foot four.

"I'd say he was maybe five foot six or so? About like Sara?" Sara Newton worked at the Mi-Wuk office, and sometimes helped out at Summit. "And medium build, not heavy, but not skinny. Would that make him about 150?"

Dan agreed. "Yeah, maybe."

"Oh!" Doris lit up with excitement. "And he was driving a huge car with dark windows. Very new and shiny. That's what made me so suspicious."

Dan looked at her quizzically. "Because?"

"That's what drug dealers drive," Doris said. Then she thought for a moment. "But he didn't really look or act like a drug dealer…" she added.

Dan nodded. "So where is this package?"

"I put it in the closet out back," Doris said. "Just in case."

Doris led Dan to the closet and showed him the package. It was small and rectangular, wrapped in craft paper and tied with twine. On the top Dan could see his name, written in a very clear script in dark ink.

Dan carefully picked it up and held it in his hands. He could feel the weight now, and his fingers probed along the edges and sides of the package. There was a narrow ridge around three sides of the package on both top and bottom. The fourth side had no ridge, and Dan then knew what was inside. He put the package back in the closet.

"Are you going to open it?" Doris asked.

"Later," Dan said. He didn't want to explain any more to Doris.

"Do you want me to call the Sheriff's office?" she asked.

"I don't think so," Dan answered her. "I think I know what this is. But I want to make sure first. I'll take care of it, Doris."

"You DO know what it is?" she asked.

"I am guessing, but I don't think it's a bomb," Dan replied. The less he said to her, the less she would be responsible for anything that happened later. They heard the outside door open, and Doris turned. "I'll go see who this is," she said coldly.

"Okay," Dan agreed. "I'll be with you in a minute."

Doris left to go out front and Dan reached back into the closet to feel the package. It definitely felt like two small books, wrapped together. He turned the package over in his hands. Nothing inside moved. The bottom was just as neat as the top. Dan put the package back in the closet one more time and went to join Doris in the main office.

The rest of the afternoon, Dan kept himself busy. He wrote up a report on his activities that morning, and proofread it twice before sending it down to Steve Matson. Then he called Steve to talk to him about it.

Sara Newton answered the phone, and Dan chatted with her for a bit before asking to talk to Steve. Sara sounded as young and full of life as ever, and Dan was touched when she expressed her concern about him. He assured her that he was fine and that he was being careful.

Steve Matson was not quite so interested, and after getting Dan on the phone, he was quick to work through the report and wrap up the call. Dan could hear himself trying to prolong the conversation, but Steve was simply too busy to let that happen. Apparently there was something else that was even more important to Steve Matson today.

And then Dan heard another group come into the station, and he went out to greet them. He was particularly careful to answer all their questions, and took the time to tell a couple of good stories while he was at it. He kept that up for the rest of the afternoon.

At ten minutes to five, the phone rang and Doris answered it. Dan heard her telling the caller to hold, and then she handed the phone to him. She hadn't spoken more than ten words to him all afternoon.

"Hello?" Dan said.

"Hey, Courtwright!" It was Bryan Lafferty, and he was not happy. "What the hell gives? I saved your fucking life out there, and I'm getting hammered for it!"

"What do you mean?" Dan asked him. Doris, in the background, was closing things up, and she was making plenty of noise while she did it.

"I just spent the last three hours talking to your friends from the Sheriff's office," Lafferty explained. "They're talking about arresting me for that pot plantation up behind Cedar Ridge, and I don't have a damn thing to do with it." He paused. "And you know that."

Dan considered this. He wasn't sure, but he did suspect that Bryan wasn't really behind the pot plants.

"Are you hearing me?" Lafferty asked him. "I got two kids I am trying to raise, and those guys are threatening me with ten years of jail time."

"Bryan, I wrote a report on what happened, as I saw it," Dan said. "I'm sure that the Sheriff's office is just following up on all the possibilities here. If you don't have any connection to that pot farm, they will figure that out and clear you."

"Bullshit!" Lafferty exploded. "All those guys have to do is plant one cigarette butt up there and my ass is toast. You know it, and I know it. And they're gonna stick me with this because they can't get anyone else."

"No, Bryan, they are not going to plant evidence out there." Dan assured him.

Lafferty gave a humorless laugh. "Man, you really are a Boy

Scout, aren't you? Cal Healey would do anything to get me into his fucking jail. Listen. This is important. I am serious about my two kids. They really don't have anybody else. You've gotta help me on this."

"Bryan, I really can't do anything. This is really a question for an attorney," Dan explained. "I wrote my report. I wrote it as accurately as I could. I did not make any accusations about what you did yesterday. But that is now out of my hands. It's up to the Sheriff as to what to do with it all. Unless you have more information?" Dan left the question hanging.

"Shit." Lafferty was disconsolate. There was a long silence while he considered what Dan said. "Okay, look," he continued. "I know some stuff that I haven't told you. But if I tell you about it, you have to help me. I had nothing to do with those pot plants, and you can't let them put me in jail for it."

"Bryan, it's an official investigation," Dan said. "If you have information about it, you have a legal obligation to tell us. And if you are innocent, then the more information we have, the easier it will be to show that."

"Yeah, right," Lafferty sneered.

"Do you have an attorney?" Dan asked. "Maybe you should talk to him about this …"

"Yeah, at $250 an hour," Bryan said. "I already owe him $750 for this afternoon. And I can't afford to keep doing that. Look, I really need to talk to you about this. Can I just come up to the ranger station now? I can be there in twenty minutes."

Dan glanced at Doris, who was now standing by the door, ready to leave. Did Lafferty really have any new information? If so, it was worth a small risk. "Sure, okay. That's fine," he said.

"I'll be there in ten," Lafferty said, and hung up the phone. Dan shook his head slowly and looked at Doris. "See you tomorrow," he said.

"Are you going to open that package?" she asked him, staring at him over the top of her glasses.

"Maybe later. Don't worry. I'll be careful," he assured her.

"Or are you just waiting for me to leave, so that if it explodes, I won't be here?" Doris studied him.

Dan smiled. "Nope," he said. "It's not a bomb. Just go home, Doris. That's what I am going to do pretty soon."

Without saying another word Doris turned and walked out the door, closing it and locking it carefully behind her.

Dan checked his watch. He had enough time to open the package before Lafferty got here. He pulled it out of the closet and looked at it again. It was very neatly wrapped. The new brown paper was crisply folded and tight.

The twine was knotted tightly, and Dan slipped his pocket knife underneath the twine and sawed swiftly, cutting it through. He then took the blade of the knife and delicately cut the tape where it was holding down a flap of paper.

Looking inside, Dan could see the gold-covered edges of the two books. He slowly pulled open the paper and saw the gold filigree on the covers. One was red; the other was pink. Each had a tiny but primitive lock. He knew what they were. He knew that if he opened them now, he would probably have to tell Frank Oliver about it, and Oliver would insist that Dan not open them.

But if he waited, by the time that Bryan Lafferty had left, it would be too late to call Frank Oliver. And then Dan could wait until the morning—until after he had opened and read Rebecca Ritter's diaries.

He heard the noise of a car pulling into the parking lot, and slipped the books into the bottom drawer of his desk. Then he went to meet Bryan Lafferty

Bryan Lafferty had pulled hard on the door, and then realized that was locked. He put his hands quickly into his packets and waited for Dan to come open it for him. It was as if the door handle had burnt his hand.

Dan unlocked the door and ushered Bryan into the ranger station. Instead of talking to him over the counter, Dan invited him into the rear section of the office where they could both sit down. And they wouldn't be visible to anyone at the front door, who might try to interrupt them.

Dan sat down at his desk and waved Bryan into the chair across from it. Almost before he sat down, Lafferty started to talk.

"Thanks for letting me do this," he said. "I really appreciate it." This was a new Bryan Lafferty. The sarcasm and smart aleck comments had disappeared.

"So what's the story, Bryan?" Dan asked.

"You've gotta to help me with this," Bryan answered. "I'll tell you everything, but you have to promise that you'll help me. I can't go to jail. I need to be here for my kids."

Dan rocked back slightly in his chair and folded his hands in his lap. "Bryan, I can't make any promises like that. If you tell me that you murdered somebody, or committed a crime, I can't promise that you won't be prosecuted."

Bryan's hand shot up in denial. "No. No! I haven't done

anything!" he swore. "That's the whole deal here. I am getting railroaded, and I haven't done anything!"

Dan nodded to show he understood. "Okay," he said. "So what do you know? What can you tell me that's so important?"

Lafferty took a deep breath to compose himself. "I think I know something about who was growing that pot there," he said.

Dan scanned his desk and found a pen, and then pulled a tablet out from a stack of papers on the left-hand side of the desk. When he was ready, he directly his gaze back to Bryan Lafferty, and nodded to show he was ready for him to continue.

"So look," Lafferty explained. "I spend a lot of time in these mountains, and I am pretty good at it. So when I saw a guy wandering around up here … first I just thought he was going for a hike, and maybe even that he was lost." His hands now were folded in his lap, working nervously against each other.

"Where did you see him?" Dan asked.

"Out there in that canyon," Bryan answered. "He was walking along, but going pretty fast. Most people, when they walk around out there, are stopping and looking around. They're tourists in the woods. This guy wasn't a tourist; he was a commuter."

Dan allowed a small smile to cross his face. It was a good description.

"So he was walking, on his way somewhere," Bryan continued. "And so I followed him. That's when I saw that little farm he had down there … and that's when I started to pay a little more attention."

"Did you tell anyone about this?" Dan asked.

"No," Bryan replied. "Just my kids, to tell them to stay away from there."

Dan raised his eyebrows in a silent inquiry. Bryan leaned back and looked at Dan. "Hey, I have enough trouble with people in these hills without looking for more," he said. "And the last thing I need is for your pal Healey to start poking around my place …" He left the sentence hanging.

"So that's it?" Dan asked.

"No, there's more," Bryan admitted. "I followed this guy back out."

Dan interrupted him. "He didn't see you?"

Bryan Lafferty chuckled. "Man, I live in these mountains," he said. "If I don't want to be seen, nobody sees me."

"So where did he go?" Dan asked.

"Back out to Cedar Ridge," Bryan explained. "Once he got out of the woods it was a little harder to follow him." He paused. When he saw Dan start to ask another question, he raised his hand and continued. "But a few minutes later I saw a car drive out of there. A black Lexus, maybe three or four years old?"

Dan wrote this down, but he knew it wasn't enough to help. "So we are supposed to look for someone who lives at Cedar Ridge and has a black Lexus?" he asked Lafferty.

"Why not? You'll find out who ran that pot farm!" Bryan answered. "But I don't think the guy actually owns a house in Cedar Ridge," he grinned.

Dan sighed. "Bryan, this isn't helping much." He was disappointed that Lafferty was taking so much of his time to tell him so little.

"Okay, okay," Bryan agreed. "There's more. See, I think the guy is the son or something of someone who owns the place. Because he is never there when they are there. And I can tell you which house it is, too. Because a few weeks later I saw that car parked in front of one of the houses. You know the one that has the ugly bear statue in front of it?"

Dan shook his head. "Sorry—I don't spend much time there."

"Well, there's a house there that has one of those stupid chainsaw-sculptured bears in front. And this guy was staying two doors down. His place has bright yellow shutters on the windows."

Dan remembered someone once telling him about a house with yellow shutters. Apparently it was not a popular design decision in the neighborhood. "So that's the house?"

"Yep," Bryan nodded.

"Okay," Dan said. "I'll get this over to the Sheriff, and we'll check it out. And if it all checks out, then you should be in the clear."

Bryan Lafferty sat in the chair and made no move to get up. Dan decided to wait. He knew that sometimes waiting was the best way to ask a question.

"You're a decent guy, Courtwright," Bryan said.

Dan smiled a thin smile. "That's what some people say. Not everyone."

"Do you really think that they are going to leave me alone now?" Lafferty said.

Dan thought this over. "I can't promise they are never going to arrest you, Bryan. But if this is good information, I'll put in a good word for you."

There was another pause, and Lafferty still didn't move. Then he put his hands, palm down, on Dan's desk. At first Dan thought it was to lean on the desk as he stood up, but Lafferty didn't stand up. Instead, he took a breath and looked back at Dan.

"I know some other stuff, too," he said. "About Rebecca Ritter."

A cold shock wave went through Dan, and he tried hard not to show any reaction. "What kind of stuff do you know about that?" he asked, not quite successfully trying to keep a slight quaver out of his voice.

"I know where she went after Wire Lakes," Bryan said. "Well, not completely, but I know where she headed."

Dan waited for him to continue. He couldn't decide if he should ask Lafferty where Rebecca went, or how Lafferty knew.

"I kind of followed them," Bryan admitted. He held up his hands in innocence. "Hey—there was a restraining order, so I never got close. Really."

Dan nodded. "So if there was a restraining order, why did you follow her?"

"I'm pretty good in these mountains," Lafferty continued. "I think you saw that. So I didn't break the restraining order. I just followed them at a distance. I am really good at that." He waited for Dan to acknowledge his boast. When Dan nodded, Lafferty continued.

"And I knew where they were headed. They told everyone about it. They left out of Crabtree, and I knew that I couldn't do that, or people would notice. So I just went out of Gianelli, and crossed over. I camped up on the ridge the first night, and I could see their camp down at Toejam Lake."

"So you didn't actually follow them?" Dan asked. "How do you know it was them?"

Bryan stared at Dan for a moment. "You know, you never saw Rebecca, or you wouldn't ask that question. I could pick her out on a mountain a mile away." He seemed to be lost in thought. "You could tell it was her just by the way she walked ..."

Dan considered this. "So you're sure it was Rebecca and Todd at Toejam. Then what?"

"The next day they broke camp and hiked to Wire Lakes," Bryan explained. "It was easy to track them. Rebecca was wearing a new pair of boots, and the pattern was really clear any time she stepped on dirt. And since she was behind Todd the whole way, all I had to do was follow those bootprints."

Dan knew that the trail they followed would have led them through Whitesides Meadow, with plenty of dirt and even some mud. The tracks would have been easy to follow. "So what did you do when they got to Wire Lakes?"

"That's where it got harder," Bryan admitted. "That goes up over some granite, and I just guessed that they were headed for the lakes. So that's where I went, too. And they were there. I had to be a little careful, to make sure that I didn't get spotted. But I was careful, and I just camped up above on one of the granite ledges. They never knew I was there."

"Probably just as well, no?" Dan asked. "You would have ended up in jail if they had …"

Bryan shook his head. "Only if Todd saw me, not Rebecca …" He paused. Dan wanted to ask why, but didn't want to interrupt Bryan's story. "So anyway," Bryan continued, "that afternoon Todd takes off with his fishing rod, and Rebecca just hangs around the lake, sunbathing and swimming."

"And you just watched her?" Dan asked.

"Yeah," Bryan answered. "I couldn't take the chance of having that turd, Todd, see me, so I just stayed up on the granite above the lake. And watched her. She was beautiful."

"You know, that's not exactly normal, Bryan," Dan suggested.

Bryan's eyes clouded over for a moment, and then he shot a glare at Dan. "You have no idea," he said. "The only people who knew what was going on were Rebecca and me. I loved her more than I have ever loved anybody, and she knew that."

Dan regretted raising the issue, and tried to get Bryan back on track. "Okay, sorry. So you were there at Middle Wire Lake …"

"Yeah …" Bryan was remembering. "Todd came back, and they had a fire. I could see that from where I was. And then I went to sleep. That night I heard them have an argument or something … lots of yelling. And the next morning, by the time I woke up, I couldn't see Rebecca anywhere. Todd was there, packing up in a hurry. I figured that she had walked out on him, so I really wanted to find her. But I had to wait for him to get out of there, so I could follow her tracks."

Dan continued to take notes while he followed Lafferty's story. He looked up to see Bryan watching him, waiting for him to finish.

Dan finished scribbling and pointed the pencil at Bryan to show he was ready.

"It was harder to track them now," Bryan continued, "because Todd's prints were all over the top of Rebecca's. And because there was so much granite. But I guessed that she was headed east up over the hump and down into the canyon that takes you to Deer Lake, and so I could just keep Todd in sight from time to time. It took a bit of guessing, but I figured it out."

He took a deep breath and let it out slowly. It was very quiet in the office now, except for the occasional noise of a distant car on the highway.

"He was a jerk, you know?" Bryan continued. "He was really moving fast, trying to catch up to her. And I damn near ran up his ass one time, when he was stopped and trying to figure out where she went. I think he saw me, but I don't think he realized that it was me. He just noticed another hiker … and I turned off the trail like I was heading off to take a leak or something."

Bryan looked intently at Dan. "And this was weird, because when he started hiking again, I could see that he was trying to cover up her tracks with his. I mean, he was walking funny, in shorter steps, and I couldn't figure out why. And then I finally got to the trail, and I saw what he was doing. Any time there was dirt, you couldn't see her tracks, only his bag-ass feet all over them." There was venom in his voice when he talked about Todd.

"So did you see Rebecca?" Dan asked.

"No, she was still ahead of us. But by the time we got down to Deer Lake, and there's that trail that goes around it to the east and then straight down towards Wood Lake?" Bryan glanced at Dan to make sure he was following this. "I think they were close together then, but he was still behind her. And he was still walking to cover up her tracks. I could see that. And then they crossed the creek, and somebody fell in. I think it was Rebecca. There was a lot of water on the far side, on the trail."

"So did they go up or down, once they crossed the creek?" Dan asked.

"They turned left, to go up to Wood Lake. And then they took that side spur—the one that goes up off the trail and into Karl's Lake? I had to be careful there, because there's a lot of open country in there, and I had to drop back a bit so they wouldn't see me. And they were going a lot slower now, so I had to be really careful. At one point I could hear them yelling at each other, and I had to just sit down and wait. So I know that they were headed in to Karl's Lake, and I followed them as best I could. But I lost them."

"What do you mean?" Dan asked. "Did they go to Karl's Lake?"

"I think so," Bryan said, nodding. "But the trails there are all granite and cairns out there. And with all that rock, the sounds echo from different directions. I mean, for a while I thought they had gone to Coyote Lake, so I went that way, and spent most of the afternoon trying to find them. Only they didn't. So then I had to go back to Karl's, and I found a few tracks there. The trail forks there so that one section goes to Kole Lake, and it's all granite in both directions. I never did see them again. It got dark, and I thought I would try to find them by looking for their campfire. But I lost them."

Dan was startled to hear the dark pain that came through in Bryan's voice. "So what did you do?" Dan asked.

Bryan shook his head sadly. "I figured that one way or the other, they had to come out past Grouse Lake. So I went there and camped and waited. And they never came out. I waited about four days, and finally gave up, and hiked out. And that's when I heard that Rebecca was missing."

"Why didn't you tell anybody about this back then?" Dan asked.

"Are you kidding me? With the restraining order?" Bryan was incredulous. "They would have slapped my ass in jail and thrown away the key. Hell, they tried to do that anyway!"

"So when you heard that Rebecca was missing, what did you think? Did you ever think about going to look for her later?"

Bryan gave a half-hearted laugh. "Look, I knew the score. She was way beyond me. I never really had a chance with Rebecca. So there wasn't any point to looking for her. I figured that if she wanted me to find her, she'd let me know …" He paused, then added sadly, "That was when I thought she was still out there somewhere, having her adventures […"

"And the last place you saw them was on the trail to Karl's Lake?" Dan asked.

Lafferty nodded, but it was clear that he was lost in thought. "Well, that's where I heard them." He paused. "There was something odd about how they walked up that trail out of the creek, though. I could see it, because I could see Todd's fat-ass boot prints. He was taking a big step, and then a little step. And he was still covering up her footprints. I think she must have hurt herself when she fell into the creek, and was limping. That's why one step was longer than the other."

Dan thought that made a lot of sense.

chapter 28

Once Bryan Lafferty had left, Dan made a quick call to the Tuolumne County Sheriff's office and reported what he had learned about the pot farmer from Bryan Lafferty. The deputy on duty assured him that the information would be passed on immediately to Cal and the rest of the team working on the case. Dan left a message for Cal to update him on any new developments.

Then Dan sat down, opened up the desk drawer, and pulled out the diaries. He studied them for a few minutes, and then decided that he would take them home to read. He kept them neatly wrapped in the brown paper, and carried them out to his truck to drive home. But during the drive he wasn't really thinking about the diaries. He was thinking about Bryan Lafferty. He wondered how much of what Lafferty had told him was true. The best liars always include some truth in their stories, because they know it makes them more believable.

So the question that Dan kept considering focused on Bryan Lafferty's account of the backpacking trip. Had Lafferty told him the whole truth and nothing but the truth? If so, then Todd Walters had lied to the Sheriff, and that raised a whole series of suspicions about him.

But the other possibility was that Todd had told the truth, and Lafferty had lied. If Rebecca really had left Todd at Wire Lakes, and Bryan had followed her down to Leighton Lake and killed her, then his story made a perfect cover for why he was down there and what he knew about it.

The one thing that Dan could not ignore was Bryan's comment about Rebecca's limp. If she had hurt her foot in the fall, it would explain why she was missing one of her boots—because she had taken it off to tend to her sore foot or ankle.

That was something Bryan could not have learned later. He had to have deduced it from what he had seen sixteen years ago. And that meant that one way or the other, Bryan was telling the truth about seeing Rebecca after she left Wire Lakes. Which made him the last person to admit to seeing her alive.

Dan stopped in at the Twain Harte Market to get half a chicken, a Caesar salad, and a baked potato to eat for dinner, and drove back to his house. He opened a bottle of cheap Shiraz, poured himself a glass, and sat down to eat. The chicken was overcooked, and greasy enough that Dan didn't want to open the diaries there at the table while he ate.

That's when he realized that he must have left the salad somewhere in the store, because it wasn't on the table, and it wasn't in the bag. He walked out to his truck, just to make sure he hadn't left it there. Nope. It wasn't going to be a very balanced meal after all.

He tossed the leftovers in the trash, washed the grease off his hands, and let himself drop into his overstuffed sofa with the two diaries. He clicked on the old lamp on the end table, which gave a dim and very golden glow to the room, and opened up the cover of the first diary.

He checked the dates on a few pages, and realized that the pink one was earlier, and the darker red one followed. Both were slightly larger, taller, than the note she had left with Todd. Each page began with a clear date on the top, and he started to read a few pages near the end of the second diary. The dates were only a month before

Rebecca had left on the backpacking trip with Todd. Rebecca's handwriting was very clear and easy to read. And Dan recognized the stylized curlicues so many young women he had known used twenty years ago.

Dan didn't know what to expect in these books, but he didn't expect to feel so awkward about reading them. They were painful at times, a young girl writing down her thoughts, sometimes in a clear and heartfelt way. Other times it seemed as if she were playing at writing; the words rang false and overly dramatic.

He found Todd's name on one of the pages, and read that Rebecca didn't think she was in love with him at all. She liked him, that's all. She knew that her parents approved of Todd as a good, moral, all-American kid, but Rebecca didn't think he acted that way with her. He was strong, both physically and in his opinions, but she didn't share some of those opinions.

And she was afraid he would expect her to sleep with him over the summer, before they left for school. He was already talking about it. She wasn't interested.

Near the end of the second diary, she wrote about a double date with Lori and another boy. Todd had teased Lori and said some very ugly things. Rebecca was resentful, and refused to allow Todd to kiss her that night. They argued, and Todd said he would never call her again. Rebecca was furious.

A few days later, they were discussing the trip to Wire Lakes. There was even an itinerary and a packing list of what she would have to carry. And that was where the diary ended.

Dan tried to remember his own life at that time, and generally failed. What would a girl at his high school have written about him? He couldn't imagine. He had to admit that he couldn't even imagine what Kristen Gallagher would write about him today.

He opened up the pink diary at the first page and began to read. The handwriting in the earlier diary had more frills, and Dan had the sense that Rebecca was less serious about writing in it. She included conversations with her dog, a corgi, and just as many conversations with God. She wrote about school, and Dan took notice when Bryan Lafferty made an appearance. She thought he was funny, and he had been nice to her after class one day.

Much of what she wrote had to do with living in a place where she could see the trees, and walk in the mountains. She took occasional trips up to Pinecrest Lake, where friends had a cabin. After reading about three of these trips, Dan realized that she always found time to leave her friends, and wander off on her own. She said it was the only way she really felt close to God.

On the third trip she was furious that her friends had become worried and reported her missing, and called her parents and the Sheriff. She had been up on Dodge Ridge, watching night fall, and only returned well after dark. The next day she wrote a poem:

"Trees are sleeping

Frogs are peeping

Stars in the sky

The moon so high

And God watches over us all."

Dan closed the book. There was only so much teenage angst that he could swallow at one gulp. He poured himself another glass of wine and went out onto the front porch, resting his hands on the railing. There were frogs here, too, that were peeping. He was relieved to see that there was no moon visible. Next door, from the flickering bluish glow coming through the windows, he could see that Walt was watching television.

The rest of the street was quiet, and very dark. Dan checked his watch. He had about two more hours before he would likely fall asleep on the sofa. Tomorrow morning he would have to call Frank Oliver and tell him about the diaries. And turn them over to the FBI. He tossed the rest of his wine out into the yard and went back inside to read.

One of the major events Dan hoped to find in the diaries was the night that Bryan Lafferty was arrested. He found it, near the end of the pink diary. But Rebecca seemed oddly calm about the whole thing. Only a few pages earlier, she had described Lafferty as "sweet." And she certainly didn't write anything about changing her mind about him, even after he broke into her bedroom in the middle of the night. She had not been terrified, apparently. In fact, she said, Bryan had been great about the whole thing—very calm.

And she never mentioned it again, except a few pages later, to say that she was sorry he was arrested, but there really was no other option.

Dan read further, looking for any more mention of Bryan, but he was distracted by another long entry that covered pages of the diary. Rebecca had been invited to fly over the Sierra by "Dr. B," who was a small plane pilot. She was very excited about it, and for days wrote entry after entry about how wonderful it was going to be to see the Sierra from the point of view of God, who made it.

The reality did not live up to her expectations. While she enjoyed seeing the many lakes that dotted this section of the Sierra, she was disappointed that she felt so distant from them. The noise in the plane was deafening, and instead of feeling a sense of wonder and exploration, in the end she felt only vaguely interested and somewhat disappointed that she couldn't get out and walk among the trees and lakes that she loved.

And then they landed at the airport in Minden, Nevada. Dr. B insisted that FAA regulations required him to rest for four hours, and so he had checked them into a hotel there. Only once they got to the room, it was pretty clear that Dr. B was not interested in resting—only in getting Rebecca into bed. She had resisted, forcefully, and eventually had to threaten to scream if he did not leave her alone.

He did that, refusing to speak to her at all in the hotel. The flight back was done in silence, and Rebecca wrote bitterly about her disillusionment.

And about Dr. B. He was "such a jerk." And about her own stupidity: "Stupid stupid stupid!!!!"

But Dan wondered if Dr. B had regrets about that day, or worries that Rebecca might accuse him of attempted rape. From what she wrote, that seemed unlikely. But did Dr. B know that? Did he fear for his reputation, and decide to do something about it? Where was he during the week that Rebecca disappeared in the mountains? So who was Dr. B? And where was he now?

Dan continued to work his way through the rest of the two diaries, without being able to find anything that would indicate that Rebecca was suicidal in any way. And while she talked about leaving home with enthusiasm, her tone was never one of desperation. She was furious with her parents at times. She never really mentioned Bryan Lafferty again. And Dr. B continued to call her every once in a while, when her parents were away. The last call was only five weeks before the backpacking trip. Rebecca told him to leave her alone.

Dan closed the books and turned off the light. The dim glow from his computer screen in the other bedroom provided enough light for him to navigate through his house. On one level, he was frustrated that he couldn't see more, couldn't find more to help him come up with a solution to what happened to Rebecca. But he had tried. And now he felt a certain sense of relief that it was no longer his problem.

It was now all up to the FBI.

chapter 29

Dan woke up to the sound of a deer crunching the apples on the tree outside his window. He had put a fence up three years ago, but it never seemed to matter. The deer always found a way into the yard, and always just at the point that the apples were starting to get ripe.

He looked at his alarm clock. It was 6:15. Too early to get up, but maybe too late for him to fall back to sleep. He closed his eyes and allowed his mind to wander through what he knew about Rebecca Ritter. There were so many possible suspects, but who would kill a young girl like that? Bryan Lafferty had given him the answer about her boot. She must have stopped on the ridge beyond Leighton Lake to take off her shoe and rest her foot. And someone had pushed her over the edge. He was slowly falling asleep when he woke up with a start.

It was 7:20, and he was running late.

By the time he got up to Summit Ranger Station, Doris' car was already in the parking lot. He strode briskly into the office and was met with a stare from Doris.

"I see that you are still with us," she said. "That's a relief."

"Yep," he responded. "Alive and kicking. It's tough to get a couple of books to explode when you want them to …"

His attempt at humor didn't amuse Doris. "Well, I am happy that you are safe, even if you were reckless."

It was time to try tactic number two. "Thanks, Doris," he said softly. "And I did know that it was a couple of books. So I wasn't really being reckless."

Doris turned away without further comment to download the messages off the phone, but her manner showed that she was not going to stay angry with Dan.

Dan went into the back office and picked up the phone to call Frank Oliver. He wasn't going to enjoy this conversation, but he decided to get it over as quickly as possible and hand the whole problem of the diaries over to the FBI.

Oliver answered on the first ring. Dan explained that someone had dropped off a package last night at the ranger station. He explained that since it had his name on it, he had taken it home and opened it up. And he explained that after opening the books, he realized that they were the diaries from Rebecca Ritter. Now he was calling Frank, first thing in the morning, to tell him about it.

"So you already opened these up?" Oliver asked.

"Yes," Dan admitted.

"And can I assume that you read through most of them?" the FBI agent continued.

"I read through a lot of them," Dan admitted, without offering anything more.

Frank Oliver was silent. Dan waited. He saw no reason to make this easier on the FBI agent, not after the conversations they'd had in Sonora.

Finally, Oliver broke the silence. There was a slight edge of exasperation to his voice when he asked, "And did you learn anything?"

Dan wasn't sure if he really wanted to go into great detail with Oliver about anything in the diaries. It would be easier to let the FBI agent figure it out for himself, and Dan could really step back from the case. He wanted to do that. But he found himself explaining about Dr. B and the flight over the Sierra.

"So who, exactly, is Dr. B?" Oliver asked.

"I don't know," Dan answered, truthfully.

Frank Oliver thought this over. "Okay …" a longer silence followed. Dan was happy to let it run.

"I hear you had a bit of an adventure the other day with a pot farmer …" Oliver changed the subject.

"Yeah," Dan agreed. "I guess you heard about that from the Sheriff?"

"I heard about it from the DEA," Oliver corrected him. "They heard about it from the Sheriff. Sounds like you were a little lucky."

Dan thought this over. "Yeah, I might have been," he said.

"And do you think this had anything to do with the Rebecca Ritter case?" Oliver asked him.

"I don't think so," Dan said.

"Neither do I," said Oliver.

Dan tried to remember another time that Oliver had ever agreed with him, and failed. It was a strange sensation.

"So you have a lead with this Dr. B," he heard Oliver say. "And I should probably read through those diaries myself. It never hurts to have a second set of eyes on them."

Dan wasn't sure, but it sounded as if Oliver was thinking out loud, and including Dan in the investigation.

"Look, I know you have a of lot stuff going on up there," Oliver continued. "But could you follow up with Lori Marchand up there, and ask her about Dr. B? She seems like the most likely person to know …"

And Dan found himself saying, "Sure. And I could ask a few other people who were here at the time, and see if they know." He was thinking of the di Contis.

Frank Oliver asked a few more questions about the diaries, and stunned Dan by announcing that he would drive up to Sonora to pick them up.

"When do you want to do that?" Dan asked.

"Today," Oliver answered.

It took a moment for that to sink in. "Okay," Dan responded. "Do you want me to just hold them here at Summit? We're a good ways past Sonora."

"That's fine," Oliver assured him. "I'll get there before noon." And he hung up the phone.

Dan placed the handset back on the phone and thought about this. If Frank Oliver was going to drive up and collect the diaries, then he had certainly changed his attitude about this case. Dan wondered who had called him, and what they had said. It must have been impressive.

Dan found himself feeling relieved that he was turning the whole thing over to the Feds. He was only going to ask a few more questions, to help them out. He was happy to help, but it wasn't his problem, and he wasn't going to have to deal with the politics that came with it. He even felt a little sorry for Frank Oliver.

And right now, he told himself, he still knew more about this case than the FBI agent in charge of it.

By the time he got off the phone, things were getting busier out in the main office. Doris was writing up permits and answering the phone at the same time. When Dan walked out to join her, she told him that Cal Healey had called, and asked Dan to return the call. And no, he hadn't said it was urgent.

A couple of vans pulled up in the parking lot, and Dan heard the sounds of highly excited young voices carry through the closed glass doors of the ranger station. It looked like a troop of Girl Scouts had arrived.

Dan put the note about Cal's phone call in his pocket, and prepared himself for the onslaught. A young woman climbed out of the second van and took charge of the group. Within a minute or two she had the girls lined up to use the restroom, while she came into the office to talk.

"That's quite a group there," Dan said with a smile.

The woman shook her head slowly, her ponytail flopping briskly from side to side. "You have no idea," she said. "I've been trapped in the van with them for almost three hours!"

Dan chuckled and asked what they needed. The girls were going to camp at Eagle Meadows that night, then hike into the back country for their first overnight backpacking trip ever.

While he started filling out the permit, Dan asked if they might like him to give an orientation to the area, and notes on the rules and regulations for camping and the wilderness.

"That would be wonderful," the Scout leader enthused. "They hear this stuff from me, but it would be really great if they could hear it from you, as well."

Once the girls had all visited the restroom, Dan joined them outside for a talk. For the next twenty minutes he gave them his standard lecture on what to do, and not do, in the Wilderness areas of the National Forest. The girls were respectful and attentive, even when they were occasionally giggling. And they had a few questions.

This was what Dan loved about talking to kids. So many adults seemed to think that they shouldn't ask a question, for fear they might show their ignorance. These girls peppered him for another ten minutes about everything from bears to chipmunks.

And when they had run out of questions, one of the older girls, who must have been at least ten or eleven, invited him to join them for s'mores around the campfire later that night.

Dan laughed and assured them that if he was in the area, he would be sure to stop in and say hello.

"And eat s'mores," the girl insisted.

Dan laughed again and agreed. "Yep. I'll have a s'more."

The Scouts drove off and Dan walked back into the office. Doris handed him a note. Cal Healey had called again.

Dan walked into the back office and dialed the number for Cal. The Sheriff got straight to the point.

"Do you know anyone named Chester Fowler?" he asked Dan. The name sounded vaguely familiar, but Dan couldn't place it. "Why do you want to know?" he asked Cal.

"Because he's been reported missing, and we're trying to find him."

Dan shook his head. "I'm drawing a blank, Cal."

"Would it help you to know that Chester Fowler is about five ten, 190, and is African-American?"

"Oh, yeah!" Dan remembered. "Todd Walters' friend. So he's missing now? Did Todd report him?"

"No," Cal replied. "The First United Methodist Church in Turlock reported him missing. He didn't make the Bible study group last night."

Dan chuckled quietly. "Churches take Bible study a little more seriously these days …"

"He's the pastor," Cal explained. "And he's ex-military—never misses anything for any reason. He called last night to say he was going to be late, then never showed."

"Okay," Dan reconsidered. "So what do you want me to do?"

"Well, first of all, I wanted to see if you agreed with me," Cal answered. "This is the guy we saw with Todd Walters."

"Seems like it," Dan agreed.

He heard a sigh from the other end of the phone line. "So I guess I will have somebody run over and see if we can track down Todd and his friend …" Cal Healey didn't sound enthusiastic about it.

"Let me know if you want me to do something," Dan offered, then reconsidered. "No, if you want me to do something, ask Steve Matson. And then he can tell me about it."

Cal gave a dry laugh. "I don't think we'll ask for your help on this one. But if you see either one of these guys, let me know, okay?"

"Sure," Dan agreed. "But I am going to be here at the station pretty much for the rest of the day."

"So you're not planning on visiting any pot farms?" Cal asked.

"Nope, just giving out permits to Girl Scouts," Dan answered.

"Well, that's a better use of your talents, anyway," Cal needled him.

"Hey—speaking of that, did you check out Bryan Lafferty's story about that house up there?" Dan asked him.

"We're working on it," Cal said. "We do know who owns that house …"

"And does his story check out?" Dan pressed.

"Maybe. So far." His dislike of Lafferty was obviously making Cal cautious.

"Okay, well, keep me posted on that one, will you?" Dan asked. But he didn't wait for an answer. It occurred to him that Cal might know about Dr. B. "Back when Rebecca Ritter disappeared, do you remember a doctor in town? Rebecca calls him Dr. B in her diaries."

There was a long silence. "So you have Rebecca's diaries now?" Cal asked him.

"Yeah—sorry," Dan admitted. "I think Anson Ritter must have dropped them off for me late yesterday. So I read through them a bit. Frank Oliver is picking them up later today."

"So did you learn anything?" Cal asked.

"I'd like to track down this Dr. B," Dan said. "But I don't think there is anything that helps us solve the case. Teenage girls have a lot going on."

"Tell me about it," Cal replied. "I have one at home … Dr. B, huh? It's not ringing any bells for me, but I'll ask around."

"Frank Oliver suggested that I call Lori Marchand about it," Dan said.

Cal thought this over. "Why don't I give Lori a call," he said. "I can also ask her if she has seen Todd Walters or his friend."

"Go for it," Dan agreed. He hung up the phone and joined Doris back behind the counter. She was talking to a group of young people looking for a campsite. As Dan listened to their conversation, one of the campers mentioned that they were a church group.

Dan's mind went back to the conversation about Todd Walters and his friend. Dan wouldn't have picked out Chet Fowler as a minister, he realized. He wondered what their connection was. Maybe it had to do with the military service? Dan wondered if he could hand that over to Frank Oliver, and ask the FBI to check on that.

The phone rang and Dan answered it. "You are not going to like this." It was Cal again. "He wasn't a doctor; he was a dentist."

"Dr. B?" Dan asked.

"According to Lori, he was a dentist in town for a few years. She says he was very interested in Rebecca, but moved down to the Bay Area a long time ago ..." Cal said. "She thinks his name was Barret or something."

"Can you track that down for me?" Dan asked.

"I already did," Cal replied.

"So what's the answer?" Dan asked. "And why did you say that I wasn't going to like this?"

Cal responded, "Because his name was Glenn Bartlett."

"The guy who found the body." Dan didn't ask it as a question.

"Yep," Cal agreed. "The guy who found the body."

chapter 30

Frank Oliver walked into the Summit Ranger Station at exactly three minutes before noon.

Dan had been watching the clock for the past half hour, thinking that it would be slightly pleasant to be able to greet the FBI agent with the news that he was late. Something about Frank Oliver just grated on his nerves.

But Oliver wasn't late. He walked into the station, nodded curtly to Doris, and immediately pointed to the back office, suggesting to Dan that they should walk into the rear office to talk. Dan paused for a moment, tired of the arrogance of Frank Oliver, and then followed him into the office. Dan was trying hard to keep Oliver from ruining his day.

Oliver held the door open for Dan and then closed it behind him. After a quick glance around the office he waved Dan towards the only good chair and waited for Dan to sit in it. It was the chair in front of Dan's own desk. Frank Oliver remained standing.

Dan took his time. He didn't like the way that the FBI agent had assumed control in an office that wasn't his. Dan sat down, leaned back a bit in his chair, crossed his right leg over his left, and checked his watch. He could see Oliver looking around the office for the diaries.

"So where are they?" Oliver finally asked with carefully controlled exasperation.

Dan didn't answer. He uncrossed his legs and leaned forward, reaching across the top of his desk for the paper shopping bag with the diaries.

Oliver strode quickly over to take them from Dan. He pulled the books out of the bag and began scanning the room for a place to sit. The only chair left was the wooden hardback chair that Doris used for her bad back.

Dan let the moment drag as long as he could before offering, "I'll go back out to the front desk …"

Oliver nodded and then waited impatiently for Dan to get up. The two men moved awkwardly around each other to exchange places.

As Dan was leaving he turned to glance at Frank Oliver. He could see Oliver's hands shaking slightly as he opened the first diary. He wondered why they were shaking. To Dan it seemed more like worry than excitement.

He considered what the FBI agent had to worry about. Dan could not resist the temptation to ask, "Are you okay?" Oliver looked up, and in that glance Dan saw that something was definitely not okay.

"Yeah, sure. Why wouldn't I be?" Oliver responded.

Dan shrugged and answered, "No reason. Just asking to be polite."

Frank Oliver nodded curtly and made a show of returning to his studies of the diaries.

Dan shrugged and left him alone. He closed the door to the back office and turned to see Doris leaning on one elbow, looking at him over her glasses. She wrinkled her nose at him.

"Bad day?" she asked.

Dan gave a sad smile. "I wonder if he ever has a good day," he replied.

Doris thought this over. "And he's the one who is handling the Ritter case now?" Dan nodded.

"It looks like he doesn't want much help," Doris noted.

Dan shrugged. "He's the FBI. They don't need help." He knew Doris would appreciate the irony.

"You mean like the way he got those diaries from you?" Doris asked.

Dan allowed a wry grin to pass over his face. "And most of everything else on this case," he agreed.

Doris considered this for a moment while she shuffled some papers. "And are you just going to let it go, and let him take it all over?" she asked.

Dan shot her a surprised look. "I don't have a choice, Doris. I've been told it's not my job; it's his."

Doris looked up at Dan and smiled. "And you don't see anything you can do about that?"

Dan held his hands up in surrender. "Nope, not much!" he said.

Doris folded her hands in front of her bosom and looked Dan straight in the eye. "Well, you're wrong," she said. "It's lunchtime. Did you see him bring in anything to eat? Neither did I. And you are about to go over to the deli and get a sandwich." She paused to let Dan agree with her.

He stayed silent, but didn't argue with Doris.

"Why don't you pick up two sandwiches, and offer him one?" She didn't take her gaze off Dan's face.

Dan looked away and made mumbling noises. He sure as hell didn't see any reason to buy Frank Oliver lunch, and he could just imagine the reaction from the FBI agent. He wished Doris would let this one drop.

And she almost did. And then, after a couple of minutes, she said in a curiously quiet sing-song voice, "It's lunchtime. And little boys are always grouchy before they get their tummies full …" She looked over at Dan.

He burst out laughing. "Okay, you win," he said with a grin.

"I'll ask him what he wants."

Doris held up her hand. "Never ask a hungry little boy what he wants to eat. You can never make him happy. Just wait until he is hungry, and then put something it front of him. He'll eat it," she said.

Dan agreed. "Okay … so what do I get him?"

"Get two sandwiches you like, and let him pick which one he wants," Doris suggested. "And nothing too weird," she warned. "Just turkey or ham. And get some chips and drinks. And cookies, too! Make it a full lunch."

Dan was still chuckling as he walked out the door to get in his truck.

chapter 31

Dan opened the door to the back office and saw Frank Oliver studying Rebecca Ritter's diaries and writing out notes on a yellow legal pad.

"I thought you might like something to eat," Dan said. "I got turkey or ham …"

Oliver pointed to an open spot on the desk and said, "Doesn't matter …" He then turned back to the diaries.

Dan waited. He pulled the sandwiches out of the bag and held both of them toward Frank Oliver. "You choose," he said. It was more of an order than an invitation.

Oliver looked up again and stared at Dan. Dan met his gaze, and Oliver took a deep breath. "Okay, I'll take the turkey." He paused, then added, "If that's all right?"

"Great," Dan assured him. He pulled up Doris' old wooden chair to the other side of the desk and put the deli bag down between the two of them. "I've got chips here, and a soda or bottled water …?" He looked up at Oliver, again waiting for the FBI agent to choose. When he didn't, Dan continued, "and I have an apple, a banana, and a couple of cookies."

"That's a lot more than I usually eat for lunch," Oliver remarked.

"Mountain air," Dan said cheerfully. "Always makes you hungrier up here. I bet we finish this all."

Oliver took another deep breath and put down his pen. He

began to unwrap his sandwich while Dan pulled the rest of the lunch out of the bag. Dan placed both drinks on the desk between them, and waved for Oliver to choose. While Oliver reached for the soda, Dan pulled open the bag of chips and pointed the open end toward Frank Oliver.

Oliver was eyeing his sandwich. "This looks good," he said. "They do a good job," Dan replied. He waited until Oliver had taken a huge first bite out of the sandwich and then asked, "So how are things going with the diaries?" When Oliver could not respond, he added, "Are you clear on all the people and places?"

Oliver continued to chew, while shrugging his shoulders. Dan interpreted that to mean that the agent was not completely confused by it all. Dan took a bite of his own sandwich. The two chewed in silence for a while … but Dan knew it would be hard for Frank Oliver to take another bite without giving him some kind of response.

He was right.

"I think I've got most of it," Oliver said. "They're in the police reports, too."

Dan nodded and grabbed a handful of salt and vinegar chips. He offered the bag to Oliver, who took a few for himself. Dan waited for the agent to take another bite before speaking again.

"More info about the prom than I ever wanted to know," Dan said.

Frank Oliver nodded his agreement while chewing. He reached for the soda bottle and took a swig.

"Did you see that stuff about Dr. B yet?" Dan asked. Oliver shook his head and leaned forward to take a few potato chips.

"It's near the end of the first one," Dan explained, pointing to the diary on the desk that lay closed. He suspected that Oliver had not yet read it.

Frank Oliver nodded again and took another bite of his sandwich. "And the descriptions of Bryan Lafferty are in that one, too," Dan added.

Oliver swallowed and looked at the older diary. "I'll get to that one later this afternoon," he said.

Dan drank from his bottle of water and looked out the window. "It must be hard being a teenage girl, at least a pretty one," he said.

Oliver looked up at him questioningly. "Well, there are at least two stories in there that are something between sexual harassment and attempted rape," Dan explained. "Can you imagine having to deal with that all the time?"

Oliver shrugged. "No charges filed? We are well past the statute of limitations ... and I'll bet they are he said/she said kinds of things." He looked at Dan.

Dan nodded.

"Just a teenager finding out that the world is a little more dangerous than it should be ..." Oliver summed up. He was now polishing off the last bite of the first half of his sandwich.

"Yeah," Dan agreed. "I was just thinking about motive. If she were going to file charges: that could be important."

Oliver wagged his head back and forth as he chewed on some chips. "No mention of that in the police report. Did they not check them out?"

"Well, the Bryan Lafferty thing was big news around here, and that's in the police report. Charges were filed there, and they even got a restraining order on the kid," Dan answered. "So she did file charges there, or at least her parents did, and I think the Sheriff's office checked that out pretty carefully. Lafferty is still their prime suspect for this thing."

"He's the stalker?" Oliver asked.

Dan nodded. "But if you read that section of the diary, I am not sure those kids were telling the whole truth to anyone."

"There's a surprise," Oliver said dryly. He was now surveying the table, his eyes making contact with a chocolate chip cookie. Dan handed over a cookie and took one for himself.

"At least, she doesn't seem very upset with Lafferty, either before or after he supposedly broke into her room. Sounds like maybe she knew what was happening the whole time."

Frank Oliver leaned back in his chair and savored the chocolate chip cookie. "Of course, it doesn't matter so much what she thinks, as what he was thinking …" he said.

Dan agreed. "We should talk about that sometime. He came by here and gave me a lot more information about this whole thing."

Frank Oliver looked at him suspiciously. "Who? Lafferty? Like what? When did he do that?"

Dan took his time and filled in the FBI agent on all that Bryan Lafferty had told him. Oliver took pages of notes, but he asked very few questions of Dan during the conversation. When Dan was finished with the story, Oliver was still writing on his yellow legal pad. It took another couple of minutes for Oliver to finish his notes.

He looked up at Dan. "So you don't think Lafferty is our prime suspect in this?" he asked.

"Oh, he was involved. He was around when it happened," Dan corrected. "He was in the area, and he was paying attention to Rebecca. But I don't think he killed her, or did something to cause her death."

Frank Oliver took this in. "Okay," he said. "So who do you think did it?"

Dan leaned forward. "I don't know," he said. "I just don't think that Lafferty had any motive or any anger toward Rebecca. So I don't see him as a good suspect, even though he lied during the initial investigation."

"Which leaves Todd … whatshisname," Oliver continued.

"Walters," Dan reminded him. "And if what Bryan Lafferty now claims is true, then Todd Walters lied to the initial investigation, too."

"Isn't this guy a war vet? Paraplegic?" Oliver asked.

"Yeah, he's had a tough time of it," Dan agreed.

Frank Oliver considered this as he looked at the desk in front of them. A lonely apple was all that remained of the lunch. Dan pointed to the apple to offer it to Oliver.

"Go ahead," Oliver said, offering it to Dan.

"No, thanks," Dan said. "But if you really don't want it, I'll offer it to Doris …"

"Go ahead," the FBI agent agreed. "So what was the other harassment about?"

Dan nodded. "A guy she calls 'Dr. B.' Took her for a flight in his plane, and couldn't keep his hands to himself. It's not much fun to read."

Frank Oliver sniffed. "That doesn't sound like much of a reason to kill somebody …"

"Yeah," Dan agreed. "But if she threatened to tell people about it? That couldn't be good for a doctor …" Frank Oliver shrugged, to show Dan that he wasn't impressed.

"I did find out one more thing," Dan said. "I found out who Dr. B is. It turns out that Dr. B was a dentist who was living up here at the time. He moved away a couple of years after this. His name was Glenn Bartlett."

Dan looked at Frank Oliver to judge his reaction. Oliver looked up at Dan. "The guy who found the body?" he asked.

"The guy who found the body," Dan confirmed.

"So where is he now?" Oliver asked. He hand was already moving towards his notepad and pen.

"Down in the Bay Area," Dan said. "I've got the Sheriff's office trying to figure out exactly where he is, but they told me they lived in Livermore. I found an office there, but it's closed right now …"

Frank Oliver's eyes rested on the phone in Dan's office. "Can I use this?" he asked.

"Sure," Dan agreed. And then he remembered. "And if you are going to get some help tracking people down, I have one more name for you: Chester Fowler."

"Who's he?" Oliver asked, his face twisted in confusion. "I haven't seen his name anywhere …"

"He's someone who has been spending a lot of time with Todd Walters recently, and now he's missing. It might help to find out what their connection is."

Oliver grunted, and wrote himself a note. He began punching numbers into the phone while he talked to Dan Courtwright. "We will track this guy Bartlett down this afternoon and try to figure out what his story is," he said. "And let's pick up Walters as well. I'd like to talk to him, too." He paused, and Dan waited expectantly. "And I'll ask somebody to run a quick check on Fowler, too."

His voice changed as his phone call was answered. He waved to Dan and turned away to talk quietly on the phone. Dan walked back out into the office and closed the door behind him.

Doris gave him a short, smug smile. "Sounds like you boys were getting along in there," she said.

Dan smiled. "I'll never forget the power of a full belly, Doris."

"So are you going to help him?" Doris asked.

"It sounds like he's going to want that," Dan answered.

"It sounds like you both want that," Doris added.

Dan looked out the window at the trees surrounding the parking lot. He could see the breeze moving the branches, casting gently moving shadows on the blacktop.

"Yeah, I guess that's right," Dan agreed.

chapter 32

But that wasn't exactly what happened.

For the next four hours Frank Oliver set up a command center in the back room of the Summit Ranger Station. He seemed to be able to talk on two phone lines at the same time, because Dan and Doris had a hard time finding an open line. And when the phone did ring, it was almost always for Frank Oliver.

By three o'clock Doris was making some exasperated noises every time it rang. And the old fax machine that they still used for permits was now beeping and printing on a regular basis. Dan and Doris took turns delivering these into the back office for Oliver to review.

But the FBI agent didn't share much with either of them. And they had enough to do with the people who walked into the station that they didn't have much time to ask him any questions.

At 4:45 Doris announced that this was one of the most frustrating days she had ever spent in that office. Dan didn't disagree. They could hear Oliver talking to someone on the phone in the back room, and it didn't sound as if he were happy.

Doris sighed. Dan noticed that she was looking at the topo map on the counter, and it seemed as if she might be looking at the area around Leighton Lake.

"See anything important there?" he asked Doris.

Doris shook her head. "No, I was just thinking about those

photos." She paused. "It's all so sad."

Dan agreed. "That's how it felt when we were there. It was depressing to be in a place that is so beautiful and wild, and then knowing that you're there because somebody got killed."

"And I can't even imagine what this must have been like for the Ritters," Doris said. "God, it must have been horrible, not knowing, but with terrible suspicions."

A commotion in the back office interrupted their conversation. The door flew open and Frank Oliver came out, his eyes quickly fixing on Dan.

"I found Glenn Bartlett," he said. "He's someplace in Baja California called Moolahay or something. He flew down there in his private plane, and the plane is still at the airport. He's supposed to be doing free dental work in some tiny village a couple of hours from there."

"Oh, my," Doris said. "Is that the man who found Rebecca?"

Frank Oliver quickly turned to look at Doris. He stared at her without saying anything for a few seconds, then turned back to Dan. "We should talk back here," he said, and turned around to go back into the rear office. Dan gave Doris a consoling look and followed Oliver.

"The police down there say that they will keep an eye on him, and make sure that he doesn't leave," Oliver said.

Dan nodded. "Okay. But you don't have to worry about Doris." He was angry at the way Oliver had ignored her. "She is a professional, and she was here when the Bartletts brought in those photos."

Agent Oliver stopped and looked at Dan as if he were a moose that suddenly had appeared in the office. "I have to worry about everything," he snapped. Dan saw no purpose in arguing the point. The FBI agent was wound so tightly that there was nothing to be gained.

Frank Oliver continued, "I've read these diaries. The packing list in the last diary is just what Todd said Rebecca had in her pack." He looked up at Dan expectantly. Dan shrugged. He was still thinking about Doris outside the office.

"Todd Walters said that when she left him at Wire Lakes, she had switched some of the stuff around, so that she had enough food and equipment to go out on her own. And she had left him without enough food," Oliver reminded Dan. "But when he listed everything that she took …" He left the thought hanging.

"It was what she had started the trip with, based on the list in her diary?" Dan finished the sentence for him.

Frank Oliver sat back in Dan's chair and squeezed his lips together with his left hand. "So why did that seem important to Todd? Why would he lie about it?"

"Because if Rebecca didn't do that," Dan noted, "if she didn't pack up a bunch of stuff and walk out on Todd, then she and Todd were still together later that day."

"It makes Mr. Lafferty's story a little more credible …" Oliver said.

Doris knocked on the door, and Dan opened it. "Steve Matson is on the phone for you, Dan," she said.

Dan left Frank Oliver and went out into the front office to take the call from his boss. Steve wanted to know how things were going. "Okay," admitted Dan. Steve suggested that Frank Oliver might be a bit difficult to work with.

Dan chuckled. "Just a bit," he said.

"Well, he's under a lot of pressure right now," Steve said. "Do what you can for him."

"That's exactly what I'm doing," Dan reassured him.

"Thanks, Dan," Steve said. "Just between you and me, this may be his last chance there. He's been given this case, and it's his case to solve." He let this sink in. "But he's not exactly the agency's golden boy…"

"Got it," Dan replied. And he did. That was why Frank Oliver was so tight. He was on thin ice, and this case was just adding weight to the problem.

Dan hung up the phone and returned to the back office. He found Frank Oliver staring at the two open diaries in front of him.

Oliver looked up at Dan. "The paper isn't the right size," he said. Dan stared back blankly.

"The note she wrote," Oliver explained. "It's not the same size as these diaries."

"Different diary," Dan answered. "We don't have the diary she kept on the trip itself. These are from before that."

"But these two are the same," Oliver said. "And if she always bought the same kind of diary, then the paper on the note is not the right size."

"So maybe she bought a new size of diary…" Dan started.

"She started every page with the day and date at the top of the page here," Oliver noted.

"And the note she wrote didn't have either one," Dan remembered. "As if somebody cut off that part of the page…"

Frank Oliver met Dan's gaze. "Where is Todd Walters right now?"

Dan shook his head. "I don't know, but we can have the Sheriff try and pick him up."

"Let's do that," Oliver agreed. "And I am going to have my forensics team look at that note. I bet we can prove it was cut." He looked at his watch. "But that won't happen until tomorrow."

"Do you want to wait and pick up Walters tomorrow?" Dan asked.

"How hard is he going to be to find?" Oliver asked.

"I don't know," Dan admitted. "They know where he lives. They've been looking for him anyway. He spends a lot of time at the

VFW hall. So if he's at either of those places, it shouldn't be hard."

The FBI agent began rummaging through the papers on the desk, looking for something. "That guy Fowler was in Afghanistan as a chaplain. Looks like he was there the same time that Todd Walters was there," he said.

"Did they know each other?" Dan asked.

"Hard to say," Oliver shrugged. "Fowler was attached to a Medevac unit."

Dan thought this over. "Maybe they met when Walters got wounded."

Oliver sat back, obviously frustrated. "Yeah, maybe." He didn't seem to think that it mattered very much.

"The number's right on the phone, if that's what you're looking for," Dan said.

Oliver glanced to confirm this and said, "Thanks. Anybody in particular I should ask for?"

Dan smiled. "It's a small county. And it's after five o'clock. Just call it in. If they have any questions, I'll talk to them and work it out."

Frank Oliver made the call, and asked to be notified as soon as Todd Walters was picked up. He hung up the phone, and sat back in his chair. Dan could see that he had something on his mind, but he was still surprised when Oliver turned to him and asked, "Want to get something to eat?"

It was a little early for Dan to eat dinner, but he didn't want to turn down the invitation. It might mean that Frank Oliver wanted him around when they questioned Todd Walters. At the very least, it meant that Oliver was feeling a little more collegial toward Dan. And that was a feeling Dan was happy to encourage.

"Sure," he said. "What do you want to eat?"

"I saw a pizza place on the way up here," Oliver said. "Is it any good?"

"Yeah, sure," Dan said. "It's just a couple of miles down the road. I've just got to lock up here. I'll meet you there in ten minutes."

chapter 33

By the time Dan got to the restaurant, Frank Oliver was already sitting down at a table and staring at the menu. Dan picked him out on the far side of the dining room, and sat down across the table from him.

When the waitress arrived, Oliver immediately turned to her and ordered a medium pepperoni pizza and a diet soda. He looked expectantly at Dan.

Dan was half-expecting to share a pizza. That was what he normally did here. Instead, he asked for a house salad and a small cheese pizza. He would probably take some of it home. And he ordered a beer.

Dan recognized the waitress, but didn't remember her name. She remembered that he drank Sierra Nevada. He could sense Frank Oliver making mental notes, and he didn't care.

He sat back in his chair and asked, "So what do you think?"

Oliver considered this question for far longer than Dan thought he would. The waitress had time to bring them their drinks, and promise Dan that she would be right back with his salad.

After she left the table, Frank Oliver cleared his throat.

"Right now everything points to Todd Walters," he said. It was a question as much as it was a statement.

"If you're right about those diary pages, it does …" Dan agreed.

Oliver nodded, and his left hand went up to cover his mouth.

Dan wondered if he were worried about people reading his lips, the way football coaches cover their mouths on the sidelines. Frank Oliver gave a quick, deep sigh and spoke to Dan. "This is kind of a make or break case for me," he said.

"What do you mean?" Dan asked.

Talking with the FBI agent was always a slow process, and this was no different. Oliver waited for a moment. "I'm under a lot of pressure," he said. He was clearly struggling with what to tell Dan. "They are talking about laying some people off …"

Dan saw no reason to hurry the conversation along. Mandy (That was her name! He would have to remember it next time) came back with his salad, and he began to eat. Once he had a mouthful of lettuce, he looked up expectantly at Oliver.

"I need to nail this one down," the agent continued, "to keep my job."

Dan nodded. He swallowed and said, "It seems to me like you're doing fine," he said.

This elicited a snort from Frank Oliver. "Doing fine isn't going to cut it," he said hotly. "I've been told that I better nail this down tight enough to put someone away for a long time, or else …"

Dan considered this. "It's going to take a pretty solid case to convict someone in a case this old."

Frank Oliver didn't answer. He took a long sip from his soda and looked out the window. He stared long enough that Dan turned to see if he was looking at anything in particular. He wasn't.

Dan let him sit in silence until the pizzas arrived. When they did, Oliver ordered another large soda. As they dug into their pizzas, Oliver spoke again. "So what do you think happened? Your best guess?"

Over the next half hour, Dan worked through the evidence and explained each piece as well as he could. Frank Oliver asked him questions on a few points, but generally let him proceed.

When he was finished, the FBI agent said, "So you think Todd Walters probably pushed her over the cliff?"

"Maybe pushed, maybe bumped. Maybe felt guilty because she jumped," Dan said. "I don't have enough information to know what happened out there, but I think he was there. And I think he tried to hide that fact, which makes me more suspicious of him."

Oliver nodded.

"But I sure wish I could explain Glenn Bartlett being the guy who found the body," Dan continued. He looked at Oliver for help.

Oliver shook his head. "We've got to talk to both of those guys," he said.

Dan stood up to go the restroom. "I'm pretty sure that the Sheriff will get hold of Walters soon," he said. "It's up to your guys to track down Bartlett."

Mandy returned to the table. "Is everything okay?" she asked.

Dan smiled and nodded. Was she just being nice, or was she trying to get his attention? At any rate, she was too young for him. Dan excused himself and walked to the restroom. But it was occupied.

As he waited, Dan noticed the photos on the wall of the hallway: Little League and softball teams that had been sponsored over the years by the restaurant. There were lots of cute kids there, and the photos went back quite a few years. He wondered if Kristen Gallagher was in one of them. What year would that have been? And then he remembered the Girl Scouts. He glanced at his watch. He still had time to stop and visit them, but he would have to leave soon.

Back at the table, he handed Frank Oliver a twenty-dollar bill and explained, "I almost forget that I promised I'd stop in and visit a Girl Scout troop at their campsite."

"Sure," Oliver said. "I'll call you tomorrow with any news."

"Are you going to stay up here tonight?" Dan asked.

Oliver shook his head. "No, I'll go back to Modesto. I like sleeping in my own bed. And I can get some work done down there, too."

Dan held out his hand, and Oliver stood up to shake it. "Keep me posted," Dan said. "And let me know what I can do to help."

Frank Oliver held onto his hand a bit longer than usual. He stammered a bit, then mumbled "Thanks."

Dan left him to pay the bill, and walked out to his truck. The sun was on the horizon, and the trees had a golden glow to them. It was a perfect temperature. The highway was empty in both directions, and Dan eased out onto the road and headed east. In his rear view mirror, the sunset was turning the few clouds in the western sky a deep orange.

chapter 34

He drove up the highway with the windows down. Instead of driving the speed limit, Dan drove a good ten miles an hour slower. It was too delicious an evening to hurry. He wondered if Kristen had ever been a Girl Scout.

As he drove by the Summit Ranger Station, he noticed an SUV in the parking lot, and wondered if he should stop. In the single second it took him to make the decision, he saw a young man wave his arms and yell. If Dan's windows had been up, he would not have heard the cry. But they were open and he did.

"Hey! Help! Stop!"

And he couldn't ignore it.

He slowed to a stop and turned around on the highway. As he slowly eased into the parking lot, the young man raced over to him.

"There's no pay phone here!" the young man accused. He wore blue jeans and a t-shirt with some kind of grisly rock and roll image on it. And he was still waving his arms.

"What's going on?" Dan asked him.

"We found this guy," the young man replied. "He's all tied up."

Dan followed him over to the SUV in the parking lot. The door was open on the passenger side, and Dan could see someone sitting there. But there was something odd about it. The man's arms were tied behind his back. His head was down, in a position that Dan could only assume was very painful.

Dan turned to confront the young man. The young man held his hands up helplessly, innocently. "He's in handcuffs! We couldn't get them off."

Dan turned back to the SUV. Now the man's head was up, facing Dan. Dan recognized the face.

"Chester Fowler?" Dan asked gently.

The man's eyebrows shot up in surprise. He nodded, and added, "I am happy to see you, sir."

Dan bent down to help him out of the car. Fowler gave a groan as he stood up. "We have been looking for you, Mr. Fowler. Your church reported you missing."

"The sheep are looking for the lost shepherd," Fowler chuckled. "Well, I am grateful for that."

Dan helped him over to the bench in front of the Summit Station, where he could rest more easily. The handcuffs were firmly attached, and Dan didn't see any way to get them off.

"Can you tell me what's going on here?" Dan asked.

"I am a prisoner of my own good intentions," Fowler said, shaking his head back and forth.

Dan noticed Fowler's knees. The pants were dirty and torn. Dan imagined that the knees inside were scraped, too.

"We found him at Donnell Vista," the young man said. He had been joined by a friend about the same age. "He had tape over his mouth, but we took that off."

"He was in some bushes," the friend added. "But we heard him moving around in there."

"We thought it might be a bear or something," the first young man added.

"I'm sorry to disappoint you," Fowler said to the young men. "But I am grateful that you found me."

Dan called in to the Sheriff's office and reported that he needed assistance. Chet Fowler tried to interrupt him to say that he didn't need an ambulance. "The EMTs on the fire truck will have the tools to get these handcuffs off," Dan explained. "I don't."

There was an awkward silence, and Dan asked if Fowler would like some water to drink.

"I'm afraid I would explode," Fowler replied. "I am very much looking forward to using the toilet once I get these cuffs off."

Dan glanced at the young men. "There's a restroom here," he said. "I could help you in there ..."

"And how long before help arrives?" Fowler asked.

"About an hour or so," Dan answered.

Another long pause. Dan sensed that Fowler was too embarrassed to ask for help.

"Come on," he said. "I'll help you." He motioned for the young men to help get the minister on his feet.

"Thank you," Fowler replied. "Thank you very much."

Dan led him into the restroom and closed the door. He unbuckled Fowler's pants and pulled them and his underwear down, then helped him sit on the toilet.

"I'll wait outside," Dan said.

"That won't be necessary," Fowler said with a laugh. Dan could hear that he was already relieving himself. "Good gracious but that feels good."

Dan waited for Fowler to finish, then asked him a question. "So did Todd Walters do this?"

"You have me at quite a disadvantage," Fowler replied. Dan waited.

"Todd is carrying a very heavy burden," Fowler continued. Dan waited, but the minister offered no more.

"A burden that he's been carrying for about sixteen years?" Dan asked.

Was it a nod? Fowler didn't respond directly, but Dan thought he detected a nod of agreement.

"Can you help me up?" Fowler asked.

"Of course," Dan replied. He gently pulled up the minister's clothes and buckled his belt for him. But before they went back outside, Dan wanted to ask another question.

"I need to know where Todd is," he said. "I am worried about him. And I am worried about others. If he did this to you, someone he knows and trusts, I am worried he'll do something worse to someone else. I need to know if he has a gun. Is he armed?"

"He is a very troubled man," Fowler agreed.

"Does he have a gun?" Dan asked again.

"He did when I saw him," Fowler responded. "That's why I am in handcuffs."

Dan turned to open the restroom door, still holding Fowler with one hand. "So where is he?" Dan was getting angry, feeling that Fowler was holding something back.

"I wish I could tell you where he was, or what he will do. But I can't." Fowler paused. "I don't know. He didn't tell me."

Something about that last comment struck Dan. Todd Walters had told Fowler something, at some point.

"You were in the Medevac unit for Todd, weren't you?" Dan asked. Fowler nodded.

"And he thought he was going to die, didn't he?" Dan pressed.

Chet Fowler stopped short of the door and looked at Dan. "I think Todd expected to die the minute he threw himself on that IED." His eyes stared directly into Dan's.

Dan met his gaze. "Did he want to die? Did he tell you what happened up here back then? Did he tell you about Rebecca Ritter?"

"I can't tell you what he said," Fowler answered, shaking his head. "That's confidential. But I will tell you that he was very upset. And he wanted to get some things off his mind."

Now Dan was sure that Todd had told Chet Fowler about Rebecca and how she died. He wanted desperately to force Fowler to tell him more. But that was in the past, and there were more urgent matters to deal with right now. "So where is Todd now?" he asked. "Where did he go?" He wanted to shake the answer out of the minister, to make him somehow produce the answer.

Fowler shook his head. "I don't know. He didn't tell me. He wasn't interested in talking to me by then." He looked up at Dan. "He just told me to get out of the car, right into the bushes, and drove off."

"And how long ago was that?" Dan asked.

Fowler thought this over. "Maybe half an hour ago?"

"Which way did he drive out of the parking lot when he left you?" Dan pressed.

Chet Fowler thought this over for a moment, and then answered, "He was coming back this way." Fowler used both of his hands to point out on the highway towards Sonora.

Had Todd passed him on the highway? Dan tried to remember. He didn't think so, but he wasn't sure. Still, it made sense. There was a whole network of roads through the Stanislaus National Forest, and Todd could have taken any one of them. Once off the main highway, he could hide out for days, maybe even weeks if he had food. Or he could steal it from others.

Dan climbed into his truck and got on the radio. He reported the information he had: that Todd Walters had left Donnell Vista about thirty minutes ago, heading West on 108. That he was armed and dangerous. And Dan asked for as much backup as he could get.

It would be at least another half hour before any of that backup would arrive. And in that time, Todd Walters could be getting away. Dan started his truck, and asked the two young men to stay with Chet Fowler until the paramedics arrived. They promised to do so, but Chet approached Dan's truck.

"I'd like to go with you," he said. "I might be able to help."

Dan looked at the minister, who was still wearing handcuffs. It wasn't a hard decision. "If I find him, I'll call it in, and maybe you can help then. But right now, I'm going to ask you to stay here."

The minister started to protest, but Dan rolled his window up and drove his truck out onto the highway. It was getting dark, and there was a lot of territory to cover.

chapter 35

If he had gone off-highway, there were four or five roads that Todd Walters might have taken. From the ranger station, the first turn-off was for Herring Creek. Dan slowed down. Herring Creek Road ran in a large loop for miles up into the mountains. Should he take it? It would be the most logical and organized way to search, taking each road in turn from beginning to end.

But Dan knew all too well that the longest and most complex road system off the highway was the one to Niagara and Eagle Meadows. And he suspected that Todd knew this as well. It would be the most likely choice for someone who was looking for a place to hide. Dan sped up again and drove past the intersection.

The light was fading, and the headlights on Dan's truck came on a few minutes later as he drove through a particularly dense section of forest near the Cascade Creek turn-off. He glanced down the road as he drove by, but didn't slow down.

He did the same at Mill Creek on the right-hand side, and pushed on toward Eagle Meadows Road. He knew why now. The little girls there were on his mind. He had no idea what Todd Walters might do.

As he slowed down to pull into Eagle Meadows Road, Dan got on the radio and called in his position. He suggested that the backup units check the roads that he had passed on the way. They were still well behind him.

Cal Healey from the Sheriff's office came on the radio. "Hey, Dan, you should probably switch to another channel," he said.

Dan thought this over. At first the request made no real sense, but then he realized that Cal was sending him a message. Of course Todd Walters had a radio scanner in his SUV. He would be able to track their radio traffic and understand the search.

"Message received, Cal," Dan responded. "But I am having trouble with my radio. Let's stay on this channel."

"You got it," Cal replied. "We're on our way."

Dan began to formulate a plan. "There's a group of NRA guys at Eagle Meadows," Dan reported on the radio. "About ten of them, with more firepower than most Marine combat units, so I would imagine that might not work out the way Walters would like. I'm guessing that if he gets that far, he'll turn around pretty quick."

"Roger that," Cal replied. "We're approaching Sugar Pine now, so we'll hit Herring Creek first."

Dan's truck started to slide wildly in a tight turn, and a flash of white panic shot through him. A pine tree loomed suddenly on his left, and Dan was not sure how he missed hitting it. But the gravel on the road held, and he came out of the turn with a resolution to slow down. The forest was very dense now, and it was dark enough that Dan couldn't see very well outside the beams of his headlights.

He passed the first Y in the road and kept left, toward Niagara campground. If he could find someone there, they would be able to tell him if Walters had passed that way.

Dan slowed as he entered the Niagara campground, and stopped in front of a group gathered around a firepit. He didn't bother to get out of the truck, but called out to the group, "I'm looking for a blue SUV, jacked up high, that might have driven through here. Did you guys see anything like that?"

One of the men walked over to Dan. "Yeah, about ten minutes ago. Headed over that way." He pointed down the road toward Eagle

Meadows.

Dan shot out a quick "Thanks," and roared off again.

He picked up the radio and called in the information. "Suspect seen heading east out of Niagara campground," he reported. "So if we can get units up to the Eagle Meadows turn-off, we should have the whole area blocked off."

"Roger that," Cal replied. "I'd advise you to wait for backup."

Dan knew that Cal was right. The smart thing to do would be to wait. But he also know that those Girl Scouts were further down the road, and he didn't want to give Todd any more time than necessary to develop a plan. He drove out of the campground and started weaving his way through the dark forest toward Eagle Meadows.

chapter 36

Dan flicked on his high-beams, but it didn't help much. The road twisted and turned through the forest, and his headlights were pointing well off the road most of the time. He leaned forward on the seat, trying to peer into blackness to see what was around the next bend.

The road wasn't in great condition, with a combination of stretches of washboard, a few large potholes, and lots of smaller rocks that weren't big enough to take out the bottom of his oil pan, but were big enough to knock him silly in the cab. He could feel his teeth vibrating inside his head.

Dan's wheels were sliding on the gravel in the corners, and he began to lose track of time and distance. His focus was only on the road, his truck, and his need to get to Eagle Meadows.

A tight left turn threw his rear wheels into a slide, and Dan struggled to keep control. He slid to the right toward a large log that lay parallel to the road. A shot of icy adrenaline raced through him as the truck hit the gravel bank on the edge of the road and banged to a stop.

"Shit." Dan was furious with himself. He gunned the engine and shifted into four-wheel drive to try to get the truck back on the road. It shuddered and shook, slowly easing forward, but slipping sideways at the same time. Dan coaxed it as best he could, his every nerve sensitive to a slight change in feel and sound. Was the traction improving? The truck began to tilt even more to the right, and Dan feared it was going to roll over.

And then, with a lurch, it clumped back out on the road, bouncing hard.

Another chill, this time of relief, rolled back down into his gut, and he sent the truck forward again. It was making an odd sound on the right-hand side—a kind of shrill rattling or vibration.

Dan wanted to keep driving, but worried that the noise could mean he was rubbing a fender into the tire. If that were the case, it would cut through the tire quickly, and he would be stranded.

He stopped the truck and jumped out. In the dark he couldn't see well, but it didn't look like the body of the truck was damaged. He felt with his fingers along the side of the truck from front to back. He couldn't feel anything that would explain the noise. But the tail lights showed something in the back.

Pieces of a small tree were caught in the rear wheel well. Dan yanked out the pieces he could see and felt around the tire. Nothing there. He ran back around to the driver's side and climbed in. As he drove off the noise was gone.

He was driving more cautiously now, trying to leave himself a margin of error. The road rose as it climbed the ridge, and as he neared the top the forest thinned out. Dan could see large trunks lying on the ground in the glow of his headlights.

Off to the right a flash of light caught his eye. Before he could react, something smacked against his windshield, and he instinctively ducked. His first thought was that it was odd a rock would hit his windshield up here. Pain sprayed the right side of his face, and his second thought was that he had been shot.

chapter 37

White pain flashed across the right side of Dan's face, and he instinctively bent his head down and to the left. There was something in his right eye. Dan feared it was glass from the windshield, and as he bent over he blinked several times to try to get it out.

Another smack hit the windshield. Dan crouched down behind the dash and tried to think. His right eye screamed in pain every time he moved it. The glass was still in it.

Dan reached up and turned off the headlights to the truck, then turned off the engine. That would make him less of an obvious target. He pulled at his eyelid, trying to make space for the glass, hoping it would fall out.

Another shot, this one clanging into the front of the truck. A hiss told Dan that it had probably put a hole in the radiator.

How could Todd Walters see him to shoot? Did he have night-vision goggles in his SUV? Dan tried to twist his head to look, his right eye still closed tightly in pain.

Shit. His foot was on the brake, and the rear of the truck was bathed in red light. He yanked his foot away from the pedal and lowered himself down on the floor. He could hear his breath, gasping, as he lay there.

No more shots.

Dan waited. The pain in his eye was excruciating, but now he began to realize that his arm, pinned underneath him, really hurt.

And his right leg was beginning to cramp up from avoiding the brake pedal. He eased his body around until the pressure on his leg relaxed, and took a deep breath, his eyes closed.

He heard nothing outside the truck. No shots, no noise from another vehicle. There were odd creaks and groans from the engine as it cooled down.

He took another breath. His right eye was firmly clamped shut, and it was still killing him. He was afraid to move it for fear the glass would do more damage.

With his left hand, he reached up and grabbed the mike for the radio. He pushed the button and called in.

"I have located the suspect," he explained, struggling to make his voice sound more or less normal. "We're on the road to Eagle Meadows, about a mile or two past Niagara. Suspect is armed, and has fired on me. I am wounded."

It was Dispatch that responded, confirming his information.

"I have this guy trapped," Dan continued. "He can't get out of here without driving right past me. But I need some backup."

Dispatch confirmed that backup was on its way. So was an ambulance.

Dan reached under the seat and pulled out his sidearm. He lay back down, the pistol cradled on his chest. It was pitch black in the truck. Dan closed his left eye and rested.

The radio crackled on again, asking Dan about his injuries.

"Not life-threatening," Dan replied. "But I can't see very well. The side of my face is cut up from windshield glass. I have glass in my eye."

Dispatch responded with a confirmation that backup was thirty minutes away. So was an ambulance.

It occurred to Dan that Todd was probably listening to all of this on his scanner. That thought sank in. As it did, Dan realized that he not only had Todd trapped, but that there was still one way for Todd to get out. And it led right past Dan's truck.

Dan would be a sitting duck.

He held the pistol more tightly in his right hand. If he opened the door of the truck, the courtesy lights would give Todd a clear shot again. He couldn't remember how to turn them off. He thought about smashing the lights with his pistol. Or maybe trying to unscrew them?

But weren't there also lights in the sides of the door? Dan couldn't remember.

In the distance, Dan heard Todd Walters start up his engine.

chapter 38

Dan struggled to fight his way off the floor of the truck. He banged his head on the steering wheel, and finally pulled himself back up onto the seat.

He paused. He could still hear the engine of Todd's truck.

Dan slowly eased his head up above the dashboard and used his left eye to try to find Todd Walters.

There were orange lights over there in the trees. How far was it? Dan estimated a hundred yards or more. Way too far for his pistol. Dan watched as Todd Walters slowly drove along in the forest, with only his parking lights on.

Which direction was he heading?

With a chill of fear, Dan realized that Todd was coming back down the road toward him. And as he got closer, Todd would be able to turn on his headlights and light up Dan's truck like a football field.

A puff of breeze drifted through the cab of the truck. The dust had settled out of the air, and the scent of pines was clean and clear.

Dan realized that the windows of the truck were still open. He could climb out, without giving away his position.

He checked Todd Walter's location. The lights were slowly getting closer, occasionally blinking on or off as Walter passed behind a tree.

Dan rolled his body up to the passenger's side window of his truck and leaned out. It was pitch black on the road. Dan thought about trying to keep his pistol with him, then gently tossed it out on the dirt of the road. He put his hands and arms through the window, and then slowly pushed himself out.

There was an awkward moment when Dan felt his thighs on the edge of the window, and his hands were still off the ground. It would be a very silly position to die.

He squirmed and wiggled and felt his body start to fall forward onto the ground. His thighs scraped along the window and then his hands touched the road. And then his arms, and then he was rolling in the dirt.

Todd's truck was now much closer, and Dan could see the lights more clearly now.

His hands searched frantically for the gun. It had to be right there in front of him. A finger on his right hand sensed it, and Dan grabbed it and scrambled off the road on all fours, tumbling into the dirt and bushes. He rolled up against the trunk of a cedar and edged around behind it. He could smell the dust from the road as he breathed in big gasps. He hoped that it wasn't visible to Todd Walters.

Todd's truck slowed, and Dan heard Walters shift the truck into neutral and set the parking brake. Fifty yards away? Did he see the dust?

Dan waited. The truck rumbled quietly, menacingly.

Dan looked down at his legs to make sure that his feet weren't in the light of the headlights. The toe of his right shoe was clearly illuminated in the glare of the lights. Should he move it? The motion might catch Todd's eye. Or Todd might have noticed already.

A shot blasted, and Dan jumped involuntarily at the noise, pulling his foot back as he did so. Even now he couldn't tell if the tree was really big enough to hide him. But the shoe was no longer in the light.

Had he been spotted? Dan slipped the safety off his gun and tried to ease himself to the far side of the tree. In a fire fight, Dan was completely outgunned by Todd's rifle. And who knew what else Todd had in his SUV?

Dan realized that as Todd Walters drove forward, the angle of the SUV's lights would change, and Dan would have to move to stay covered. The tree didn't seem big enough. He was afraid to put his arm down, afraid that he couldn't keep it out of sight. Afraid that it would give his position away. He tried to shift himself using his feet and shoulders to lever his butt around, and started to fall over.

Another shot rang out, and this time Dan heard it bang against his truck.

Good. Walters thought that Dan was still in the cab.

Dan sat back and took another breath. How long had he gone without breathing?

The SUV began to rumble forward again.

The headlights were now lighting up Dan's truck completely— bright enough to bathe Dan in the reflected light. Through his left eye he could now see the bush that he had crashed through, and the side of the road. He squirmed over again as the SUV crept forward, trying to stay out of the light's path.

Dan tried to catch his breath and think calmly. The soft bark of the cedar seemed to comfort him. As long as he kept the tree between himself and Todd Walters, he couldn't be shot. Not even an AK-47 could hurt him through the trunk of the cedar. And Todd wasn't about to get out of his SUV.

"Like two kids playing a game of tag around a picnic table," Dan thought. Except the consequences of getting tagged were deadly. He pulled his feet up underneath himself and slowly slid upright. He wanted to be in a position to fire at Todd as he drove away. This was certainly a situation where deadly force was authorized.

The SUV was now only a few feet away. Todd Walters was

slowly easing it forward, and as Dan turned his head to the other side of the tree, he could see the red glow from Todd's tail lights.

The SUV jerked to a halt, tailpipe still rumbling.

Dan started to peek around the back of the tree, when another shot nearly deafened him. Again he thought he heard the clang of the bullet hitting his truck.

Todd had to be facing away from him now, aiming at the truck. But on this side of the tree, Dan was at a disadvantage. His right eye was still closed tightly, still screaming at him. And to get into position to see with his left eye would expose his whole head.

Dan rolled back to the other side of the tree and peered around the trunk. Todd was no more than ten feet away, holding a rifle over his head, pointing it down into the floor of the cab of Dan's truck.

"Freeze!" Dan screamed as he stepped out from behind the tree. "Freeze or I will blow your brains out right here!"

Todd slowly turned his head to look at Dan, still keeping his rifle above his head.

"Drop the weapon!" Dan yelled. "Drop the weapon now! Drop it."

Todd's eyes focused on Dan, then on the pistol Dan held.

"Push the rifle out the window, butt first," Dan told him. His right eye was now watering so much that it was hard for him to see.

The butt of the rifle came out of the window, and Todd lowered it by the barrel until the butt hit the ground.

"Drop it!" Dan repeated.

Todd let go of the rifle and it fell over into the dust of the road with a heavy thud.

"Keep your hands high!" Dan instructed him. "Keep them where I can see them!"

But Dan couldn't really see them. The dust and exhaust were swirling around the SUV, and the combination of pain and stress wasn't making things any easier. Dan's left eye was almost as blind as his right.

He stumbled forward, down into the ditch on the side of the road, then lunged back up to grab at the SUV.

Todd Walters didn't move. His hands were still up above his head. Dan could see that much.

"Now," Dan said as he held his pistol to Todd's head through the open window. "Now we are going to just sit here and wait."

chapter 39

His eyes were still nearly blind, and Dan used the back of his left hand to wipe them. He looked into the cab and noted Todd's joystick system for driving the SUV. He wondered if he should turn off the engine, or have Todd turn it off. But that would require allowing Todd to move his hand right next to the joystick. Or reaching across Todd to do it himself.

The engine stayed running.

It was going to be a while before the backup arrived, and Dan knew that Todd's arms would get tired. He told Todd to grab the roll bar over his head, to ease the strain.

Todd nodded and wrapped his fingers around the huge steel bar. Then he let his head fall back against the headrest of the seat and gave a long sigh. It was a sigh that Dan hoped symbolized his surrender.

Dan looked at his hand. He could see his pistol was still shaking, slightly, from the adrenaline. Or was it the vibration of the SUV?

No, Dan decided. It was the adrenaline.

The scanner in Todd's car came to life. The first backup car was now driving onto Eagle Meadows Road. It was odd hearing the radio in stereo, the one in Dan's truck still alive and repeating the message.

Beyond the headlights and the radio, the forest was black and empty, surrounding the two men like the still waters of a lake.

"You wouldn't have made it out anyway," Dan said to Todd.

Todd shrugged a shoulder. There was a long silence. "They're still a long ways away," Todd said. He waited for Dan to respond.

Dan waited, too. He thought about reading Todd his rights, arresting him. That could wait for the Sheriff. Right now he was satisfied with making sure that Todd didn't do any more damage.

"I wasn't trying to kill her," Todd said quietly.

"Uh huh," Dan grunted. "An accident, right?"

"It doesn't matter," Todd continued. "She was pissy. I just gave her a shove to scare the crap out of her." He paused.

Dan could hear his breath rasping while he held the gun to Todd's head.

Todd continued, his voice rising a bit at the recollection. "Only she didn't scare. She just went right over the edge." Another long pause. "That sure fucked things up."

Dan wondered if what he had just heard was admissible evidence in court.

Todd turned his head and peered around his upraised arm to look at Dan's face, then turned back to face the windshield.

"I'm going to put my arms down now," Todd said in a very controlled voice. "I don't think you're going to shoot me for that."

Dan pressed his gun forward into the back of Todd's head and grunted, "Keep your hands up. You just tried to kill me, you son of a bitch."

Todd waited, then moved his hands down to rest on the steering wheel. "Yeah, but now I'm unarmed and facing away from you," he said calmly. "You won't shoot me like this."

Dan had to admit that Todd might be right. He wasn't sure. "Keep your hands where I can see them," he said to Todd.

"You'd have to explain too much later," Todd said. "You know it and I know it."

Dan didn't reply. His mind began to run through the possibilities.

What would he do if Todd tried to drive away? Would he shoot him in the back of the head? It seemed too close, too final. And unnecessary. Plus, Dan knew that Todd was right; it would lead to an endless inquiry. He could shoot the tires of the SUV, but would that stop Todd? Or would he just drive away on the flat tires over the dirt road?

Dan rubbed his left eye again, trying to keep what remained of his vision. He didn't dare rub his right eye.

"You know what?" Todd asked him. "You're going to have to kill me, because I am not going to just sit here and wait for everybody else. So you can shoot me if you want, but I am going to drive away now."

"Stop!" Dan yelled.

But Todd's right hand slowly reached for the joystick and began to move the SUV forward. Dan started walking alongside, keeping his pistol aimed at Todd's head. But the SUV slowly picked up speed, and Dan knew that soon he wouldn't be able to keep up.

He also knew that he wouldn't kill Todd this way, with a shot in the back of the head.

As the SUV sped up, Dan swung his pistol over and fired a shot at the joystick. The SUV gave a lurch and sped up even faster. Dan fired again and then stumbled into a pothole on the road and fell down in the dust.

The SUV rolled quickly down the dirt road, its tail lights casting a glow through the dust behind it. It growled and thundered down the road, squeaking over the bumps. Dan rolled into a sitting position and aimed at the dark area below the left tail light.

Before he could fire, the SUV gradually veered off the right-hand side of the road with a huge thump, and slammed into a tree.

Dan kept his pistol trained on the tail lights as best he could.

"Shit!" he heard Todd yell. "You gotta help me!" His voice no longer had the calm control of just a minute ago. Now there was a note of real panic.

"Help me!" Todd yelled again. "Please!"

Dan got up from the dirt and looked at the SUV, now a good hundred feet away. He had no idea if Todd had another gun in there. And he decided that he wasn't going to find out. He slowly backed away toward his truck. He stumbled over the rifle on the ground, then felt his way toward the passenger side door.

A slight buzz of static greeted him.

"Please!" he heard Todd's voice, now quieter and more desperate.

Dan picked up the mic and called in the situation. He warned the dispatcher that Todd might still be armed, and asked her to tell the officers to approach with suitable caution.

And then he sat down in the dirt of the road, leaned against the tire of his truck, and waited for them to arrive.

chapter 40

That seemed like a good idea until Dan began to think about Cal arriving, driving into range just as Dan had done a few minutes before. The only person who could stop that was Dan.

"Crap," he thought. He stood up, still keeping his truck between himself and Todd Walters. There seemed to be no movement from Walters' SUV. Dan pointed his pistol at the back of the SUV and slowly edged out from behind his truck.

In the distance he could hear the rumble of the SUV's exhaust, and was grateful that it would cover the sound of his own footsteps as he approached.

Dan walked down the road slowly, staying on the side of the road, hoping that he would not be noticed, hoping that it was dark enough to hide him. At each step he was poised to dive off the road.

He tried to calculate where a potential blind spot would be for a driver in the SUV, but with big side mirrors, that was hard to imagine. Instead he slowly moved forward, sure that he was glowing ever more clearly in the red tail lights.

But there was no movement from the cab of the SUV. Either Todd Walters was completely oblivious to Dan's approach, or he was waiting very patiently and carefully.

Dan stepped off the right-hand side of the road briefly, into the shadow of a tree, and waited. Would that draw Walters out?

Apparently not.

Dan pushed softly through the bushes on the side of the road, and came out from the other side of the tree. Still no movement. But was that a sound?

As Dan listened, he realized he was hearing the noise of another vehicle approaching. It spurred him to action.

He jumped out from the bushes and into the roadway, and then ran the last forty feet diagonally across to the left side of the road, hoping to give Walters only a hard-to-hit moving target, and changing his position from one side to the other of the SUV while he did it.

He jumped behind a tree only a few feet behind Walters' SUV, still waiting for a shot to ring out. But he heard only the rumble of the motor. Had the other cars stopped to assess the situation?

Dan slowly eased around from behind the tree and pointed his pistol at the SUV. Inside, nothing moved. He thought he could see Todd Walters inside, leaning back against the headrest of the seat. Not moving.

Dan stared intently, trying to focus his blurry vision, finger on the trigger of his gun. He crept forward by inches, keeping Walters' head firmly in his sights.

There was still no movement from inside the SUV. Dan was now only a few yards from it. He couldn't be sure. Was that Walters' head? Dan aimed carefully.

Dan took four quick steps forward and reached the side of the SUV. Inside, Todd Walters was sitting at the wheel, his head leaning back against the headrest, his hands folded in his lap. He looked almost peaceful, bathed in the red lights of the SUV.

And then Dan realized that the red color didn't come from the tail lights. Walters' body was covered in blood. His face was white. Dan checked Walters' hands again, and saw that the left hand was tightly wrapped around the right wrist.

"I'm going to die," Todd Walters whispered.

The voice jolted Dan and he leapt back, keeping his gun aimed at Walters' head. Todd Walters stayed motionless in his seat.

Dan heard yelling from somewhere off to his left. Shouts, orders. Cal and his team had arrived. Dan waved his left hand to them, encouraging them to come forward, never taking his failing sight, or his gun, off Todd Walters. He heard someone yell at Walters to get out of the car, and then repeat the order.

"He can't," Dan explained. "He can't get out of the car. He's wounded." Dan heard, saw, and then felt someone come up beside him.

"We've got this, Dan," he heard someone say. Was it Cal? There were suddenly people surrounding the SUV, voices yelling, giving orders.

"He's bleeding a lot!" Dan heard himself say. "He's bleeding, so be careful!"

The voices began to change in tone. There was less yelling, more calm and deliberate direction. Dan found himself being led away from the SUV, back toward his own truck. He began to hear the questions they were asking him and realized that some of them came from EMTs.

"I'm fine," he kept repeating.

And they kept asking more questions.

chapter 41

Very late that night, actually early the next morning, Dan was in the hospital talking to Bob Roberson.

"The good news is that there is no glass in your eye," Dr. Roberson was saying. "The bad news is that there is a pretty serious cut in your cornea. I know it feels like there is something in there, but what you're feeling is that cut."

Dan nodded to show he understood. "I wish I had known that a few hours ago. It sure felt like there was glass in there. So what does that mean?"

"We'll have to keep an eye on it," Roberson said, oblivious to the pun, "but it should heal with time. We'll get you set up with some antibiotics and make sure that you take care of it. But you should heal." He paused. "You get to wear an eyepatch for a while, but that will come off in ten days or a couple of weeks or so."

Cal met him in the waiting room.

"So what's the news?" Cal asked.

Dan explained the diagnosis to Cal. He was still having a hard time focusing with only one eye.

"So are you cleared to go home, or do you have more stuff to do here?" Cal asked.

Dan wasn't sure, but a nurse looked over from the reception desk and said, "We're through with you here, Mr. Courtwright. Take care of that eye."

"Come on," Cal said. "I'll give you a ride home. You're a crappy driver as it is, but with only one eye you'd be a positive menace on the road."

Dan looked at him in surprise. "What?"

"Well, hell, you put some dents in your truck tonight, that's for sure. And that's before you got hurt," Cal grumped. "Of course, those could have been intentional. It's about time you got a new truck."

Dan gave him a tired smile. "This has been a damned long night," he said.

"At least you'll get some time off," Cal suggested as they walked to the parking lot. "Of course, you don't work that hard anyway …"

Dan slowly sank into the seat of Cal's car. "Fuck you, Cal," he said.

But Cal was right. The next day Steve Matson told Dan that he was not to show up for work for at least ten days, which left Dan with a lot of time on his hands. Unfortunately, that came with some restrictions. He found it hard to read or spend much time on his computer with only one eye, and he wasn't eager to drive very far, either.

Cal stopped by and brought him some food from Maggie— more food than he could eat in days. Doris did the same, and Steve Matson called and offered to pick up some groceries or anything else that he needed.

This last request Dan turned down, since he didn't want to go into detail about what he needed around the house with his boss. That was easier to do with Doris.

Doris also called to forward a message from Gail Moreno. "She says that you never got your s'mores, and she feels bad about that. She wants you to know that she and her Girl Scouts are going to be sending you a package in the mail."

Dan laughed. "I can hardly wait," he said. "I haven't eaten a marshmallow in at least ten years."

Doris didn't laugh. "She also says to thank you for what you did. She said to thank you very much. And to tell you that you are a hero, and all her girls know it. And I think you are one, too."

"Thanks, Doris." Dan was embarrassed by the comment, and hurriedly got off the phone.

Frank Oliver called. "Nice work up there," he said. Dan swallowed his surprise and said thanks. "Nope," replied Oliver. "Thank you. My boss is very happy that this thing is off our hands."

Which didn't really sound right to Dan, but he let it go.

"You know, one of our guys did track down Glenn Bartlett," Oliver continued. "They had quite a little chat." He left the topic hanging and Dan knew he was expected to ask for more info.

"So what did you find out?" he finally asked.

"Well, I think that's a need-to-know kind of thing," said Oliver. Then, after a pause, "Turns out he still thought a lot about Rebecca Ritter. He didn't want his wife to know, but that's the reason he kept backpacking up in that area. He was still looking for clues for what happened."

"And he found them," Dan replied.

"Yep. Well, anyway, thanks. I gotta write all this stuff up," Oliver said.

"Better you than me," said Dan.

On the second day home, the phone kept ringing. And one of those calls was from Kristen Gallagher.

"How are you doing?" she asked. And she sounded like she meant it. That was nice. Really nice.

Dan explained that he was fine, except that he couldn't do much, and he had to wear a patch over his eye.

"So … you're bored?" Kristen asked. "Have you tried talking like a pirate?"

Dan laughed out loud. "I don't think that would help much," he admitted.

"I was thinking you might be bored. And I thought you might need some food, too. Should I pick up a few things and bring them over to cook for you?"

Dan's first impulse was to say yes. Then he reconsidered. "Kristen, I would love to see you. And I would love to eat a dinner that you've cooked. But I have to be honest here. I've already got about six meals from Maggie and Doris, and I can see my next door neighbor heading this way with a casserole pan," he admitted. "I've got more food here than I can eat in a week."

Kristen burst out laughing. "You have a whole harem of women cooking for you!"

"Yeah, but with all this food here, there's too much for me to eat on my own," Dan said. "So can I invite you to dinner? You said you always like it when someone else cooks for you." He waited anxiously for her answer.

"Are you sure you're feeling good enough to have guests?" Kristen asked.

"Not guests," Dan corrected her. "One guest. And yeah, it would be great to see you."

"I'll be over about six," Kristen said. "Maybe we can have that date after all."